I hate (love) Brussels Sprouts

by

Tara Ford

Susie Satchel is back and that can only mean one thing – tears.

© Tara Ford 2018
All rights reserved

ISBN-13: **978-1985091054**
ISBN-10: **1985091054**

No part of this publication may be reproduced, stored in a retrieval system, or transmitted in any form or by any means, without the prior permission in writing of the author, nor be otherwise circulated in any form of binding or cover other than that in which it is published and without a similar condition including this condition being imposed on the subsequent purchaser.

Cover design by Jacqueline Arbromeit
http://www.goodcoverdesign.co.uk/

Other titles by Tara Ford

Stuff the Turkey

Calling All Neighbours

Calling All Customers

Calling All Dentists

Calling All Services

Acknowledgements

Once again, thank you to every one of you who continues to support me in my work. I want to particularly send my heartfelt thanks to those of you who have kindly left a review on Amazon. They are hugely appreciated and a vital tool to learn from, whether the reviews are good or not so good.

Thank you to my family for being so understanding when I'm 'major-busy' but maybe emptying the dishwasher once in a while could be helpful?

I hope you will enjoy reading this but if you don't, please let me know why.

Thank you!

Tara Ford

http://taraford.weebly.com/

Twitter: @rata2e

Facebook: Tara Ford - Author

For everyone
at
Kerriford Place

*** 1 ***

Miss you too, bestie. At last! Woohoo! Was it good? I can't wait to hear about it. Hope you'll be coming down in the summer hols and bring him along. Sounds like a whole new book is beginning in your life – never mind a new chapter! Go girl. Love ya, Clair xxx

I smile at my phone as I read the message a second time. Clair – she's my best friend and I've missed her dreadfully since she left. She now lives in Devon with her childhood-sweetheart, Archie, and has a fab job down there too. We used to live together in my flat but now I live alone... well, I say alone but to be honest there's a hunk of a man sleeping in my bed at this present moment and he is the most gorgeous thing you ever did set your eyes on... well, my eyes at least. He's tall (obviously when he's standing up – not when he's lying in bed. Or is he still tall when he's laying down? Hmm, I wonder) and handsome with piercing blue eyes and neatly cropped, brown hair. He's ultra-fit and muscular too. Anyway, before I get carried away with his sensational looks, what I'm trying to say is that although I do officially live on my own (and I desperately need to find someone new to share my flat with me, due to the mortgage payments and bills which I can't manage on my meagre little income), I do have a new boyfriend, Ryan (in bed), and things are going from strength to strength. So much so that... well, you never know, he may end up being my new flatmate/boyfriend (not that I'm pushing for it in the slightest – I wouldn't dare rush things after what I've been through in the last year). Flatmate/boyfriend – would it work? Hmm, I'm not sure, but like I said, I'm not rushing into things and especially as there is a slight problem which I need to clear up first.

I probably need to explain myself, but I'll make it brief. So, last Christmas I was with Kallum who turned out to be the biggest load of garbage I've ever known. I kicked him out along with the turkey, which, incidentally ruined my fabulous glass-heeled boots (until Jett managed to fix them, but that's part of another story). Then the next day I met up with Jett (having not seen him for years – I grew up with him) and we hit it off immediately. I mean, really hit it off in a big way. I mean, full-on. But he died a few days later after we'd fallen in love at first sight (again, the other story). They were such dark days for me. Then Ryan (who had asked me out before Christmas, but I had to say no because I was with Kallum) started to pop up here and there. Sadly, I sent him a stupid, drunken *facebook* message explaining all about my disastrous relationships and the death of my second boyfriend in a week, which I hope to this day he will never see. I'm surprised that he actually wants to be with me after the humiliating clown episode at school as well (another story) but he just thinks it was funny. Huh – trust me, it was far from being funny for me. I broke my little heart to be honest. Unfortunately, I seem to have done nothing but make one mistake after another as far as Ryan's concerned. Some of those messes, I have managed to get away with and some... or should I say one, in particular, is yet to be resolved – the *facebook* message.

Confused yet? I know I am. The only thing I do know for sure is that I still need to delete the message from Ryan's *facebook* app on his new phone, and even more so now that we are together as a proper couple (whatever a *proper* couple looks like). I have tried to delete the message on his phone once but ended up dropping his old mobile (which I stole from him) down the loo in a gents' toilets in a restaurant. Major fail. Poor Ryan couldn't understand why his swish, top-of-the-range phone was leaking water when he found it on the table at the restaurant. Of course, I had no idea why and was unable to enlighten him on how or why his phone should suddenly start dribbling water while resting on a table in a restaurant. I do feel bad about what I did, just for the record, but I was desperate to delete the message. Sadly, I failed at the deletion bit and Ryan had to buy a new phone because his old one died a soggy, possibly urine-saturated death (he doesn't know that, obviously).

So, that's about the long and the short of it and where we're currently at.

He's so lush, Clair. Hope I can bring him to meet you. You'll love him. Ha ha, before I close that last book there is still one more thing to do. I still haven't been able to get rid of the message. Xx

Forget it. It's just a drunken, silly message – so what! I'm sure he won't care. Don't worry about it xxx

But I do. You didn't read it – it was absolutely awful, Clair. He can NEVER EVER see it. He's got standards. Xx

Then you'll just have to try and get his phone again but for God's sake don't go anywhere near a bloody toilet! xxx

Ha ha, don't worry – I won't be going anywhere near a toilet... in fact, I think I've got an idea – it has just come to me - maybe Ryan will be near a toilet, not me! I'll let you know how I get on xx

???

Explain later. Night night, love you xx

I peer across to Ryan, who is sleeping peacefully beside me. He's super-handsome and looks so angelic with his long dark eyelashes sweeping down on to his cheeks – they are so long that they could almost touch his cheekbones. An image of his phone, resting on the coffee table in the living room, pops up into my head. Then another, darker vision crosses my mind... A devilish insight into solving my dilemma. I'm going to sleep on it though as it's quite a bizarre concept. Extremely strange and wild. In fact, I think Clair would kill me if she knew what I was thinking.

***

"Good morning, did you sleep OK?" Ryan has just padded into the kitchen, bleary eyed and even more attractive with his hair sticking up all over the place. It's the first time I've seen him first thing in the morning. Bless him – does he know how gorgeous he looks? I doubt it, he's not the vain type.

"Out like a light," he mutters, pulling a chair from under my small round dining table (well, I can't even really call it a dining table as it's more like an oversized bistro table, it's that small). Ryan eyes me with a mischievous look. "We had a good night..."

"Yes," I reply, feeling a little abashed. Does he mean the evening was good or... well, you know what I mean... the night time stuff? "Yes, it was good... err... do you want a coffee?"

"I'll have a quick one then I'll have to be off." He pulls a sad face. "I could come back later if you're not doing anything... we could... relive last night."

So, he's talking about the night time stuff, I'm sure of it. The playful look in his eyes gives it away if not his words. "Sure, why not. I'm not up to much today, just the usual catch-up with washing and ironing – all the mundane stuff really."

Ryan nods his head. "Yep, I know what you mean. OK, well I'll be all done by..." He peers at his watch, "about one o'clock – do you fancy going out for a Sunday lunch somewhere?"

"I'd love to," I say as I smile sweetly and turn to make him a coffee. "My treat this time though."

"No way – you always provide the coffee, and last night, a place for me to sleep, so our trip out this afternoon will be my way of saying thank you."

"But..."

"No buts – my treat." He rises from the chair and walks over to me, wrapping his arms around my waist. I shiver as he kisses the back of my neck. "I wish I didn't have to go," he whispers into my ear. "I want to make love to you again..."

Oh my God – how I haven't just poured boiling water all over the worktop I'll never know. "I... err..." I manage to place the kettle back on its base and turn around to face him. "Maybe... later?"

He smiles and kisses me softly on the lips. "Later." He pulls away and leaves the kitchen. I hear him head towards the bathroom. Oh God, he is such a smoothie. I'm not kidding you, my body is aching and screaming out for him – *come back and let's do it right now, right here, on the floor, over the worktop, across the sink, anywhere, I don't care where.* I blush from my own thoughts as images flicker through my mind. I'll just have to be patient and wait for him to return from the football match.

He's a sports teacher during the week and a kid's football coach and team manager at the weekends – he's always very busy. I met him through school, as I am a teaching assistant at one of the primary feeder schools and our two schools have strong links. So strong in fact, that we all have Christmas dos together, which is where I first met him, and he asked me out, even though I was dressed as a turkey (that's yet another story). I can't be all that bad you know if he wanted to date me while I donned a pair of plastic turkey feet, a feathery turkey suit and even my legs were covered with a prickly heat rash which he thought was just make-up to make it look like I had turkey legs (yes, once again, the other story). Obviously, I had to turn him down as I was in a relationship (huh – if you could have called it a relationship) with Kallum at the time. But I can tell you, I was pretty gutted to say no to him and also flabbergasted that a good-looking man like him would be interested in me. I do tend to doubt myself, but I think that comes from over two years of being with Kallum, who made me feel a bit worthless, to say the least.

Anyway, I digress – which is an annoying trait of mine – oops, sorry. Ryan has just come out of the bathroom and he appears at the kitchen door looking refreshed and raring to go. He gives me a wink before disappearing to the bedroom to get dressed. Well, I assume he's getting dressed... I daren't follow him in there otherwise he will not be managing his football team this morning... or getting dressed.

I place his coffee on the table and sit down with mine, pondering over the household chores I have in store this morning. The jobs seem far less tedious now that I have the afternoon to look forward to.

"I'll drink the coffee quick and then I really have to go." Ryan joins me at the table, picks up his mug of coffee and drinks it in short, swift slurps as fast as he can. "I'm running a bit late – I've got to get home to change first."

"Don't mind me," I say with a smile. "You get going."

He stands up and adjusts his untucked shirt. "Right, I'll see you this afternoon." Leaning over me, he kisses my lips softly again.

Argh – it drives me crazy. I want to kidnap him, lock him in my bedroom and kiss him all day long (probably a bit more than kissing to be honest). "OK, I'll see you later." I pull myself up and escort him to the front door where he does it again. I swear, one more time and he's going to be seized and used for my own pleasure. Then he does it again. "Go," I say, breathing in his scent. "You'll be really late at this rate." Or you'll be tied to my bed and sexed upon (I don't even know if that's a word – sexed) to within an inch of your life.

"I'm going. I'll see you later Susie Satchel..."

And again, he kisses me softly. For goodness sake, I wish he would stop that – it's the way he does it that is so insatiably desirable. I'm a young woman, I have hormones and emotions. He can't just keep kissing me in such a seductive way and think he can get away with it. "Bye," I manage to splutter as saliva swills around my mouth. "See you later."

He steps out of the front door and walks away, turning his head around to give me an alluring smile one last time before he disappears down the road to where he left his car last night (annoyingly, there was nowhere for him to park outside my flat by the time we got home).

Phew, thank goodness, he's gone. I would not have wanted to be blamed for him not getting to the football match or for me not getting my clothes washed or ironed ready for work tomorrow. It was a close call, it really was. I've only slept with him the once but already I can tell we were made for each other and fit together like a jigsaw puzzle – literally. I fancy him like crazy. Like no one before. I'd even go as far as saying, he leaves Jett (God rest his soul) standing.

*** 2 ***

What a lovely afternoon I've had – we've had. We went to a local carvery for a Sunday lunch, followed by the chef's special, sherry trifle. Now, we're back at mine and we have both slumped down on to the sofa, bloated and weary. We're like an elderly couple, ready for a snooze. "Thank you," I say for the umpteenth time. "I've really enjoyed this afternoon."

"Yes, it's an excellent restaurant. I'm so full though – I can hardly move."

I giggle and peer at him, half lying across one end of the sofa. "Do you need a nap?"

He nods and smiles. "Shall we?"

"Shall we what?"

"Shall we go to bed and we can both have one?"

"Oh," I say with an air of demure. "Yes, come on then." Dragging ourselves up from the sofa, we plod through to the bedroom, partially undress and climb into bed.

Ryan reaches over and cuddles into me, closing his eyes instantly. "Just an hour, that's all. OK?"

"OK," I whisper and close my eyes too.

It wasn't an hour, it was more like three. OK, so only two of those hours were spent sleeping (a little more than we had anticipated – we must have been tired). I'm sure you can imagine what activity took up the other hour. It was obvious that it would happen and it's all his fault because he kisses me like he does.

So, anyway, the time is now 6.45pm and we're just getting up. I pull my dressing gown on and head out of the bedroom as the kettle is calling. "Coffee?" I call back, knowing full well that the answer will be, yes.

Ryan joins me in the kitchen and we sit at the table slurping sweet, hot coffee. He pulls his phone out from his pocket and begins to thumb over it. "Better text the team to make sure we're prepared for tomorrow."

"Oh?" I query, while peering at his mobile. It drives me insane to think that my stupid, drunken *facebook* message is in his phone, only a couple of taps away. I would literally die if he ever read it, it was that bad. Luckily, we're not friends on *facebook*... yet. We haven't got that far but I'm dreading the day when he says we should connect on there. Even luckier, he doesn't really use *facebook* a great deal so I'm slightly relieved by that because it means that my stupid message is in his 'other messages' folder which means that he wouldn't necessarily come across it unless he searched for it.

"Yes, we've got the year eleven leaver's Olympics do this week."

"Oh, yes, of course. I almost forgot." I'm not sure how I could have forgotten because two of our year groups have been invited to go and watch – which includes me, yippee. There are just two weeks and three days left at school before the summer holidays start, although, you can't really count the last three days, so it's just two weeks left.

Since I've worked in a school, I've noticed that the majority of the staff are on a constant countdown cycle and will use any excuse to *not* count down the odd days at the beginning or end of a week, hence, just two weeks left of the term. I cannot wait for the holidays as I will be seeing a lot more of my parents, taking a trip to Devon to see Clair and her boyfriend, Archie (he's very nice) and possibly/hopefully see a bit more of Ryan, if he's up for it.

"How could you forget – you're coming to watch with Mrs Pearson and your class."

I grin sheepishly. To be honest, I had forgotten completely but then this new relationship with Ryan has rapidly gone from zero to one million in a matter of weeks and I've been a bit blown away by it all. I haven't even seen my mum and dad in as many weeks which is unheard of. Mum keeps texting me to ask how I'm doing and if I'm OK. Then she sends another text saying, 'Do you need money?' or 'Are you struggling financially, honey?' I haven't quite plucked up the courage to tell her, or Dad, that I have a new boyfriend. Not that they would mind, don't get me wrong, but I think they would worry too much, what with my past two boyfriend experiences in one week. Blimey, that last sentence sounds like I've been around the block (boyfriend-wise) quite a few times – it wasn't like that, honestly. Anyway, I'm digressing again – I really should stop that.

"I said I'd *almost* forgotten, not that I *had* forgotten about it," I lie as I screw my nose up and smile sweetly. "There's so much going on at school, at the moment, and I never realised it could be so manic at the end of the school year."

"Tell me about it. This bloody Olympics day has taken up all my spare time just lately, I doubt I'll be doing that one again – and I certainly won't be listening to any of Amber's bright ideas either."

"How is she?" I ask, suddenly acquiring an overwhelming interest in her. I haven't said anything to Ryan about her, but I recently saw her with a new boyfriend, which was quite a relief to me, I can tell you. You see, Amber used to be totally infatuated with Ryan to the point that she would not leave him alone and she lived in some sort of a fantastical world where she believed that he felt the same way about her as she did him. Unfortunately, Amber did nothing to gain any respect from Ryan because she made a complete fool of herself at the Christmas do with her licentious behaviour towards him.

"Don't know... she hardly talks to me these days. She's gone all weird."

"Weirder than she was before?"

Ryan nods his head nonchalantly. "Yeah, she's always giving me these freaky bog-eyed looks and she smirks at me a lot but says nothing."

"Hmm, that's odd... I mean, after how she was at Christmas." I can't tell him she's got a new boyfriend – it's not my business to do so and anyway, so what if she has, Ryan wouldn't care. I really don't understand why she has got to be so off with him though – that's a bit unfair. I do have her as a friend on *facebook,* but I've hardly ever spoken to her, apart from the one time, after the Christmas do, when she thanked me for looking after her while she was chucking-up in the toilets and then she commented about how she'd never been looked after by a turkey before – funny – not. Anyway, I think she hates me now because she was told that night, that Ryan was going to be stuffing the turkey (me) and she got all upset about it. Then, I discovered she had a boyfriend when I went on a short holiday with my parents because she was there too – I was gobsmacked to see her at the same caravan site as me. And the worst bit was that my parents ended up telling her practically my whole life story, which upset me massively as I then worried that Amber would go back to school and tell Ryan everything. Thank goodness she didn't because it would be super-awkward to now drop in the fact to Ryan, that I actually had two boyfriends in the Christmas week, when he wanted to date me as well, and one of those boyfriends died. Can you see how bad that looks? Can you understand why I have got to get rid of that message on Ryan's *facebook* account?

"I know, I don't get it. It's like she has some sort of secret she's keeping from me."

Oh God – I feel sick. My mouth opens but I can't think of anything to say. She's keeping *my* secret, I'm sure of it. Is she waiting for the right time to tell him? "Does..." I splutter the word out but am unable to continue as my heart races.

Ryan peers at me amused. "Does?"

"Sorry, my throat seems to be a bit croaky and sore." I cough, feigning pain. I rub my hand over my throat and gulp.

"Are you OK?" Ryan peers at me perplexed, possibly due to my sudden ailment.

"Yes, fine... I think." Again, I cough and squeeze my fingers around my throat.

"Do you need another drink? Water?"

"No, no – I'll be fine." My face is flushed but it's been caused more by the fear of Ryan finding out about Jett (the dead boyfriend – the other story) than the actual coughing. I don't know why I've got in such a state about it all really – it's not as if I was seeing Ryan at the time but I guess it's because I opted out of telling him about the extra boyfriend at Christmas and have only told him about my life with Kallum. So now it seems a bit too late to throw in boyfriend number two as an afterthought. Oh God, why have I got myself into this mess? I feel like Amber will forever hold this over me and forever have a little secret waiting in the shadows for that day when she can use it against me. I've heard she can be quite a bitch when she wants to be.

Ryan has been watching me intently for the past minute or so. "Are you sure you're OK?"

I nod and smile at him waveringly.

"What were you going to say anyway?"

"I..." I do need to know so I'm just going to come out with it, even if the answer is not what I want to hear. "I was only going to ask if Amber knew about us, that's all."

Ryan shakes his head. "No... it's got nothing to do with her at all." He reaches across the table and takes my hand in his. "Don't worry about her – she is not a threat to you in the slightest and I don't care if she knows or not."

"No, I'm not worried or threatened by her... I just wondered, that's all. I'd imagine she'd be really funny with you though because she'd think it was true about what she was told at the Christmas do."

"Oh, that. You mean the stuffing-the-turkey bit. Well, she can think what she likes, I really don't care. All I care about is you." He leans over and kisses me, and suddenly I feel so much better. Maybe one day I could tell him the truth and explain why I didn't want to tell him in the first place. If we stay together for any length of time, one day he'll understand, I know he will.

Clair always says I'm daft for keeping things hushed or covering things up and she insists that I stop telling lies because they'll eventually swallow me up in a big black hole of fabrication. It's all right for her to be judgemental and say things like that because she doesn't tend to get herself in the pickles that I do. I'm sure I'm a magnet for mess-ups. How else do I get out of them than to tell little white lies though? And they are only little white lies – I'm sure I've never gone a darker hue of white. Yet, Clair's motto is, 'It's better to get hurt by the truth than comforted with a lie'. Easy for her to say.

*** 3 ***

Ryan left at half past ten last night but not before he whisked me back off to the bedroom for another... well, you know. It was intense, I can tell you that much. I truly think I'm falling in love with him – OK, I've already fallen in love with him. Although, that word, 'love' hasn't been mentioned yet (apart from in the 'make love' sense), which is a first for me and a stark contrast to my last two boyfriends who declared their undying love for me within the first week. Sadly, Jett told me he loved me on the very night he died which was terribly heartbreaking. I felt that I loved him too which was even sadder. Anyway, what I'm trying to say is that it seems like this relationship is taking a much slower pace. I had been seeing Ryan for three weeks before we slept together and like I've just said, that 'love' word hasn't been spoken of... yet. Maybe this is how relationships are meant to be. Perhaps this is how relationships are built to last – I don't know but I sure am enjoying finding out.

I'm off to school now and as I drive through the busy town, stopping and starting in the traffic, my thoughts drift back to thinking about Ryan's phone and the message. I know he thumbs some sort of pattern over the screen to unlock it, but I haven't yet managed to watch him so that I can memorise it. But, and this is a big but, if I can pull off my cunning little plan to get into his phone, then I won't need to know how to unlock it because he will tell me how. Mwahahaha.

I've been so wrapped up in my thoughts that I didn't realise I'm at school already. I park in my usual spot and fight my way through the crowds of parents and up the path towards the reception. There's a good atmosphere at school now and I think it's because *everyone* is doing the countdown until the summer holidays. Both the staff and the children all seem to be on a high.

I say a quick good morning to the office staff as I pass by and head to the toilets to put my things in my locker. Jade is in the toilets, fiddling with her hair which, unusually, she has tied up in a bun today. She's a lovely girl and the first person I became friendly with at school – she's a teaching assistant, just like me.

"Morning," she says with a big smile as she peers at me through the mirror. "How was your weekend?"

She knows all about Ryan and she knows everything else too. For some reason, I blurted it all out to her one day and we became firm friends soon after (no one will ever replace my bestest friend of all, Clair, though – I know, I know, 'bestest' isn't a word but she is my bestest). I've been out clubbing with Jade and her friends several times and I even learnt how to pole dance (maybe I should show Ryan what I can do... OK, I don't have a pole at home so maybe I won't).

"Very nice, thank you. I saw Ryan again." I grin through the mirror.

"You're both becoming a bit of an item, aren't you?"

"Yes, I really like him." I place my bag inside my locker and heave a sigh. "Only two weeks left."

"And three days," Jade adds.

"Yes, but we don't need to count those."

Jade shrugs and pulls a couple of strands of hair down, on to the sides of her face, from her bun.

"It looks nice," I say. "Makes you look a lot younger." I let a little giggle out. "You look about twelve now."

"Thanks – I always wanted to look twelve, ever since I was thirteen." We both laugh and head out of the toilets together. "Oh..." Jade stops and turns to me. "You haven't forgotten the meeting this morning at eleven, have you?"

I peer at her puzzled, searching my brain for an answer because once again, I have forgotten yet another thing and I have no idea what she's talking about. I say once again because I have had several episodes of not having a clue what's going on at school because I live in la-la land. These bouts of 'forgetfulness' (OK, maybe they're not bouts of forgetfulness and more like spells of complete oblivion as to what's going on around me) have got me in some sticky situations, including the humiliating clown incident (yes, you know I'm going to say it – another story). School is so fast paced, and I haven't even been here a year yet so I'm sure someone out there *must* be able to forgive me for not quite having got my head around everything yet.

Our Headteacher, Mr Reynolds, even dished out a school calendar and the whole school plan to me. Well, to be perfectly honest, he practically threw them at me when he was having a passive-aggressive moment, when I went through a bit of a sticky patch with him... I mean, well, it was his attitude that was sticky – not me. And then I think I made matters worse by falling off the platform at the pole dancing club, right in front of him, but again, it was an accident and not my fault and it's yet another story.

"You're giving me that vacant look again Susie."

I snap back to the present moment. "What... oh, sorry."

"You're such a daydreamer," says Jade, shaking her head despairingly. "You do know what I'm talking about, don't you?"

I straighten up, pushing my shoulders back. "Of course, I do... it's the meeting at eleven..."

"Where?"

"Err... I can't quite remember where it is... I'll have to check my diary..."

"With who?"

"Sorry?" I stare at Jade through a foggy cloud. "With who? Err... that will be..."

"You don't have a clue, do you?" Jade laughs.

"Yes, I do. It's with... was it Mr Reynolds?"

"Blimey – well done."

That was a complete guess but I'm not telling Jade because she's already eyeing me with narrowed, suspicious eyes. The meeting could have been with a number of people, thank goodness I choose the right one. I grin assuredly. "Thank you – I am getting better at this you know. I'm pretty much on the ball these days."

"OK, so what's the meeting about? Just testing you now."

A cold shiver runs through me – I haven't the foggiest – I do not know. "Oh, err... wasn't it something to do with..."

Jade scans my face which makes me uncomfortable – have I got 'liar' written all over it? "With what?" she quizzes.

"You know, I just can't remember right now. I will check my diary though." To be honest, there's nothing in my diary otherwise I would have seen it... and remembered. But then, have I even remembered to look in my diary recently? No.

"Susie, how could you not know – you're a nightmare. I know you don't have a clue."

I sigh as we begin to walk slowly down the corridor. "OK, I admit, I don't have a clue."

Jade huffs and pats me on the shoulder. "I knew you wouldn't, so it's a good job I'm telling you. Can you imagine old Reynolds' face if you didn't turn up?"

"Oh God, yes. He hates me enough already."

Jade lets out a giggle. "I have to say, your first year has not got off to a great start, has it?"

"No, it hasn't... but surely it can't be my fault." We arrive outside my classroom as the children are walking in from the playground. "Right, I'd better go," I say, before mouthing a 'good morning' to my teacher, Mrs Pearson as she follows the children into the classroom. I smile at Jade and turn away.

"Wait," she says, grasping my arm, "don't you want to know where the meeting is?"

"Oh God, yes." I whisper, not wanting the children to overhear me. "Where?"

"Conference room, eleven o'clock, don't be late."

I nod at her and smile. "Thanks, I won't be late."

Jade gives me a wink and walks away (She's quite a good winker – for a girl. I, on the other hand, can't wink at all well. I usually end up looking like I've got something stuck in my eye, but I do appreciate a cool wink from someone else). Darn, I didn't ask her what the meeting is about, and I can't for the life of me think what it might be. Oh well, I guess I'll have to wait until eleven. I like meetings (not with Mr Reynolds though) because they can be very interesting sometimes and it's a chance to meet up with all the other teaching assistants. I don't see them all very often as it's such a big school and everyone rushes around all over the place, all the time. I suppose I could see some of them at break times, but I tend to stay out of the staffroom as there are some people I would not want to bump in to.

Two people to be precise. Two of the teachers to be even more exact. Miss Sarah Chambers and Miss Jane Hodges to be perfectly honest. I have my own pet names for them, Sultry Sarah and Juicy Jane which at several points were both extended to incorporate their constant behaviour problems. Sarah became, Sultry-Stirrer-Sarah which also morphed into Sultry-Slapper-Sarah and Jane was Juicy-Joker-Jane, then Juicy-Flipping-Jane and eventually made it to Juicy-Jumped-Up-Jane.

Ryan's sister, Rachel, incidentally, has names to go with their surnames too. She knows them well as she's a teacher too but not at this school. Anyway, it was by chance that I met Rachel one day, before I was even going out with Ryan (another story – God, this is boring now), and we got talking about schools and stuff. She said that she knew them, and she told me what her names were for them and we had a bit of a giggle. She's very nice but I've only ever met her once and I don't even know if she knows that me and Ryan are together now as Ryan tends not to talk about his family too much. Maybe I should ask him if Rachel knows about us as he seemed very close to his sister when I bumped into them both in a shop just before Christmas – while I was still hooked up with that Kallum-waste-of-space. And to think that I wasted over two years of my life with him.

Anyway (digressing again), as you may have guessed, I do not like Sarah or Jane one iota. Not even a smidgen (not sure which is smaller, an iota or a smidgen but you know what I mean). They have been pretty mean to me in the past, but once again, and I'm sorry to bore you senseless but, that's another story.

*** ♃ ***

I'm here. I'm on time. Well I never – I'm the first. That's awkward. Mr Reynolds is sitting at the head of the conference table thumbing through sheets of paper. He looks up as I enter the room, peering over the top of his reading glasses with his dark, beady eyes. Yuk – I hate him. I'm sorry if that sounds a tad spiteful but he's just the most obnoxious man I've ever met.

"Come in," he grunts and indicates to the chair next to him with his crooked little finger.

Oh my God – I don't want to sit right next to him. I don't want to be anywhere near him. "I... I was just..." Oh gosh, how can I get out of this? "I was just going to apologise for being late but..." I scan the table exaggeratedly. "But I see that I'm the first to arrive so... I really must pop along to the toilet quickly – I'll be right back." I give a wry smile and exit the room sharpish.

As I enter the toilets, I see that all the teaching assistants are in here. I'm sure they've been hiding out waiting to see who goes in the conference room first. Ha – well, it's not going to be me. I dart into the nearest free cubicle and take a deep breath as I sit down. I don't really need to use the toilet but I'm staying in here until I hear the others leave, then I know I will be the last to go into the meeting. I can be so cunning sometimes and I can hardly be frowned upon by Mr Reynolds now because I was the first one there... initially.

There's an air of excitement and lots of chatter coming from the women on the other side of my cubicle door. I don't think any of them noticed me slip into this toilet, so I can sit it out until they're all gone. And it sounds like they are starting to leave already.

Once I am sure that they have all gone, I flush the toilet unnecessarily (I guess it's more out of habit) and exit the cubicle. I walk over to the mirrors and peer at my reflection while I run the tap, needlessly. Then I leave the toilets and head back to the conference room. I open the door and step inside...

Oh God – no. Why?

"We saved your seat," says Jade, peering at me from across the room, with a glint in her eye.

"Mine?" I mutter, shaken by the sea of expectant faces staring at me.

"We are now waiting for you, Miss Satchel."

Mr Reynolds' voice grates on my nerves. "Oh, sorry, I..."

"Please, will you sit down," says Mr Reynolds, an irritated tone rising in his utterance.

I can't believe they've done it to me. Why? I'm sure they've done it deliberately. How could they?

Jade watches me as I walk around the table to the top end where Mr Reynolds is. "Mr Reynolds said that was your seat so we saved it for you." She grins sheepishly.

I can't help it, but I shoot a steely glare at Jade and she gives me a helpless shrug back. I'm sure it's not her fault but I'm truly broken. I hate Mr Reynolds so much that the mere thought of sitting next to him repulses me. Shuffling around the back of his chair, I pull out the one on the left of him and drop down into the seat, staring sullenly across the expansive table.

"Now, ladies and gentle-*man*..." Mr Reynolds peers over at our one male teaching assistant and grins at him with a sickly look of comradeship. "Today is the day you have all been waiting for this term."

My ears prick to attention, as I wonder what he's talking about, even though I'm feeling nauseous by the sickly-sweet smell of his aftershave wafting over me.

"I have it here." He waves a piece of paper in the air and looks around the table at everyone, smugly. "Now, I'm sure you all want to know who your teacher is next year and which year team you will be working with, so I will go around the table, one by one."

Ooh – I hadn't even thought about next year. So, it's plainly obvious that we don't stay with the same teacher year on year. I don't know if that's a good thing or a bad thing, to be honest. I've never really thought about it but then I am new to all this school stuff. On second thoughts, it's a shame because I've only just got used to my teacher, Mrs Pearson. She's very good at what she does and has helped me to learn the job, immeasurably.

"When I've finished reading the list, if you have any queries, please see me individually after the meeting." Mr Reynolds begins to read out the teaching assistant's names and the teacher who they will be working with. There are a few whoops and yippees and one or two say, 'Oh...OK' like they're unhappy with their partnering. I'm getting apprehensive as Mr Reynolds works his way around the table because, of course, I'll be the last to know, but then again, you know what they say, 'save the best till last'...

Finally, Mr Reynolds has got around to me. "And Miss Satchel... you will be with..."

Did I hear that right? My face has suddenly gone hot and I know I am staring out across the table like a rabbit in the headlights.

"Miss Satchel?"

I turn my head towards Mr Reynolds – he's staring at me with an odd expression. His eyes have narrowed to slits and there's a hint of a smirk in the corner of his mouth.

"Are you feeling all right Miss Satchel?"

I snort a kind of, 'yes, fine' and smile waveringly. I feel utterly sick. I'm doomed. How could he do that? He knows what went on before. Why has he done that? How can I complain? He would have the upper hand then. What a complete bast...

***

Hi honey, how are you? I haven't seen you for so long. Must be 3 weeks! Are you OK? Have you got a flatmate yet to help with those bills? Do you need any help with money, honey? Oh, ha ha, that's funny and it rhymes. Love Mum xx

Yes, very funny Mum and no, I'm fine for money and yes, it's been a while. I'll pop round one evening this week, I promise. Love you xx

Love you too, honey xx

I'm sitting in my flat, staring at the TV screen, not having a clue what I'm looking at. I wish Ryan was here, so I could spout off to him about how life's not fair but he's busy preparing for their Olympics event tomorrow.

Hi Clair, hope you're OK, didn't hear back from you. You'll never guess which teacher I'm with next year. Xx

I don't expect a reply, especially if Clair is on a late shift tonight. She's a nurse and although I admire her for doing it, I don't envy the long, unsociable hours she does.

You've just caught me on my break! Oh God, it's not that bloody, Jane, is it? Thinking of you and I want to know what your idea for Ryan is – NOW! Why will he be near a toilet? Meant to text you sooner but you know what I'm like. I compose messages in my head and then think I've done them. It's not until I step into reality that I realise I haven't actually sent the message, lol xx

Yes, I do know what you're like, but I know you're not as bad as me. I've got my head so far up in the clouds that I'm reaching the exosphere! Xx

Exosphere? Is that a word? Lmao xx

Yes, I read about it on a science poster at school. It's the highest part of the earth's atmosphere... I think! Lol xx

So, is it Jane? Xx

No, Sarah. She's a worse bitch than Jane. I hate Mr Reynolds – he's done this deliberately! You should have seen the filthy little smirk on his grotty, old face when he announced it.

What a nasty piece of work he is then! Look, Suse, I've got to go back to work now so I'll catch up with you soon. Rise above it – I know you can. AND make sure you send me a text back, so I can read it later – I WANT TO KNOW YOUR IDEA FOR RYAN xxxx

No, I can't tell her. I shouldn't have said anything to her – especially as she's a nurse. My idea is a little bizarre, but I don't see any other way of sneaking into Ryan's phone's apps without him being suspicious. He's already a bit overly protective of his new phone but I expect that is my fault anyway as his last one did end up down a toilet (but remember, he doesn't know that – right?).

It's just a stupid idea really. I'm going to spy on him whenever he reaches for his phone so that I can see what the unlock pattern is and then, when he's asleep, I'll be able to access the facebook app. Simple. Love you Clair xxx

I hate lying to her but after thinking it through a little deeper, I decided that the best course of action is not to tell anyone. Not a soul. I'm not even sure it's going to work yet.

Anyway, back to the dire matter in hand – Sarah. Sultry Sarah, oh my God, she's my teacher next year and we're in year five. I am convinced that Mr Reynolds had an evil glint of sadistic satisfaction in his eye when he told me I would be working with her. How can he possibly think it will work? Or, and I've only just thought about this, maybe he knows it *won't* work and it is his malicious little plot to get rid of me. I hate him. I hate him. I think he hates me too.

***

It's a gorgeous day today. There isn't a single cloud in the sky and the warm, gentle breeze caresses my face as we walk the children to Ryan's school, Hightown Secondary. Our children are going to watch some of the track and field events today but also, have a go at a Gladiator's Olympics assault course as well which Ryan and his team have been working hard at preparing for today. Thank goodness the weather is on everyone's side otherwise it would have been a nightmare for Ryan and his staff if it had been raining. I will no doubt see Ryan a lot today, but we've already agreed to keep things low-key for now, which I am more than relieved about. There's no way I want his colleague, Amber, to know we're seeing each other.

To my surprise, it is Amber who is waiting for us at the school field gates. She welcomes the children on to the field, says hello to Mrs Pearson and then her face drops as she sees me at the end of the line. "Oh, hello Miss..."

"Satchel," I snort at her, as I walk past.

"Of course, it is – Miss Satchel, how are you?"

"Fine, thank you. How are you?"

"Great – just great, thanks." She looks me up and down with an air of self-importance. "Any fancy costume fails of late?"

"Sorry?" I snap as we begin to traverse the field. I don't mean to snap at her but since I bumped into her on holiday, I can't help feeling that she's all out to humiliate me in any way she can. I'm not kidding you, I would love to be bitchy right now and tell her who sleeps in my bed.

"Costume fails – turkeys, clowns, that sort of thing."

I think I hate her almost as much as Mr Reynolds. "No, I've had quite a dull time of it lately." Huh – if only she knew that Ryan and I share breakfast together and all kinds of other things. If only she knew how close we've become and how sexy he is naked. I would so love to tell her but I daren't for fear of the repercussions – she knows too much about me (thanks to my mum and dad, although they were just defending me, I suppose – that's the other story). "How's your boyfriend?"

Amber practically swoons when I mention her boyfriend. I've only ever met him the once, but I suppose he seemed nice enough. "Oh, it's going fantastically well – his parents absolutely love me."

"Good for you." Good for her – huh, to be honest I think she's rushed in there a bit. I mean, meeting his parents and going on a caravan holiday with them so soon (that's where I first met her boyfriend, but I'm sure I've mentioned that already).

"Of course, I haven't told Ryan about my new fella yet – I don't want to go upsetting him, you know." She lets out a pathetic little giggle and places her fingers over her lips. "So, pinky promise – yes?" She winks and taps the side of her nose in some sort of a covert code.

I stare aghast, my jaw dropping at her words. Is she serious? Does she really, *still* believe that Ryan would be upset? Has she *still* got this obsessive infatuation with him? Seriously? I snap my mouth shut and shake my head. I can't seem to find any words to follow that comment. "Hmm," I mumble, trying to wipe the stunned look from my face as we arrive at the tents.

"See you around, Miss..."

"Satchel," I grunt. "Miss Satchel. Remember? Sa...tch...el – Satchel."

"I do know your name," she retorts, "I was just calling you, Miss – it's what we do in schools. Chill out Miss Satchel – you'll give yourself a hernia." She bounces off in her expensive, trendy trainers, across the field to the third tent where Ryan and the rest of his staff are talking.

I'm sure my blood is boiling and my face scarlet because she has just made me look like a paranoid idiot in front of Mrs Pearson and the children. One little boy is whispering to his friend and then they both start to giggle. They are laughing at me. I know it. I must be acting unreasonable. I need to chill out. Amber is right. Oh my God.

Could I really give myself a hernia? What's a hernia anyway?

*** 5 ***

Surprisingly, it turned out to be a lovely day. I managed to get close enough to Ryan, several times, to smile at him, knowingly. He winked at me once too which made my heart skip a beat, I'm sure. He messaged me at lunch time (although I didn't know where he was), to ask if he could see me tomorrow evening and did I fancy going out to the cinema or getting a take-away and slobbing out. I said yes, obviously, and I didn't mind which one we did, although I do like the idea of a take-away and slobbing out. I'm such a slob-out kind of girl at heart.

So, I've just returned home from school now and I'm going to change quickly and then visit my parents. I'm toying with the idea of telling them about Ryan, although Mum will probably get over excited and want to invite him round for Sunday lunch or something stupid like that. Or even worse, one of Dad's barbecues. My dad has an apron fetish and some of his barbecue aprons are really not the sort of thing you want your new boyfriend seeing when he meets your parents for the first time. You know, first impressions and all that kind of stuff.

Is that it? I would have thought you'd come up with a really elaborate plan like the last one, lol xx

Clair's not stupid you know. But I can't tell her because... well, my plan might not even be legal. Cautiously, I send a reply. *Yes, that's it, I'm afraid. Nothing as extravagant as the men's toilets! I'll let you know how I get on xx*

You must, do not forget, also, do you want to ask him if he would like to come to Devon over the hols to meet your wonderful, best friend? It's up to you but let me know either way xx

Thanks, Clair, I will. I'm off to Mum's now to tell them the news about me and Mr Ryan Bagshaw xx

Bagshaw? Oh God Suse – couldn't you have picked someone with a different surname, lmao! So, you work at Baghurst, you're a Satchel, he's a Bag-shaw... for God's sake, don't tell me he works at Bagsville School or something like that! Xx

Ha ha, very funny! No, he works at Hightown (no baggage there!). Now go away, I'm busy. Love you xx

Love ya more xx

Mum and Dad live in a quaint little cul-de-sac on the other side of town which is where I grew up. Jett (my boyfriend who died) lived next door with his grandparents (long story) and we grew up together. Then he disappeared when I was a kid and returned 15 years later (last Christmas), having turned into the most gorgeous man I'd ever set eyes upon (I had only just split up with Kallum the day before – dumped on Christmas day, can you believe it – when I met up with Jett again). We fell for each other instantly, our desire for each other was insatiable – within five days he was gone. Killed by a drunk driver. He's the one I haven't told Ryan about.

Anyway, it's not like me to have not seen my parents for three weeks so they are either thinking that I've got these financial problems which Mum keeps going on about (why that would make me stay away from them, I don't know), or I'm having a Jett-grieving spell again. Mum worries too much really and if there's nothing to worry about, she'll find something to fret over – even if it means she has got to take on the neighbour's worries as her own (she's very close to her neighbours) just so she can have something to trouble herself with. So, I'm now on my way to allay any uneasiness Mum might have.

I pull in to my parent's drive and see the living room curtains twitch. Mum is at the door before I've even got out of my car. "Honey... oh, honey. How have you been – it's been so long? Far too long." She has flung her arms around my shoulders and is squeezing the life out of me, like I've just returned from an around-the-world expedition.

"It's been three weeks, Mum, not three years."

"Yes but..."

"Can we go in before you crush me to death?"

"Oh honey, I've missed you." She peers into my face as she lets me go. "Is everything all right?"

"Yes Mum, everything's just fine."

Brushing her hand over my hair, she then wraps her arm around my shoulders and guides me in. "No little mishaps lately?"

"No, everything's just fine, like I said, please stop worrying so much. Is Dad home?"

"Not yet – are you staying for some tea?"

"If you've got enough, that would be great."

"Your dad has always got enough," says my mum, beaming at me like I'm a long-lost child.

I suppose I can understand how she feels as I am their only child.

My dad does most of the cooking so that Mum can spend her time worrying about things. It works, I suppose, and they've lived a long, happy life together. And although she can be a little over-the-top sometimes and quite frustrating, I love my mum to bits – and my dad too. "How are things going?" Mum asks with a hint of unfounded apprehension in her voice.

"Yes, good." I follow her through to the kitchen and she prepares two coffee mugs.

"Is Clair doing all right? Have you heard from her?"

"Yes, she loves her new job."

"And the boyfriend? Everything going all right with him?"

"Swimmingly," I say with a smile. "She's very happy in Devon."

"Good. Will you be going to see her over the summer?" Mum flicks the kettle on and stands with her back to the worktop, her arms folded in front of her.

"Yes, definitely. I'll probably go down for a week."

Mum nods agreeably. "And how's school?"

"It's OK – only two weeks left."

"I know, I had a look on the council website, it gives you so much information about schools. How wonderful to have such a long time off over the summer." The kettle boils and Mum turns to make the coffees. "So, what have you been up to, apart from working?"

"Not much really." Gosh, this is such a stilted conversation. It's like we don't really know each other and we're just making small talk. I'm guessing it's me who is a little tense, but I don't want to tell Mum about Ryan and then have to go over it all again when Dad gets home. I'd rather tell them both together, maybe over dinner. And besides, there will then be less time for Mum to worry about anything she can think of to worry about.

I take a mug of coffee from Mum and follow her to the living room where we sit down. As soon as I'm seated, my phone tinkles. I look at Mum and she smiles at me. "A message?" she enquires. I nod at her and pull my phone from my bag.

It's a message from Jade. *Hi Susie, hope you're OK after your shock yesterday. Your face said it all. I bet Reynolds has done that deliberately. Hope you're not too upset – Sarah might even be OK. Love Jade x p.s. sorry only just texted you but I've been so busy x*

I'm fine about it (I've got to be because Reynolds is not going to beat me – I won't let it happen) but you think the same as I do...

"Who's that, honey?"

I break off from texting and look up. "It's just, Jade, from work. She's talking about our new teachers for next year."

"Oh? Do you have new ones starting?"

"No, the TAs have been assigned their new teacher for next year. Everyone gets moved around each year, apparently."

"Who are you going to be with? Anyone nice?" Mum sighs. "I hope it won't be that girl who upset you when we were on holiday."

"You mean, Amber?"

"Yes, that's the one."

I huff and try to turn it into a cough as I don't want my mum to think I'm annoyed or frustrated with her which I am. "No Mum, she's at another school."

"How do you know her then?"

"We have links with her school. Can I just reply quickly to this?" I hold my phone up and smile sweetly.

"Yes, of course honey, go ahead." Mum drinks her coffee, while perched on the edge of the sofa, and watches me.

... about Reynolds. He hates me, and I bet he's done this to try and get rid of me.

I'm sure that's not true. Anyway, Sarah asked me if I had your number today. I didn't give it to her, but I could???

Feel free, she's going to want it from me soon anyway.

OK, I'll give it to her tomorrow... unless she catches up with you first. Have a nice evening, bye x

You too and can you do me a favour and not tell Sarah or Jane about me and Ryan. I'll tell them when I'm good and ready.

Wouldn't dream of it, Susie. Relax and enjoy him x

I blush slightly at those last words because my mum is sitting opposite me and still watching me texting.

Thanks. I will x

"So, who is your teacher? Anyone nice? I know you've been happy with your one this year – what's her name?"

"Mrs Pearson and yes she's very nice – and a good teacher too." I sigh and continue. "No, for the next academic year I've got Sarah – one of the teachers who set me up for the turkey costume... and the clown thing."

"Oh, good grief, no, honey. How do you feel about that?"

"Well, what do you think?"

"Not very happy at all, I'd imagine."

"Correct, in fact I'm sure that Mr bloody Reynolds has done it deliberately."

"Why on earth would you think that?"

"For his own amusement – he's like that. I don't like him at all. He's a hateful, mean man."

"Could you talk to Mr Reynolds? Tell him how you feel?"

"I wouldn't give him the satisfaction of knowing I'm upset about it."

"Oh dear, honey, well, all you can do is see how it goes, I suppose."

I nod and sip my coffee as Mum changes the subject completely and begins to tell me some gossip about her neighbours, which I try to show an interest in but it's very trivial stuff that doesn't concern me in the slightest.

Dad came home and beamed from ear to ear when he saw me. He went into full swing, like we were having a big celebratory meal, and decided to get his trusted barbecue out and whip up some chicken, pepper and vegetable skewers which were rather yummy. He donned one of his favourite, tasteless aprons and his chef hat, which is far too small, and I think it's probably a child's one – but he loves it all the same. We're now sitting in the last of the evening sun, which has always been thankfully bestowed upon their garden and Dad has made some fruit smoothies which are refreshing and delicious. My dad loves cooking and making things but when I asked him once why he never became a chef, he said he wouldn't enjoy doing it at home then. I suppose that could be true of many professions.

"That was lovely Dad, thank you."

"Don't mention it love."

"Now we've finished our meal and I've got you both together, I have something to tell you."

"Oh?" Mum's expression has instantly turned to one of horror.

"Nothing bad," I say, reassuringly. "It's good actually."

"You've found a flatmate?" Mum's face is softening.

I shake my head and I'm just about to tell them...

"You're selling up and moving back home?" Mum jumps in again. Dad peers at her, astonished by her words.

"No, sorry, I'm not."

Dad now looks relieved, but Mum's dejected pout tells another story. "You're back with Kallum?"

"Mum," I gasp, "no way – are you mad?"

"Well, you never know – stranger things have happened," she mutters.

"If you let the poor girl speak, we might find out, Sharon," says Dad, the irritation clearly rising in his tone.

"I'm trying to help her, John. She might be finding it difficult to talk to us."

"Mum, I *am* finding it difficult..."

"There you go," says Mum, raising her hands up righteously.

"If you'd let me finish, I was going to say the only reason I'm finding it difficult to tell you, Mum, is because you won't let me get a word in."

"Oh, I'm sorry honey. Go ahead, what were you going to say?"

I tut and raise my eyebrows. "I was going to say that I have met someone... a man."

Dad lets out a laugh. "I'm relieved you didn't say a woman. I'm not sure your mum could handle that."

"Ooh no. Let's keep things how they should be." Mum giggles.

I tut again. "Anyway, I've known him since before Christmas – he's a teacher at Hightown." I glance at Mum and Dad, trying to gauge their reaction.

"You've been seeing him since before Christmas! But..." Mum shrieks.

"No, Mum – will you just hear me out."

She slaps her hand to her chest with relief. "Oh, thank goodness for that. For a moment there, I thought..."

"You thought I had three on the go at Christmas? Seriously, Mum?" I frown at her. "Give me some credit."

"What is wrong with you, Sharon?" Dad looks a little indignant.

"I just thought... Oh, I'll shut up now. Carry on honey – I'm sorry."

"I've been seeing him for a few weeks now..."

"So that's why you haven't been round to see us," says Mum. "I said to your dad, I bet she's got a new boyfriend."

Dad nods in agreement. "She did."

"When are we going to meet him?"

"I'm not sure yet – we haven't rushed into things. It's going at a nice steady pace, so I don't want to put any pressure on him. I simply wanted to let you know, that's all."

"Oh," says Mum, a little glumly.

"Hopefully you will... in time."

"Have you met his parents?" Mum enquires.

"No and he hardly ever mentions them. I'm not sure he's that close to them really."

"Oh, that's a shame."

"Well, I don't know for sure Mum, but time will tell, won't it?"

"It certainly will, honey. I look forward to meeting him when the time is right. Now..." she jumps up from her chair, "anyone for another smoothie? We should celebrate your new relationship."

*** 6 ***

I've stopped off at the late-night chemist on my way home from Mum and Dad's. As I scan the shelves I feel like a criminal – maybe I am, or potentially am, but I've got to do it, I don't see any other way out. I study the products, my heart pounding in my throat. I can't do it. I can't buy them from here. What if the checkout girl knows why I'm buying them?

I've built up a sweat and my heart continues to gallop. I look guilty – I know I do. The woman standing behind the pharmacy counter is watching me. She knows I'm a criminal, I can tell. Oh my God, I've got to get out of here...

***

I've just ordered them from *Amazon* and I can get them on one-day delivery – no one knows who I am at *Amazon*, although, they do have my name and address... Would they know why I've ordered them? Of course not – I've become overly paranoid. Get a grip of yourself Susie Satchel.

So, tomorrow they will come, hopefully discreetly packaged, and then I can plan the execution. Not an execution literally, don't get me wrong, I'm not going to execute Ryan or anything silly like that. That would be totally crazy. I'm just a little crazy, not extremely crazy.

He's coming over tonight and we decided to go for the slob-out/take-away option rather than go out to the cinema or a meal. I'm pleased as it means I don't particularly have to find some nice 'going out' clothes to wear and can slip into something more casual but nice... maybe even sexy.

So, I've got a short, flowing navy-blue skirt on and a cream blouse with navy-blue daisy print. I actually look like I *am* going out. My outfit looks far too smart to be classed as casual/slob-out gear but I'm going to pretend that I've had it on all day. In hindsight, I can't really say that because, unless my name is Sarah or Jane, I wouldn't wear such a short skirt to school. It's just above my knees, so, not super short like some girls wear them. Honestly, the sights I've seen, especially when I've been out clubbing with Jade. I mean, for goodness sake, some girl's 'skirts' barely cover their panty line but then I suppose they probably aren't wearing any pants anyway. I'm far more reserved and I think Ryan knows that, so he wouldn't believe I'd worn a short-ish skirt to school. Oh well.

He is turning up in about twenty minutes and for some reason, I feel quite nervous tonight. I expect it's because I haven't seen him for a few days and hardly spoken to him either as he's been so busy at work.

I have masses of respect for teachers (OK, I suppose I respect Sarah and Jane as well – but only as teachers) because everyone thinks that they have easy jobs because they have lots of holidays. That couldn't be any further from the truth, honestly. If they are not report-writing, sprucing up their classrooms, making display material, collecting resources, making resources, resourcing resources, organizing trips, responding to parent's queries or enquiries, planning parent's evenings, planning class lessons, planning their TA's lessons or going to training sessions and meetings, they are swimming, neck-deep in data figures. And that's all before the school day starts. So, I have deep respect as you can well imagine.

I'm pacing the living room carpet, peering out of the window each time I pass it. My heart is racing, and I feel giddy – it must be love, I reckon. It's either that or the anticipation of what will happen this evening, you know, apart from obviously eating a meal, I mean the other stuff. I don't think he'll stay though as he will want to get home, ready for an early start tomorrow.

The front door bell rings and I gasp – it's him. I was so far away in my thoughts that, although I knew he was coming, it's caught me by surprise because he is a bit earlier than I was expecting. I casually go to the front door and open it with a big, beaming smile on my face.

I freeze.

My smile drops.

Oh, my giddy aunt.

No, it's not actually my giddy aunt because I don't have a giddy aunt (I don't know why I said that in my head, but it was the first thing that came to mind in my shocked state. Thank goodness I didn't say it out loud because it would have sounded stupid but I'm sure my startled expression is screaming a thousand giddy aunties. Can you imagine that?). Right now, I wish I did have a giddy aunt because she might be able to deal with this situation far better than me.

Momentarily, I'm stunned. No, stupefied is a more apt description. I can't think of any words to say. I stare, disbelievingly. Surely, this isn't really happening. Am I dreaming – or more appropriately, having a nightmare?

He shuffles from one foot to the other, hands tucked in his trouser pockets and a sheepish grin smothering his face. He's handsome. He's lost weight. There is an uncanny, sad and distant look in his eyes. I'm overwhelmed as the image before me brings back a whole heap of baggage filled with biting emotions and deep melancholy.

"Hello." He speaks softly.

I'm clinging on to the door frame, but I can't talk. My tongue sticks to the roof of my dry mouth.

"How are you?"

I peer down at his polished shoes – they're new. His shirt and jacket are new too. His hair has recently been cut. He's smart... smarter than I remembered. He looks nice. I nod and give a wavering smile. "OK – you?"

"I'm good, thanks."

There's an awkward silence as we stare into each other's eyes. Knowingly. Nostalgically.

"You look well," he says, with a smile.

"Thanks... so do you." I think I want to cry. I know I want to shout. In fact, I'm sure I want to scream. I want to get rid of him quickly. He can't stay here. I want to know though. I want time. I want it to be a different day. A different time. A different place. Just until I know. Until I know why. Want, want, want.

He looks me up and down and I know it's with an admiring eye. I know I look the best I can look at this moment. But it's for someone else. Kallum cannot just walk back into my life like this. It's killing me inside and I don't know why. It shouldn't be. After everything he did. After everything else that has happened to me since. After Jett. After starting a relationship with Ryan. My emotions are all over the place. He has got to go. And now.

"I..." he breaks off and peers deep into my eyes.

"Yes?" I'm starting to panic as time is not on my side. I wish it were for some very strange reason which I cannot comprehend.

"Are you busy?" He peers down at the ground in front of him and kicks a tiny stone away.

"Yes, sorry." Why am I apologizing? "I've got guests coming. I'm sorry." I've said it again? Seriously?

Kallum nods his head. "OK... Sorry for turning up unannounced." Now he's at it but then he *should* be saying sorry and he *should* say it a hundred million times more.

"It's OK. Another time maybe."

"Another time. Yes... right... OK." He gives a faltering smile and turns on his heels.

I close the door swiftly as if the action of doing so will make him go away quicker – leave my mind quicker. I turn around and lean back against the door, closing my eyes as I'm flooded with raw emotions. Guilt overrides everything else as I try to readjust my thoughts and gain composure.

Moments later, a knock at the door jolts me and I turn, fearfully. I can see a tall figure on the other side, through the obscure glass. Oh my God, he's back. I thrust the door open, my mouth open, ready to say, please go now.

Ryan peers at me perplexed. "Are you OK? You look like you've just seen a ghost. What were you doing against the door?" He grins at me and shakes his head, despairingly. "What are you up to, Miss Satchel?"

"Nothing, err... come in... just err..." I step aside and let him in. Did he see Kallum leave? Surely, they must have passed each other. Does he know what Kallum looks like? Oh God. "I was just err... looking at the walls... in the hallway... I might decorate..."

Ryan shoots me a baffled glance as he passes. "Does the hallway need decorating?"

No, it doesn't because I did it recently – when I was going through my bereaved, lonely and bored patch, at the beginning of the year. "Yes, it does," I lie. "I don't like the colour." I love the colour, but I guess I may have to change it now, just to prove a point. I'm so deceitful – I hate it.

"It looks fresh..." Ryan peers at the walls closer, "... and... fairly new." He turns and frowns at me. "Are you sure it hasn't been done recently?"

"Not unless the paint-fairies came in and did it while I was asleep." I shrug and try to laugh it off. "Anyway, how are you?" My heart is starting to calm down now and I think I may have just got away with it.

"I'm good – the holidays can't come soon enough though."

We're still standing in the hallway and the atmosphere is strained. He didn't kiss me when he came through the door but I'm guessing that's probably my fault as I know I must have appeared standoffish – I know I felt cold and distant for a moment. "Yes, I'm looking forward to them too."

Ryan shifts on his feet, uncomfortably. "So... shall we...?" He indicates to the door, leading to the kitchen.

"Oh, yes, go in." God, why is this so awkward – is it me?

He opens the kitchen door and walks in as I follow behind. "I thought, for a moment, we were going to stand in the hallway all night, picking paint colours."

I giggle and instantly warm to his charm again.

"Come here, you," he says, pulling me towards him. He wraps his arms around my waist and kisses me softly, on the lips. "I've missed you."

"It's only been..." I break off and think. How long is it? I should know. How stupid. Kallum's unexpected visit has really thrown me.

"Three days... if you count today." He kisses me again and I feel like melting into him. "Too long..."

"Yes..."

Somehow, we've backtracked out of the kitchen, across the hallway and in to my bedroom – and all while kissing each other, intensely. He lays me down on the bed and proceeds to undress me, in between removing his own clothes. "I hope you're not too hungry," he whispers into my ear. "Can it wait?"

I nod. "Yes... it can."

***

Wow – that was such a profound experience. Although that elusive word, love, was not mentioned, I know he felt it, the same way as I did. I'm in love with him and annoyed with myself that I almost let Kallum come between us. What was I thinking of?

Ryan jumps out of bed and heads to the bathroom for a quick shower, while I pull on my dressing gown and head towards the kettle. We're going to order a take-away, to be delivered, as I don't think either of us have the strength to walk out of the flat. My phone is on the table and as I pass it, I notice the blue light flashing, indicating a notification or message. I pick my phone up and peer at the screen. It's a text message from Kallum. Oh no, not now. Why is he doing this? Why now, after so long?

Hi Susie, sorry to turn up unannounced. You looked amazing. Could we meet up for a chat sometime? Kallum x

A kiss? He's put a kiss on the end of his message. What's he playing at? Has he forgotten what he did? Has his baby even been born yet? I listen out and can hear the shower running so I reply quickly while my heart feels like it's jumped up to my throat again. *Hello Kallum, good to see you looking so well too. What do you want to chat about? Regards Susie.* I press send. 'Regards Susie', with no kiss. It sounds formal and that's exactly how I want it to sound. But I've asked a question, oh dear, that means he'll reply. I listen again for the shower and it's still going. I don't like this clandestine texting behind Ryan's back – I'm in love with him, although he doesn't know it yet. Or does he?

About old times. Good times. I'd like to hear about what you've been up to. How you're doing. That's all. I hope we can still be friends x

Oh my God – really? Do I meet him, or not? I have no idea what to do. It could be a genuine, harmless request but why's he suddenly showing an interest in me again – after more than six months, seven months, in fact.

I'm not sure it would be a good idea. Why now? I don't get it, Kallum. Absentmindedly, I flick the kettle on and prepare two mugs of coffee.

Several minutes pass and I've just made the coffee when my phone bleeps again. *Because I love you still and can't get you out of my head x*

"That feels better... are you OK?"

I'm standing in the middle of the kitchen, phone in hand, with a gobsmacked expression as Ryan walks in. Instinctively, I slip the phone into my dressing gown pocket and grab the two mugs of steaming hot coffee. "Yes, fine. Here you are." I pass him a mug and we sit down at the table.

Once again, Ryan is looking at me mystified as he speaks. "Chinese? Indian? Pizza? What do you want?" He peers deeply into my eyes...

"Susie?"

"Yes?"

"Are you OK, you've been acting kind of weird? Has someone called you?" He peers at the pocket of my dressing gown.

"Yes... err... I'm sorry, it's just... my mum... yes, it's my mum – she's having a bit of bother..." Where is this going? "...with her..." Ryan continues to stare at me, clueless. "...with her feet..." Her feet? Where the hell did I get that from?

"Oh?" Ryan perks up and looks at me with interest now. Or is he just relieved that I'm not actually as weird as he thought I was a moment ago?

"Yes, she's got... well, she's had an accident and broken her toes..."

"Toes? More than one?"

"Yes... about three, I think."

"I bet that's painful," he says, frowning.

"Yes, she can hardly walk – poor thing." I hate myself. Why have I said all of this? I *am* weird.

"How did she do it?" Ryan sounds genuinely concerned.

I pause for a moment, realising that I'm not going to get out of this one easily. "Oh," I say, gesturing with my phone, "she... she fell down the stairs – what a silly thing she is."

Ryan nods his head, his mouth turned down. "There's not a lot they can do for broken toes. I don't think so anyway."

"No, there's not," I reply, with conviction. How do I know? I haven't got a clue, to be honest.

"Has she been to the hospital to get checked out?" Ryan sips his coffee and keeps a fixed gaze on me which is really making me feel uncomfortable. Doesn't he believe me?

"Yes."

"Well, I hope she gets better soon. So, are we having something to eat or going to visit your mum with a bunch of flowers and chocolates?"

I'm flummoxed. Honestly, I am. I'm so glad I wasn't drinking my coffee then because I think I would have spurted it out of my mouth, right across the table. Ryan is willing to see my mum? So soon? He must see this relationship as being far more serious than I thought he did. Wow. Now I feel really guilty for being such a weirdo and a liar too.

My phone bleeps again and I squeeze my pocket, as if it will stop the notification from coming through. I can hardly breathe. I stare across to Ryan and give a wavering smile.

"Is that your mum again?"

I pull my phone out and pretend to read a message but in reality, I haven't touched the screen at all. I fear that it will be another message from Kallum and if I look at it, it will somehow morph into a loud speaker message that reads itself out loud. "Yes, she's fine," I say, pretending to reply. "She'll have to keep her feet up for a few days. Dad will have to run around after her, he's going to love that. Now, what shall we have to eat?"

*** 7 ***

How do you feel? Love and kindness, Kallum x
Are you ignoring me now?
OK, I'm going to bed – let me know what you want to do, love Kallum x

It's gone eleven and Ryan has only just left, five minutes ago. The messages from Kallum kept on coming, which annoyed me massively. I've practically lied my way through the whole evening as far as Ryan is concerned. Pretending to read the messages to him about my poor mum and her broken toes, and I hate it. I hate me. And I think I might have rekindled my hatred for Kallum too. Mulling it over now, I'm thinking to myself, how dare he? Who does he think he is? Does he seriously think he can just walk back into my life and carry on where we left off?

Hi Kallum, I do not think it's a good idea to meet up for a chat (I don't think there's much to say anyway). I'm sorry I don't have the same feelings for you and have moved on with my life. I have a new boyfriend now and I am very happy. I hope you will find happiness too. Regards, Susie. There, straight to the point, formal and not a hint of hope. I press send and breathe a deep sigh. I do hope I won't hear back from him, but I can't help the tiny little nag inside my head which is harbouring some sort of revenge.

***

I'm heading towards Sarah's classroom because I'm determined to face her with a confident smile and also, give her my number. It's break time and, as I was hoping, she's sitting at her desk when I politely knock on the door.

"Come in," she shouts.

I open the door and stride across the room. "I thought you might like my number for next year," I say, with a determined tone.

Sarah gawks at me. "Sorry?"

"My phone number – for next year."

"Just leave it there." She points a pink Shellac finger nail to an empty spot on her desk.

"Oh, have you got a pen and paper and I'll write it down then?"

Sarah huffs as she turns away from her computer, scans her untidy desk, finding a scrap of paper and a broken pencil. "Here, write it on there – sorry I'm really busy."

I write my name and number on the paper, tuck the edge of it under a giant eraser and lay the pencil across the top. "There you are," I say. "I'll leave you in peace then." I casually stroll out of the classroom, feeling like her eyes are boring holes in my back. Sharply, I turn to look back as I reach the door and she is glaring at me. "Bye then – catch up soon," I say, joyfully. Her expression doesn't change, and I swiftly leave the classroom, close the door quietly behind me and scurry off down the corridor towards my own classroom, shaken but proud.

I'm not going to put up with a year of that, I can tell you. Why can't she be more civil? A little smile wouldn't go amiss. She owes me, you know, but I'm wondering if that's why she's finding it difficult to be friendly. Maybe I should start the new school year off by being ultra-efficient, a little more understanding of her desire to always be perfect (It's an affliction, I'm sure) and helpful in every way possible. If that doesn't work, nothing will. Maybe she'd be happier if I were to dress each day in a turkey or a clown costume. Maybe that would do it.

As I'm walking back to my classroom, I see Jane tottering along in her high-heeled sandals. She's wearing a flowy, summer dress (I'd say it's a bit inappropriate for school because the neck line is far too low) and an artificial flower in her hair. Who does she think she is? More importantly, *where* does she think she is? She looks like she should be in some sort of TV advert, running barefoot through a lavender field, the breeze catching her hair and blowing it into waves, behind her back. "Susie Satchel – well, well, I haven't seen you around for a while," she says, as she approaches me.

"Well, I've been here. I expect you just haven't noticed me, we've all been so busy at school."

"Hardly surprising..."

"What's hardly surprising?" I ask.

She looks me up and down. "It's hardly surprising that I haven't noticed you. You don't exactly stand out these days, do you?"

"You mean the clown costume?"

Jane lets out a tiny giggle and then sighs. "Oh dear... looking back, you've got to admit..."

"No, I don't think it was funny, Jane, and I nearly lost my job over it."

"Did you?" She looks at me, surprised. "I didn't know that."

"Well, I say, 'nearly' because Mr Reynolds didn't think I was capable of knowing what day of the week it was, let alone what goes on at school."

"Oh dear..." She looks down at my black dolly shoes (highly appropriate for school wear, I would say) and screws her nose up. "Well, you're with Sarah next year so you'll have to be on the ball. She hasn't got time for any messing about or..." Now she's looking at my tied back hair (again, I think it's totally appropriate for school). "...vagueness."

"I'm not vague," I respond, pointedly. "It's more a case of hoodwinked, wouldn't you say?"

Jane shrugs her shoulders and gives me a curt glance. "Whatever. Anyway, I've got to go – busy, busy." She walks away with her nose in the air, leaving me fuming by her remarks.

I always seem to get to a point where I have got to force myself to rise above things. I have always got to put on a strong front and pretend that I'm not phased in the slightest, by the way some people treat me. Whereas, in reality... Argh...

Fair enough. All the best to you, Susie. Kallum x

Hi Suse, when are you planning on coming to Devon? I've got a couple of day's holiday already! Let me know ASAP and I can book them off. Love you, your forever-friend, Clair xx

I'm not seeing Ryan until the weekend now, but I guess a quick phone call can't hurt. I need to know if he wants to come with me, but I haven't plucked up the courage to ask him yet...

No, I can't bring myself to call him – text message it is then. *Hi Ryan, hope you haven't been working too hard, lol. My friend, Clair (the one I used to live with), has invited me down to Devon in the summer holidays. She said you're very welcome to go too. Not sure what your plans are but, do you fancy it? Susie xx*

Within minutes of me sending the message, my phone rings. It's Ryan. "Hello," I say, nervously.

"I would love to – when?"

"Oh..." I'm taken by surprise. There's no beating about the bush with him, is there? "Well, she said it was up to us to decide when and then she will book a couple of days off."

"Cool. When do you want to go then?"

"I..." I'm not used to this spontaneity in a boyfriend. "I don't mind – I'm not doing anything else much."

"Neither am I. How long do you want to go for?"

"Oh, err..." I'm not used to having such an amiable boyfriend either. One minute he's happy to go and visit my mum (I still feel bad about that lie) and take her flowers and chocolates, the next, he's more than willing to go on an impromptu holiday to Devon with me. This is all a first for me. When I was with Kallum, I'd be lucky if he managed to turn up on a pre-arranged date, which had been set months previously. "Maybe a day or two? Could you do that?"

"I've never been to the West Country before. Whereabouts in Devon – it's a big place?"

"It's Ilfracombe, north Devon."

"OK, why don't we make a week of it and if we can't stay with your friend, Clair, for that length of time, I'll get us a charming hotel? How does mid-August sound?"

I'm speechless. Is this what normal couples do? Do they sort things out, there and then with such conviction? "Oh... err... OK."

"Why don't we just get a hotel for half of the week anyway? That way, we can still see Clair, but we could have some of our own time too." I hear

Ryan laugh down the phone. "We'll get a posh room with a four-poster bed – don't worry, I'll pay for it. What do you think? Do you like that idea?"

"Oh yes, but I'm not having you pay for it all."

"Look," Ryan's voice has lowered and turned all serious. "Do a deal with me..."

"What's that?" Oh God, I should have known this would be too good to be true.

"You spend your money on paying your mortgage and I'll spend mine on taking us on a nice holiday together – deal?"

I nod, although he can't see me. "OK..." I say quietly, humbled by his generosity. I'm so in love with this man – he's amazing. "Are you...?"

"Sure?" he cuts in.

"Yes."

"Absolutely." I hear him sigh down the phone. "I'm more than happy that you even considered asking me to go with you, Susie."

"I wouldn't want to go with anyone else," I say.

"I miss you – I don't think I can wait until the weekend to see you."

I give a nervous laugh. "I miss you too."

"Are you doing anything tomorrow night?"

"Only cooking a meal for you?"

"Then I'll be there. Is six o'clock OK?"

"Perfect," I say, feeling giddy with excitement. "Do you like spaghetti Bolognese?"

"I love it – it's one of my favourites. Until tomorrow then... goodnight and thank you."

"Thank you?" I'm puzzled, what's he thanking me for?

"For being you – goodnight."

"Goodnight and... bye," I say and then hear the end-of-call tone. Oh gosh, I love this man even more now and that's why my plan to get rid of that *facebook* message is so very important.

I have got to be truthful now and tell you that I received my little package, from *Amazon*, in the post today. Trust me, I was so relieved that it fitted through the letterbox and I didn't have to collect it from a neighbour or anything like that. At least no one has seen my face and knows who I am and that I have this little package in my possession. I hate what I'm going to do but it's the only way – I don't see any other way out and it's killing me. Honestly it is. I've become fixated on my little plan, I know that, but it's because I know it will work, guaranteed. Any other way would be very hit and miss and far too risky.

Just found a cute little, 5-star hotel, less than a mile from the city centre, and they have a suite available with sea views (from the balcony!) Sadly, no four-poster bed though. Will a king size do? How does the 17th to the 20th of August sound? We could go to Clair's on the 14th and spend 3 days with her first x

I cannot believe it. We got off the phone only minutes ago and he's already found a hotel for us, sorted out the dates and arranged our whole trip. He's more than amazing. *That sounds absolutely fantastic – I can't believe you've done all that. I'll contact Clair and let her know so she can book a couple of days off. A 5-star hotel? Won't it be expensive though? Thank you, Ryan – you are incredible xx*

Booked! X

OMG! That's insane Xx

See you tomorrow night x

Clair, sorry it's a bit late – hope I don't wake you. Ryan is coming to Devon – woohoo! We're going to come on the 14th Aug (if that's OK) and stay with you until 17th when we will check-in to our... wait for it... 5-star hotel suite with sea views!! Then we'll stay until 20th so we could see you for a little longer but do our own things as well. Hope that's OK, I'm soooooo excited! Love ya xx

OMG! I am awake and soooooo excited too. Just checked and I'm on an early on the 14th so should be around when you arrive. I'll book off the 15th and 16th OMG – can't believe you're coming. Can't wait to meet Ryan. Love you too, BFF xx

*** 8 ***

Sarah ignored me today when I passed her in the corridor. I even went to the effort of smiling exaggeratedly and saying good morning to her, but she didn't acknowledge me in the slightest. Her loss, that's what I say. God, I'm going to hate school next year.

Anyway, I'm home now and I have just cooked the meat sauce for our spaghetti Bolognese tonight. I'm really looking forward to seeing Ryan this evening as, apart from enjoying his wonderful company, he's going to show me the hotel where we'll be staying. I have mixed emotions today though, as I have also got to carry out my plan. I've got to get it over and done with. Get it out of the way so that our relationship can truly blossom without this dark cloud of culpability hanging over me and slowly eating away at my confidence. My heart pounds every time I run tonight's course of events through my head. It's got to work – nothing can go wrong. I cannot afford for anything to go wrong...

***

"Come in," I say, a huge beam on my face. At least I've welcomed him in a proper fashion this time. We don't need to ponder over the hallway paintwork tonight. Ryan walks in and gives me a lingering kiss before I've even closed the door. He's looking decidedly handsome this evening, in a pair of light blue jeans and a pink polo shirt. He suits pink, I don't know why but I think a lot of men suit pink – it's not just for the girls. I'm wearing a knee-length summer dress with a pretty palm tree print.

"You look gorgeous," he says, before kissing me again. I haven't even closed the door behind him yet and already, we're building up an appetite for the bedroom.

"Thank you," I say, pulling away from him and closing the door. "You look nice in pink."

"Do you hate men wearing pink?"

"No, not at all. It suits you."

"Some women don't like it. Amber hates it." He snorts a laugh. "If I had my way, we'd change the staff PE kits to pink, just to annoy her."

I smile and beckon for Ryan to follow me to the kitchen where I have set the table, romantically, for two. I've got a bottle of wine too and although it's a work night, I don't see why we can't have a glass or two. If my plan goes well, Ryan won't be going to work tomorrow anyway. "Have a seat," I say, sweetly.

"We're having wine? On a work night?"

"Why not... I was going to ask you if you would like to..." Oh my God, if he says no... "If you'd like to stay the night and leave early in the morning so you can go home to change."

I can see Ryan mulling the idea over in his head. He *must* say, yes.

"We should have a celebration, our first holiday together and it might help to wash down my spaghetti Bolognese – you haven't tried my cooking yet."

Ryan picks up a glass and holds it up. "Fill me up then."

Yes! Yes! He's going to stay.

"And your Bolognese smells delicious – I'm starving. If it tastes as good as it smells, there will be none left."

"Do you like garlic bread?"

"I do and if you'll allow me to breathe all over Amber tomorrow while still wearing my pink top, I'll be a very happy man."

I laugh aloud, open the bottle of wine and fill his glass, pouring one for myself too. I need a drink, trust me. "I've told Clair and she can't wait to meet you. You'll like her boyfriend too, he's very nice."

"I look forward to meeting them." Ryan takes a large swig from his wine and places the glass on the table. "Can I help you with anything at all?"

"No, it's all in hand and just about ready to serve up. Would you like it now?" My heart is racing in anticipation. Ryan nods and smiles at me. Oh God, here I go...

He ate every last bit of it and drank one and a half glasses of wine. "Shall we go into the living room?" I ask, clearing the plates away.

"That was good, thank you, and the wine has gone straight to my head." He stands up and grabs me into an embrace. "Are you the dessert?"

"No, funnily enough, I've got a toffee Pavlova. I was going to bring some in to you, in the living room. Would you like some?" I know he loves it because he told me the first time we went out for a meal (which was the last time I tried to get at his phone).

Ryan nods enthusiastically. "Yes, please." He kisses me softly. "Thanks Susie, I really enjoyed that."

"Go on then," I say, slapping his behind. "Go in the living room, I'll bring it in, in a minute."

By the time I carry two bowls of Pavlova into the living room, Ryan is sprawled out on the sofa, watching the TV. We eat the dessert while watching a documentary about the natural world and I have got to say that I do struggle to swallow mine as the fear of what I have done, washes over me again and again. Stage one is complete. That sounds so harsh – OK, so I've done a terrible thing but I'm sorry, there's simply no other way...

***

I've just woken to Ryan grumbling and groaning next to me, although, he appears to be asleep still. I note the time is approaching 1.30am and I'm guessing that it's working. We went to bed around eleven and had some amazing sex, even though I felt terribly remorseful for what I've done. I've been driven to this, you must understand. I care for Ryan far too much to risk losing him now and although Clair kept on saying that the message couldn't have been that bad and if Ryan liked me enough he wouldn't care, it's not just about that. It's about my reputation too. I know that Amber could still disclose information about me at any given moment, but I don't think I interest her enough for her to go telling anyone – well, not until she finds out about me and Ryan, at least. But then she does have a boyfriend now so hopefully that's enough for her and she'll leave me well alone.

Ryan turns over and grunts as he resettles under the duvet. I peer at him, through the darkness and feel so very bad. This feels worse than worrying about the actual message – how can I have done this to him? In the dark stillness of the night, my dreadful actions of earlier have been amplified to a new level of disbelief and horror. There's no turning back now though. As Ryan rolls back over, I hear him groan. I stare out, across the shadowy bedroom and wonder when it will really start to happen. When will be the time for stage two of my awful plan...?

It has gone past three o'clock now and I have not slept at all. Ryan has tossed and turned and continued to grumble and moan. Suddenly, I open my eyes wide and watch, through the dimness, as he heaves himself out of bed and clambers across the room and out the door. I hear the bathroom door close heavily and jump out of bed myself.

Tiptoeing out of the room, I peer across the hallway with bated breath. The chink of light coming from under the bathroom door feels like a signal. A sign that stage two is in process. The thin strip of cold, white light seeps out from underneath the door, illuminating me as if it knows that I am a villain. It highlights my silhouette in the gloomy shadows – pinpointing my whereabouts for the great universe to dish out some sort of justified retribution. I gulp back the nausea creeping up into my throat. Oh God, how could I have done this?

The toilet flushes but Ryan doesn't appear at the door. It sounds like he's being sick in there. Oh God, that wasn't supposed to happen. A minute later, the toilet flushes again. Still, Ryan does not come out.

Several minutes go by and I tiptoe back into the bedroom, wondering how long he's going to be in there. I didn't want this to start just yet – it's too early. I climb into bed and pull the duvet over me, waiting and listening while my heart races and beads of perspiration dampen my brow. Then the bathroom door opens, and I see the chink of light under the bedroom door. He's coming back to bed. I slide down further and pretend to be asleep. I wait...

Ryan doesn't return to the bedroom, but I hear him pad through to the kitchen and then back to the bathroom. I listen and wait again. My heart is beating so fast now that I'm sure it's going to explode. Maybe that will be my punishment, sent from the universe – my heart will burst into a million pieces.

Ten minutes or so pass and the toilet flushes again. Then Ryan appears in the bedroom. He staggers around the bed and climbs in next to me. He has a strange, unpleasant smell about him and his breathing is heavy. I'm frozen to the spot – I daren't move. I don't want him to know I'm awake, not yet anyway. It's too soon.

I continue to lie very still, my own breathing incredibly shallow, as I peer out across the room, willing the morning to come.

By four o'clock the first signs of light are beginning to lift the dark shadows around the room. I watch the walls, the window and every other thing in my room as slowly, colour returns, replacing the black and grey hues of darkness.

Ryan has lain motionless for the last forty minutes, with just the odd grunt or groan, but now he's started to move again. He climbs out of bed and stumbles around the room to the door, clutching his stomach as he goes. Then I hear him go into the bathroom once again.

By half past four, I've decided the time is right to go and see if he's OK. He's been in the bathroom for at least twenty-five minutes now and I've heard the toilet flush twice. I go to the bathroom and knock gently on the door. "Ryan? Are you OK in there?"

"No," a little voice comes from behind the door. "I'm not well."

"What's wrong?" I say, sympathetically (trust me, my sympathy is genuine – I cannot believe, in the cold light of day, that I have done this to him).

"I don't know... I... I've got a really bad stomach ache and... diarrhoea."

"Oh dear. Can I get you anything...?" I break off, momentarily. "Water?"

"No, I keep being sick as well – I can't even keep water down."

"Oh gosh, I'm sorry. I do hope it wasn't my cooking."

"Do *you* feel OK?" he mutters with a whimper.

"Yes, I'm fine."

"Can't be your cooking then."

I hear a shuffling noise in the bathroom and then the sound of him being sick again. The toilet flushes.

"Susie?"

"Yes, I'm still here."

"I feel so ill..."

"I wonder what it could be?" I say, guiltily.

"I don't know but I think I need to go to hosp..."

"No," I snap. "Err... no, I'm sure you won't need that Ryan. It might settle down."

"But... I've never been this ill..."

"Maybe it's something you ate at work," I try to reassure him. Oh my God, there's no way he can go to hospital – they'd know, wouldn't they? They would find out what I've done and then I'd be in big trouble.

"Could you call my doctor then?"

"Err..." Oh dear me. I roll my eyes upwards and gulp. "Ryan, listen, if it is some sort of food poisoning then you're doing the right thing..."

"What do you mean?"

"When you're sick and have diarrhoea, it's a really good sign – it means you are clearing the bad stuff out. My mum told me that. How would you feel if you made your doctor come here and then suddenly you started to feel better?"

"Hmm..."

Gosh, he sounds totally dejected – I feel awful. "Why don't you give it another hour or so and see how you are then?"

"O...K..."

"I think it will probably settle down, Ryan. Try and drink some water but just tiny sips, OK?"

"OK, I will.... Susie?"

"Yes?"

"What time is it?"

"Err... hang on..." I run to the kitchen and look at the clock. Upon my return, I lean against the bathroom door. "It's getting on for five o'clock – why?"

"Can you text my school and tell them I won't be in today. I've hardly slept all night and I can't see me getting out of your bathroom any time soon."

"Yes, of course. I'll just get my phone. Be right back." I hurry off to hide my phone away and then return, knowing that stage two is almost complete. "Can I use yours because my battery is flat, and my charger is really dodgy? Funnily enough, I've ordered a new charger – it should be here today (that's a lie but I've got to do it, I'm sorry)."

"Yes, sure. You'll have to unlock it first and then you'll find the school's staff number in my contacts."

"OK, I'll be right back. Where is it – in the bedroom (I know exactly where it is because I am fixated on the bloody thing and can't ever take my eyes off it)?"

"Yes... and Susie?"

"Yes?"

"I'm really sorry about this."

"Ah, don't be sorry. You can't help it, can you?"

"When I can get off this toilet I'll go home."

"There's no rush," I say, suddenly giddy with excitement, as if I'm just about to be set free from the iron chains harbouring my shameful conduct of the past. It's working, it's actually working. "I can leave the key and you can lock up when you go – in your own time."

"Thanks... I owe you."

"No, you don't owe me at all. Right, I'll get your phone."

A minute later I return. My heart is really racing now. I'm almost there. I'm nearly at the point where I can look through Ryan's phone, in peace. "Ryan, how do I unlock the pattern?"

"Err... it starts at the top middle one..."

"OK," I say, trying to sound calm.

"Go straight down, and then right, and then up one."

I follow his instructions and hey presto, it's unlocked. Oh my God, I've not only done it, but I also have Ryan confined to the bathroom for the near future.

"Have you done it?"

"Yes, just searching for your school. What do you want me to say?"

"Say, I'm sorry I won't be in, but I've been up all night with sickness and diarrhoea."

"OK..."

"It's done," I say, moments later, "Ryan, are you sure you don't want anything? I'm going to go and make a cup of tea, I'm gagging."

"No thanks. I'll try and get out of here as soon as possible but it won't be a pleasant experience if you need to use your bathroom."

I laugh. "Don't worry about it. Just get better." I scurry off to the kitchen, with Ryan's phone in my sweaty palm. I flick the kettle on and start the process of removing the message from his *facebook* 'other' inbox...

Result.

I know, I know it's bad but it's a result. I'm sorry.

*** 9 ***

The *facebook* message is more embarrassing than I remembered:

Hello Ryan... or should I call you Mr Bagshaw? I hope you don't mind me adding you as a friend. I just wanted to apologise for my quick exit, that day at the pool. I was a bit embarrassed, to be honest. Oops – sorry. And what you must think of me after the clown day, which turned out to NOT be a clown day after all and was in fact, a cross-country day. Well, I can't imagine what you must think about that. My entrance wasn't exactly graceful, and I had got it all completely wrong. Oops – sorry again. I don't mean to keep saying sorry, but I just don't want you to think that I'm some sort of a weirdo. From a nursing-turkey to a wired-chest to a clumsy clown, I couldn't blame you if you didn't want to accept my friend request.

I'm a bit drunk tonight (well, a lot actually) as I've been out pole-dancing with friends. Mr Reynolds hates me even more now than he did before half-term because he was at the club tonight when I fell off the stage. He saw everything, and he now thinks that I am a bad influence on the rest of his staff. He can go and get stuffed (by the cruellest means possible) as far as I'm concerned. I wanted to die actually, lol. Talking of dying – my boyfriend died at Christmas, well, not the one I was with when I spoke to you, I mean another one, ha ha. The one I was with when we had the Christmas do, left me because he got someone else pregnant. He walked out on me on Christmas day – can you believe it? Of all the days to dump someone, he chooses Christmas day! And my other boyfriend died on New Year's Eve. That sounds terrible because it sounds like I had two boyfriends in one week, ha ha. Well, I did really but it wasn't like it sounds, ha ha. I'm not a floozy or anything like that, ha ha.

It changed the world for me when Jett (boyfriend no.2) died. I feel like it was all my fault but please don't think that I killed him because I didn't. However, I've come to realise how short life can be now and I need to make the most of it. Have you got a girlfriend yet? Not that I'm asking you out or anything like that but it's just nice to chat. I hope I'm not waffling on too much but then you have got a choice of whether to accept my request or not. Ha ha – you really must think I'm a weirdo. OK, maybe I am. Maybe I'm a lonely weirdo, ha ha. Sorry. I'm going now because I've written loads and I can't even see properly now because I'm too drunk, ha ha. Lonely, drunk weirdo, ha ha. Goodbye, hope to hear back from you but if you decide not to, then I totally understand. After all, who would really want to be acquainted with a weirdo-freaky-turkey-clown with metal tits who has two boyfriends in one week and one of them ends up dead? Ha ha ha. Kindest regards, Susie Satchel.

It's terrible and I'd even forgotten about the bra wire incident, which was yet another humiliating episode. A rush of euphoria washes over me as I delete the message. It has gone. It really has vanished. Not a trace. I've done it. I've actually completed my mission. I have won.

Now, I need to make sure that Ryan gets better, so we can start our relationship afresh (from my perspective anyway). I quickly make a cup of tea and carry it through to the hall. "Are you OK in there?" I call out to the bathroom, as I can hear the tap running.

The door unlocks, and Ryan's drained, pale face appears. "Can I get back in your bed?" He sounds and looks absolutely pitiful.

"Yes, of course you can. Stay here all day if you like." I smile warmly, as the sense of accomplishment increases. I feel free. I feel like a heavy load has been lifted from me. I put an arm around Ryan's shoulder as he steps out of the bathroom, doubled over. "Do you still have a bad tummy?"

He looks up at me and nods. "A bit – not as bad as earlier, but I daren't drive home."

"Then don't – I mean what I say. You can stay here all day if you want to and help yourself to drinks... when you're feeling better, of course." And I know he will get better, eventually. I guide him back to bed and tuck him in. "Here's your phone." I pull it out from my pocket and place it on the bedside cabinet. The fear of what was inside his phone has completely gone and I feel at peace now. "I'm going to work at eight but call me if you need me – I'll have my phone on me all day."

"I thought it was broken."

"Err..." Oh God, I need to be more careful. "No, just the charger but I can usually get it about a quarter charged – it just takes a while."

"OK," he mutters and slides under the duvet, further. "Thanks for everything, Susie."

"No need to thank me – you just get better. Night, night." I leave the room, closing the door behind me and take my tea through to the living room, where I'm going to have a sit down for half an hour... and maybe even a nap. I'm mentally and physically exhausted, as I'm sure Ryan must be too.

***

I've had a super-confident day at work. I even made a point of saying, yet another, exaggerated, good morning to Sarah and Jane as they passed me in the corridor, which they could *not* ignore and *had* to respond to this time. As they passed, I had a conceited smile on my face, which makes a change for me, and which took the two beauty queens by surprise. Huh, I can give, as good as I get. There's no stopping me now – I'm an achiever. Well, maybe I wouldn't go quite that far but life is good today. I've texted Ryan throughout the day and had a couple of replies. He's still at my flat and I'm on my way home now. It's a nice feeling, knowing that there is a man waiting for me at home... I wish it could always be like that, but I know that is a long way off yet.

I've just got home and it's such a delight to see Ryan looking so much better with colour back in his cheeks... and he looks so cute too. He's wearing my pink dressing gown and lying on the sofa with a mug of coffee cupped in his hands and the TV on. He looks at home. "How are you feeling?" I ask, the guilt returning momentarily.

"Much better." He smiles at me.

"That's good to hear. Well, it's the weekend now so you can relax."

"And what better way than to be sitting here in your living room, wearing your dressing gown."

I laugh, uncomfortably. Is he being serious or sarcastic?

"Have *you* been OK today? I mean, no stomach pains or anything like what I've had?" he asks.

"Yes, I've been fine..." God, I honestly feel terrible for what I've done. "So, you can't blame my cooking," I add, jokingly.

"No, I wouldn't dream of blaming you or your cooking, but I really don't know what it was... maybe a bug? One of those 24-hour things?"

"Maybe," I reply, trying desperately not to look sheepish. "Anyway, now you're better, would you like something to eat?"

"Oh, I don't know – I haven't ventured that far yet. I've kept two coffees down though."

"Why don't you try a slice of toast?"

Ryan nods. "I am hungry. I suppose the worst that can happen is, I rekindle that close, cosy relationship I've been having with your bathroom and toilet."

I laugh again. "I'll make some toast – see how you get on with it." I take Ryan's now empty mug and go to the kitchen with a sorrowful feeling in my heart. He is so lovely; how could I have done something like that to him? How can I comfortably live with myself for the rest of my life, knowing what I've done? I have no choice – I have got to. It was for the good of all and time will heal. I'll keep repeating that to myself until I feel better about it.

***

Ryan is fully recovered and to my surprise, he has stayed here all weekend (apart from to nip home yesterday morning to get some fresh clothes). I did say to him that he could wear my dressing gown all weekend (easy access for those passionate moments) but he insisted on getting some clean clothing. It's now Sunday afternoon and we've been out doing some 'holiday' shopping, as Ryan arranged cover for his Sunday-morning football team, due to his recent illness.

We're both so excited about Devon that you'd think we were jetting off to the Maldives or some other exotic destination for a fortnight, not a week in the west country. This weekend has really shown both of us that we get on very well, share a lot of the same thoughts and passions and enjoy each other's company considerably. So much so, that I would ask him to move in, in the blink of an eye, but I don't want to rush things or spoil what we have at this present moment. I'm guessing that Ryan will just end up staying here more often until it comes to the point that he actually lives here. I'm holding out, financially, in the hope that it *will* happen as I really don't want to get another flat mate when it could turn out to be Ryan who moves in. After this weekend, it just seems the right thing to do and a natural progression in our blossoming relationship.

"Apart from Thursday night's episode, I've had an enjoyable time this weekend," says Ryan.

I'm sitting on the floor, between his legs while he plays with my hair – it's heavenly (the hair-playing bit, not the sitting-between-his-legs bit, but then again, I suppose that's quite nice too). "Yes, me too. I don't want you to go this evening."

"Trust me, I don't want to go either, but I've got so much school stuff to do that, if I stayed any longer, I'd never get it done."

I turn my head and look up at him. "I could help you?"

Ryan laughs and strokes the back of my hair softly. "I know you could – and would – but most of it involves late nights at school, unfortunately..." He breaks off, thoughtfully. "I could come over on Wednesday night... and stay again, if I'm invited. Hopefully, avoiding a repeat of my last mid-week stay though." He grins at me.

"Err..." I feign contemplation, after all, I don't want to look too keen, do I? "You're invited... In fact, you have an open invite."

"Oh, do I?" He leans over and kisses my neck which makes me shiver. "So, I can come and go as I please?"

"If you'd like to."

"I'd like to," he whispers in my ear. "I'd like that a lot." Sliding down, to the floor, behind me, Ryan brushes my hair to one side and kisses my neck again. His hands gently squeeze my shoulders and then his fingers run up and down my back, causing me to shudder. It's going to happen again, I know it is. We've had sex four times over the last two days and we're just about to start the fifth... Happy days.

*** 10 ***

If I had to work it out as a percentage, I would say that Ryan has stayed at my house, eighty-five to ninety percent of the time since the stomach upset episode (which I still feel terrible about, I have got to say). That elusive word, 'love' has still not been mentioned but maybe it doesn't need to be because I can certainly feel it and I hope he does too. There have been times when I've wanted to declare it to him, in the heat of the moment, but something holds me back each time. I don't know why, but I feel like it should come from him first, or maybe, he's thinking exactly the same thing as me – who knows. It's not overly important that Ryan hasn't declared his undying love for me – he may be one of those men who finds it hard to say. His actions speak far louder than his words ever could though, so I'm happy and secure in the fact that he cares deeply about me.

Time has been whizzing past, way too quickly but so far, I've had a lovely summer holiday. And now, looking back, I realise how much I enjoyed being at school for those last few days before we broke up. The atmosphere was heightened with excitement, both from the staff and also the children. It was a hectic time of the school year, due to the shuffling around of classrooms, the school leaver's production and other end-of-year events but it was such fun. I can honestly say that I don't mind going back to school in September, even if I will be working with Sarah – somehow, having Ryan around and the summer break have both made me feel stronger and able to cope with anything that life might decide to throw at me in the future and I do think that I get more than my fair share of life's little complications.

Ryan spent the first two weeks of the holidays at school, preparing for next year, sorting through his sport equipment, changing some things around and doing his planning. As for me, well I've spent a couple of days, visiting my parents, shopping for holiday clothes and giving my flat a spring-clean (it needed one). And now, we're on our way to Devon. It has come around so quickly.

We've been travelling for over three and a half hours now but we're nearly there. Devon is a beautiful place and I have had the pleasure of viewing the scenery while Ryan drives. He insisted on driving, saying that I'd done so much for him already, by feeding him regularly, offering him this opportunity to have a holiday in Devon and generally putting up with him. Putting up with him? I'd say it's the other way around, to be honest. He has got to put up with my dippy, forgetful ways and everyday vagueness (yes, OK, I know I was totally defensive when Jane said I was vague, but she's not allowed to insult me like that – I'm the only one who can insult me). Ryan says I make him laugh because I am so dippy, but he also says I'm cute with it. I take that as a compliment.

I peer down at my phone as the female voice in my phone's satnav directs us to turn right at the next junction. The distance left says 2.2 miles and 11 minutes. I text Clair to tell her how close we are.

Ooh goody! Can't wait – I'll get the kettle on xx Oh, and I hope you're hungry because I've made a buffet tea – go me! Xx

"Clair has made a buffet tea for us."

"That's nice," says Ryan, keeping his eyes on the road. "I'm starving."

"After all the sweets, you've eaten along the way?"

Ryan smirks. "Sweets don't count – they're not classed as substantial food."

I giggle as we turn right into a built-up area. "We're nearly there," I say, excitedly.

As we pull into a small car park, I see Clair's cheery face at the main doors of a huge building in front of us. She looks just as lovely as she always has, and her blonde hair has got longer. I jump out of the car, run over to her and pounce on her, hugging her tightly. "We're here – oh my God, I've missed you. You look amazing."

"So do you," she replies, cupping my face in her hands and kissing my cheek hard.

"You must be Clair," says Ryan, who is now standing by my side. "It's very nice to meet you." He extends a hand, offering a handshake.

"Oh, never mind that," says Clair, pushing his hand down. "Give me a hug."

Ryan looks a little embarrassed as he puts one arm around her shoulders and hugs her.

"I've heard a lot about you," says Clair, stepping back and taking hold of my hand. "And I hear you've been looking after my bestie very well."

"I'd say she's been looking after me, actually."

"Really? That does surprise me. And there was me thinking my dear old Susie could only just manage to look after herself and even then, it's questionable." Clair grins at me and squeezes my hand playfully. "Come on in," she says, as we reach the door, "Archie is just getting changed – he's just got home from work."

We follow Clair into the building and a fresh, clean smell hits me. The building houses four spacious, two-bedroom flats and Clair and Archie have one on the ground floor with a small garden at the rear.

"This is a lovely place you have here," I say, as we walk through her long, narrow hallway, lit up by open doors on each side.

"I love it," says Clair. "And we're about a 15-minute walk from the beach too."

"Sounds perfect," says Ryan, taking my hand and squeezing it gently, while smiling at me.

As we enter the kitchen, Archie is preparing mugs. He turns and smiles. "Hi Susie – good to see you again." He approaches me and pecks me on the cheek. "And you must be Ryan – nice to meet you mate." They shake hands and the atmosphere feels all friendly and exciting. "Do you guys want tea or coffee?"

"Coffee please," we say at the same time.

There's a table behind us, filled with an array of nibbles and club sandwiches. "Wow, that looks amazing Clair," I say, suddenly feeling very hungry.

"Well, I thought maybe we could have a bit of tea and then if you guys feel up to it, after your long journey, we could go out this evening. There's some really nice pubs down by the harbour and you could get food down there too, if you're peckish later."

"Sounds like a plan," says Ryan.

I nod and grin. I feel like I'm in heaven at this very moment, I'm so happy.

"But first, do you want to bring your bags in and I'll show you to your room?"

"Ooh, that would be lovely, thank you madam," I say, mockingly.

"Let them drink their coffees first," says Archie, passing mugs around. "Honestly, she's been so excited – you are all she's been going on about for the last few weeks."

"Yes, Susie has been the same." Ryan puts an arm around my shoulder and laughs with Archie.

I can see that they are going to get on well and as for me and Clair, well, we're like two peas in a pod anyway. Best friends forever – that kind of thing.

We've been given a tour of the flat, which is much bigger than I first imagined, and now we're in our room, with our bags, freshening up. We'll be having some tea in a minute and then we're going to walk down to the harbour at about seven o'clock. I'm ecstatic for several reasons. Firstly, I'm back with Clair, secondly, I'm on holiday with Ryan and thirdly, we have our own double room with an en-suite toilet and wash basin. OK, there's not a shower in there but considering that Archie has built the en-suite facility himself, I think he's done a fantastic job.

I'm sitting on the edge of the bed, placing my underwear into the bedside drawer, when Ryan pulls me down on to the bed. He kisses me upside-down which is very erotic (for some strange reason). "No," I whisper, before giggling. "We can't... not now" He kisses me again. "Get your clothes put away Ryan Bagshaw – we're having some tea in a minute and then going out."

"I'll get you later," he whispers and kisses me one last time before he moves away.

The thing is, I can never resist him when he starts. I am so deeply attracted to him, both mentally and physically and it's like I lust after him all the time, as he does me. I'm quite surprised by my resolve at the moment though, but then I'm guessing it's because we're not in the privacy of my flat. If we were, I know that we would have jumped into the bed (or not necessarily 'into') by now and be having some quite amazing sex.

***

The pubs near the harbour are indeed, very nice. So nice, in fact, that the whole area is teeming with visitors. The harbour itself is a gorgeous bit of scenery, so we decide to get some drinks and sit outside in the warm, evening sun and watch the boats bob up and down on the glistening water.

"It's beautiful here," I say, feeling the warm glow of the sun on my skin.

"It's even more beautiful on Lundy Island," says Archie, eyeing Clair with a smirk.

"Oh," I look to Ryan. "Have you heard of Lundy Island?"

"I've heard of it – never been though."

"Well, you'll be going tomorrow."

"What?" I say, surprised by Clair's words.

"Tomorrow. We've booked a trip over to Lundy Island – we're all going."

"Oh, wow." I'm giddy with excitement.

"We're getting on the ship at ten o'clock, but we need to be here 45 minutes before that, so it's a fairly early start I'm afraid."

"A ship?" I say.

Clair laughs. "Yes, the *MS Oldenburg*, no less." She looks to Archie and laughs again. "We did think about flying you over there in a helicopter, but it was way too expensive."

"That sounds fantastic," says Ryan. "Do we owe you anything for the ship?"

"No, it's all paid for," says Archie.

"You'll love it," Clair adds. "We went there a couple of months ago. If you're lucky you might even see dolphins as we cross the Bristol Channel."

"Oh wow, it sounds amazing."

"It is," Clair grins at me. "We will have an amazing time."

***

We certainly have had an amazing time with Clair and Archie, these past few days and the weather has been beautiful. Apart from our trip to Lundy Island (which was out of this world and I want to go and live there with the puffins forever), we have visited Tunnels Beaches (again, an amazing place) and the Ilfracombe museum. We've also had afternoon tea at Castle Hill gardens and we went to the Craft Hut to paint our own pottery. We've had a fantastic time with Clair and Archie and it's been so nice to see Ryan and Archie get on so well.

Clair has got to go back to work this evening and Archie returns to work tomorrow. As for us, well, we'll be checking into our hotel later this afternoon, which I'm very excited about. But we've planned to meet up tomorrow evening and then again, the following evening for a meal and drinks with Clair and Archie.

It is a beautiful morning once again and this is the first time that me and Clair have been on our own, as the men have gone to Ilfracombe Golf club (I didn't even know that Ryan liked playing golf) for the whole morning.

"Ryan is very nice," says Clair, making two coffees. "I'm really happy for you."

"Ah, thanks. You and Archie are good together too."

"Yes, he's brilliant. I can't imagine life without him now." She pauses and turns around from the kettle to peer at me. "I've been wondering, since you arrived, whether you ever managed to get rid of that message?"

"Err..." Oh God, the memories have just come flooding back. "Yes."

"How did you do it in the end?"

"I... err..."

"I want the truth," she says, lightheartedly. "No porkies."

"The message was worse than I remembered, Clair."

"Yes, I believe you but how did you get into his phone?"

I look down at the table, shamefully.

"Suse?"

"I did something really bad."

"What?" Clair carries two mugs to the table, pulls out a chair and sits down next to me. "What did you do?"

"I tricked him, into using his phone."

"OK... and?"

"Well, that was it, I pretended I needed to use his phone..."

"You're not telling me everything – I can tell by your eyes."

"I feel terrible, Clair. I did a really dreadful thing. You'd hate me if you knew."

"No, I wouldn't. You've got to tell me now though."

I sigh heavily and take a nervous sip from my coffee which burns my lips.

"It's hot be careful. Come on then, tell me. I'm not going to say anything, am I?"

"I made him ill... and when he needed to text work to tell them he couldn't go in, I made him tell me his unlock pattern, so I could write and send the text for him."

Clair looks at me surprised. "How did you make him ill?" She peers at me incredulously. "Don't tell me you poisoned him for God's sake."

"No... I... I gave him six Senokot Max Strength."

"Oh my God, Suse." Clair shakes her head at me. "Did you need to go to that extreme?"

"I didn't see any other way to do it." I can't look Clair in the eye now.

"Couldn't you have just asked to use his phone because yours was broken or something?"

"No, because I needed the time to find his *facebook* app, find the message and delete it – without him seeing what I was doing."

Clair shakes her head again. "Suse, you could have killed him – that *is* a form of poisoning."

"Is it?" I say, horrified. "Is it really?"

"Yes. You are so lucky he wasn't rushed off to hospital, where they would have discovered that he'd had an overdose of laxatives."

"Oh my God – really?"

"Really," Clair says, sternly. "Don't ever do anything so stupid again. I knew you were up to no good when you texted me, Suse." She shakes her head at me once more. "I can't believe you'd be so stupid."

I'm staring down at the table like a scorned child. I can't express how awful I feel.

"Why didn't you ask me about something like that, first?"

I shrug, unable to find any words.

"I'm a nurse for God's sake *and* your best friend. Why didn't you speak to me? You have been lucky to get away with it. Can you imagine if it had gone wrong and poor Ryan had ended up in hospital?" She pauses and scans my horrified face. "You most certainly would have ended up with no boyfriend – and that's at the very least." She shakes her head despairingly. "I can't believe..."

A tear wells in my eye and tips over, on to my cheek.

"Oh dear..." Clair reaches out to hug me. "Come here, you. Sometimes, Susie Satchel, you are danger to yourself and to others. Please don't ever do anything like that again."

I burst into tears. "I won't, I promise," I splutter, "I feel so awful for doing it. He can *never* find out."

"He won't from me," says Clair, calmly, while stroking my hair. "You are bloody stupid though."

I dry my eyes and heave a big sigh. "I've fallen in love with him."

"I can see that." She stops stroking my hair and places a hand on my knee. "Do things right, Suse, do things honestly. Please stop getting yourself into these messes and then panicking about them like you're going to be shot by anyone who finds out. Things are never as bad as you seem to think they are."

I nod, agreeably. "I know, I know, I can't help it..." I break off and peer at my best friend through watery eyes. "He hates lies and that's all I seem to do is lie."

"What have you lied to him about – the message wasn't a lie?" She peers at me inquisitively. "The message, if anything, was the truth and the truth is really not half as bad as you think it was or still is."

"No, not the message – I mean Kallum."

"Kallum?" Clair withdraws her hand from my knee and peers at me with narrow eyes. "What's Kallum got to do with anything now?"

"He turned up at my flat – "

"When?"

"A few weeks ago."

"Why?" Clair's face has screwed into a disdainful look. "Was Ryan there?"

"No, no," I say, shaking my head. "But Ryan was on his way, so I had to get rid of Kallum quick."

"Oh God, please don't tell me you killed him off and locked him in a cupboard in your flat and he's now your biggest lie ever." Clair's mouth turns up, into a smirk.

I let out a snort of laughter. "No, but... I did tell a lie to Ryan, when he arrived moments after Kallum had gone."

"Why?"

"I was flustered. I didn't know how to explain to Ryan why I was leaning back against the front door when he arrived."

"Why didn't you just tell him the truth? What harm would it have done?"

I shrug like a confused child. "I don't know... I really don't know why. I know it's stupid, but I just panic in situations and try to talk my way out of them or tell a lie."

"So, what lie did you tell him and why did Kallum turn up anyway?"

As I proceed to tell Clair, her face changes from exasperation to disbelief to despair. Her expressions are quite a picture to watch but I know that she can't understand why I get myself into these messes. I'm not sure I can understand either.

"Well," she says, drawing in a deep breath. "I imagine that you might just get away with that crazy lie. Honestly though, Suse, what a ridiculous thing to tell Ryan about your mum. And, as for Kallum, well, he needs his head testing..." She breaks off, thoughtfully. "His baby must be due soon, surely? Haven't you heard anything about that?"

I shake my head. "No... and I don't particularly want to either. I removed them both from *facebook,* so I wouldn't know when she might have it or anything else about her either. I got the impression that they're not together now though – "

"Unless he's now doing the dirty on her and wants to get back with you again," Clair adds with a sneering grin. "Look, promise me one thing before you leave today, because we probably won't get another chance to have a chat like this, for the rest of this week."

"What's that?" I say.

"Promise me that you'll stop panicking about situations and just tell the truth when things happen. None of us are perfect, we all make mistakes. You can't ever go wrong by telling the truth."

I nod and smile at my best friend. God, I wish she lived closer. I need these girlie chats a lot more than she could ever imagine.

*** 11 ***

Ryan is an extremely observant person, I'm discovering. He has just asked me if everything was OK between me and Clair, when we left. He thought there was something, not right.

"No, everything's fine," I say, a little unconvincingly. "Why do you say that?"

"No reason, particularly. I just thought you two seemed a little…"

"A little what?"

"I don't know – perhaps it's just me. Anyway, what did you get up to while we were at golf, apart from looking after me and doing my packing?"

"Oh, nothing really. Just had one of our girlie chats – I've missed them."

"I bet you have. Let's move to Lundy Island and then we can visit them more often."

I laugh. "Funny you should say that because that's exactly what I was thinking – I'd love to live on Lundy Island. It's so peaceful and away from everyone and everything."

"Apart from the hundreds of tourists it gets."

"Hmm…" I place a hand on Ryan's knee as he drives along the road. "I'm looking forward to staying in the hotel."

"Yes, me too. It was great staying with Clair and Archie but there's nothing like having your own bit of space."

I nod agreeably. It has been nice staying with them, but night times were a little awkward in the sense that we felt obliged to be ultra-quiet when it came to any bedroom antics. Thankfully (clear conscience wise), it only happened once as we were either too tired or too afraid of making a noise that it dampened our libido. Now we are free to enjoy each other in the privacy of our own hotel room – who cares who will hear, we'll never see them again.

As we approach the hotel, I can see that it was once a very grand mansion. It's set high up, on a hill and has sweeping views of the valley, Ilfracombe town, the harbour and as far out to sea as anyone can see.

"Wow," I say as we get out of the car. "It's even better than the picture you showed me."

"I know, I didn't want to show you all the pictures because I wanted it to be a surprise."

"What a surprise it is... and what a magnificent surprise. I can't believe it, Ryan. It's truly amazing."

Ryan wraps an arm around my waist and pecks me on the cheek. "I thought you'd like it."

I've already got my phone out and I'm taking pictures of the scenery – it's so breathtaking.

"Shall we go and check-in because you've got this view from your room, madam."

"Really?" I honestly can't take it all in enough. I want to freeze time at this present moment. Standing here, overlooking such beauty with the man I love, next to me, is truly like being in heaven.

"Yes, come on – you can take as many photos as you like once we have checked in." Ryan laughs and goes to collect our bags from the boot of the car.

Our suite is just as amazing and the balcony view – oh my God, I just cannot describe it. I want everyone in the world to come here (at some point – not while I'm here) and see this. This is another place I want to live, right now, in this fabulous hotel.

"Have you seen the bathroom yet?" Ryan asks.

"No..." To be honest, I haven't really looked at the room at all. As soon as we walked in, I headed straight for the balcony doors, opened them up and stepped out into the late afternoon sunshine to continue getting a fix from the view. Ryan has started unpacking already, I can hear him behind me, opening wardrobe doors and drawers. As for me, I just cannot tear myself away from the view. At this moment, I'm the happiest girl in the world and I don't want the moment to end.

"Are you going to stay there all night?" Ryan laughs. "I suppose we could put a quilt and a pillow out there and you could sleep under the stars."

"Oh, that would be amazing," I say, in a dreamy state. "I'd love that."

"I wasn't being serious." He laughs again. "Come on, let's get unpacked, get changed and we'll go into town to find a restaurant for dinner and plenty of drinks..." He breaks off, thoughtfully. "Then, when we get back, we can make love under the stars tonight – on the balcony."

I turn away from the spectacular view and peer at Ryan, incredulously. "Really?"

"I was joking again, we could leave the doors open though." He laughs before wandering off to the bathroom.

It's not that he said we should do it on the balcony, it's more the words he used. He used *that* word, love, you know what I mean? That's only the second time I've heard him use it – in that context at least. It sounds so sexy when he says it.

I drag myself inside, not wanting to leave the view. I want to be absorbed by the scenery, in some strange way. I want to stay here forever, just to wake up to it every morning. It makes me immensely happy – I'm sure I must be over-infatuated with it. Bewitched even.

We found a gorgeous little restaurant earlier and had quite a few drinks to go with our delicious meal. We're back at the hotel now, lying on the bed fully dressed, with the flat screen TV on in the background. Ryan is stroking my bare leg, underneath my summery, wrap-around dress. He leans into me and kisses my mouth. "I love being with you."

I meet his eye. "I do too." He lifts my dress higher and kisses me again.

"I love everything about you..."

"Me too..." He pulls at the ties of my dress and it comes apart. "I mean, you... no, me... oh, you know what I mean, I love everything about you."

Ryan laughs and shakes his head at me. I really know how to kill off the moment, don't I? He gets up from the bed, leaving me lying here half-undressed and trying to count how many times he said that word, while he goes to the bathroom to clean his teeth.

We are now in the throes of some steamy, unrestrained sex, which we hadn't been able to do while we were at Clair's. Ryan is being particularly attentive to my needs tonight. Somehow, it all seems serious. Then he whispers in my ear...

"Susie... I have fallen in love with you... I *am* in love with you..."

They say that there are some mind-blowing moments in our lives, which we will never forget. Well, I've just had one. Like nothing I've ever experienced before, Ryan's words were so profound and made me feel like I wanted to weep – to cry like a baby. It choked me and for the first time in my adult life, I believed every single syllable. I believed in him and I believed in me.

I believe in us.

I haven't even replied because I'm completely taken by the moment to the point of being speechless. I'm floating along on a wave of intense delectation, rising and floating back down in unison with his every move, his every breath.

"I..." I still can't speak as we both come to a final crescendo of oneness. And then silence, apart from the urgency of our rapid breath. Stillness.

"I'm in love with you too, Ryan..."

There were times when I thought I had found true love in Kallum, but I look back at those times and realise now that those 'oh so precious moments' were one-sided, crude naivety. Then there was the whirlwind romance with Jett which I now realise was based on an insatiable lust for each other. We did love each other (which was declared the night he died) but I believe it was based on a different, deeper-rooted, nostalgic kind of love. I have a strange feeling that it would not have lasted though. As I ponder over my past relationships, Ryan is sleeping peacefully beside me. I now realise that I have never loved or been loved like this before. This is real. It has a compelling unknown strength. I know that now. This revelation has rendered me into wakefulness. I cannot sleep as my mind races through endless possibilities of what the future might hold. I'm scared as well as hopeful. Scared of losing like I have lost before. Hopeful of a real beginning, yet terrified of an ending, when there may not even be one.

***

The last few days have been magical, and that's saying it mildly. We are different. Everything we do, everything we say, everything we feel – it's all profoundly different. We love each other and that has been made perfectly clear in words and actions. It's like a part of Ryan has been unlocked and he now freely tells me he loves me. And it is usually him that says it first. And with deep meaning. He's sincere and I can tell that by the look on his face and the tone in his voice. Our eyes meet, he peers into my soul declaring his love, and I can feel it penetrate my innermost being.

Each evening, we've visited Clair and Archie and either, gone out for a meal, or drinks, or simply stayed at their place, while Archie cooked up a delicious fruity chicken curry. During the days, Ryan and I have been out sightseeing, walking (loads) and visiting many places of historical interest. It turns out that we both like history and find historical buildings or places, to be of great interest. We were surprised, when we discovered, that we both seem to get the same uncanny feel for a building and can stand in them for ages, just sucking up the history. I'm so glad I'm not the only one who gets these overwhelming emotions from people of the past and their often-tragic lives.

Today is our last day and I can't help feeling down. We are going to pop in and see Clair and Archie before we leave but I want to take the balcony and its view with me. Obviously, I can't, so I'm taking as many pictures as I can, from different angles.

"Haven't you taken enough pictures of that view, babe?" That's something new too, 'babe' – it seemed to get unlocked, along with the word, love. I like it, I have got to be honest.

"Just a couple more, then I'm done." I turn and grin at him cheekily.

"But you've taken loads every single day."

"Different times of the day, different lighting and different weather – they've all been different."

"And, don't tell me... different boats on the sea."

"Exactly. And ships," I add.

"OK, and ships then."

I turn back around and take two more pictures. "There you are, I'm done." Reluctantly, I close the doors and peer through the glass, while saying goodbye to the view, in my head.

Ryan picks up both of our bags and carries them to the door. "Come on then, cup of tea at Clair's before we head off home."

*** 12 ***

Neither of us want to say goodbye and we have stayed at Clair's for much longer than we had anticipated. I have invited Clair and Archie to stay with me whenever they want to, as I still have Clair's old bedroom empty. Clair has reciprocated with an open invite for us, but she has also just asked me why I haven't got a new flatmate yet. I open my mouth to answer when, to my surprise, Ryan jumps in. "I'm hoping I might get an interview." He turns and smirks at me.

Clair peers at him puzzled. "An interview?"

"Are you looking for a new job?" I ask, wondering what he's going on about and why he's changed the subject completely.

"No, I mean an interview to be your new flatmate." He winks at me.

"Oh... I..."

"That's a promising idea," says Clair. "Why not?"

"I was joking – I doubt Susie would want me living with her really."

"I..." Oh my God, yes, I would, but I don't want to seem too keen in case he really is joking.

"Yes, she would," Clair jumps in. "You should do it. Life is too short." She turns and looks at me. "Why not, Suse?"

"I... well... he can if he wants to," I laugh it off, in an attempt to cover my embarrassment. I shoot a cursory glance at Ryan before turning back to Clair. "Anyway, we really have to get going now. We've had such a lovely time here, Clair, that it's hard to leave."

"Yes, thank you for putting us up – it's been great to meet you and Archie."

"It's been our pleasure. Come again sometime."

"Oh, we will – definitely," says Ryan, rising to his feet and giving Clair a peck on the cheek. "Thank you." He stretches an arm out to me, offering his hand to pull me up, which I take gladly.

I hug Clair for what seems like ages. "I'm going to miss you."

"Not as much as I will miss you." She kisses me on the cheek, turns me around and slaps my behind. "Go on, off you go, or we'll be here all night saying goodbye."

Clair stands at the door as we drive away, waving and blowing kisses, while Archie stands behind her with his arms wrapped around her waist. I am going to miss her so much. Even more than the balcony view, I think.

As we head out towards the motorway, I place a hand on Ryan's knee. "I meant what I said earlier." My heart is racing because this is a big step for me, if he says, yes.

"About your flat?"

"Yes."

"I didn't think you sounded too keen."

"I thought you were joking."

"I was... but you know what they say. Many a true word is spoken in jest."

"So, you would like to then, really?"

"I'd love to... but only when you are ready." Ryan flicks a glance and a smile at me before turning his attention back to the road.

"I'm ready." You know, if it wasn't for the fact that I was confined to the inside of Ryan's car, I think I would be jumping up and down by now, screaming with joy. I am *so* ready and although we haven't been together for that long, in the grand scheme of things, I want to live with Ryan – right now, today. Forever. Suddenly, the end of our holiday has become a lot less doleful. This could be a brand-new beginning.

"I am too. It's crazy, but I am ready."

My heart is honestly fluttering like a little butterfly's wings. It sounds corny but it's true. I squeeze Ryan's knee and then stroke it lovingly.

"I am so in love with you, Susie Satchel – what have you done to me?"

I laugh and flick back my hair. It feels so good to be alive today. "I expect it's the same as you have done to me," I tell him, gladly.

I'm guessing you are back today, honey. Did you have an enjoyable time? When are we going to meet, Ryan? Love Mum xx

Hopefully soon, Mum. Had an amazing holiday – I'll pop round in the week to show you the photos. Love you xx

Love you too, honey. Sounds like you did have a lovely time! You don't often say, love you xx

Ha ha, yes, I'm all loved up xx

With Ryan? Xx

Maybe???? Xx See you soon xx

Hi Clair – we're home! Thank you for everything. Love you, millions xx

Love you more and Ryan is so gorgeous, you should let him move in xx

I am xx

Woohoo! No more lies, OK? Xx

No more – I promise you xx

I delete the last two messages in the thread – not because I'm covering up or lying but because I now want a fresh start. It's all upwards from here on. Honesty is the best policy, as they say, and I'm sticking to it.

Ryan has flopped down, on to the sofa, and his eyelids are heavy. Hardly surprising after our long drive home. The traffic was a nightmare and it added two hours to our journey. "Coffee?" I say, wondering if he is going to stay awake long enough to drink one.

"Hmm... please."

By the time I return with coffee, Ryan is fast asleep. His unpacked bag lies in the hallway, where he left it and I suddenly feel an urge to empty it and wash all his clothes. After all, he brought the bag into my flat, when he could have left it in the boot of his car if he had any intentions of going home tonight. I quietly place the mug of coffee on the table and tiptoe back out of the room, closing the door softly behind me. I empty both of our bags in the bedroom and take a huge pile of washing into the kitchen. That's it – the clothes are in – he's staying. Like it or not, although, I think he'll like it. I do hope so anyway.

***

Two days have passed, and Ryan hasn't gone anywhere. His clothes have been drying on the small clothes line in my tiny garden and then, dutifully, I have aired and ironed them. We went shopping yesterday, as I had absolutely nothing in, and Ryan hoovered the flat. Now, we are just about to sit down to a meal, cooked by Ryan, in *our* kitchen. Can you believe it? We're like a little married couple – it's great.

Ryan has made a lasagna (it's another one of his favourites and I've already made a mental note of it) and it smells delicious. He brings two plates over to the table and sits down. "Hope you like it," he says, taking a sip from his glass of wine.

"It smells lovely."

"We need to have a serious chat and what better way than to do it over a lasagna."

"Absolutely," I say and giggle into my glass of wine. "So, who's starting this serious chat then?" I knew it was coming because earlier, Ryan said we should talk, over dinner, to sort out where we're going.

"I will..." He sips at his wine again. "Well, it's obvious that we want to be together all the time."

I nod. "Yes."

"And, you need someone to help you with the bills."

"Yes..."

"So, do you want to make it official?"

"Official?" I begin to eat my lasagna, peering at Ryan with interest.

"Yes, I move out of the house I'm sharing and take on half your mortgage and bills."

"Yes, let's do it."

"But we'll do it properly, like you would if I was flat-sharing."

"There's no need..."

"You might change your mind about me one day, Susie – you need a get-out clause."

"OK, if you say so."

"Agreed?" Ryan raises his glass.

"Agreed," I reply, raising my own glass to his. "There is a problem though..."

"Oh?" Ryan's handsome little face looks so worried, suddenly.

I giggle. "Yes, if we're going to do this and be a real couple, living together, you're going to have to..." I smirk at him.

"Yes?"

"Meet my mum and dad."

I see the tension fall from Ryan's shoulders. "Absolutely. I'd love to meet them."

I half expect him to now say that I will have to meet his parents, but he doesn't. Maybe, like the 'I love you' thing, he's much slower at moving things forward, even though, he's moving in with me pretty quickly. He hardly ever talks about his family and I haven't found the right moment to ask him about them. As for his sister, Rachel, he doesn't mention her much either, yet they get on very well. To be honest, I really don't know that much about Ryan's family and only know snippets about his past and a long-term girlfriend he used to have who left him for an older, rich man. Ryan says the man is just her sugar-daddy and Ryan never realised, when he was with her, how much of a gold digger she was. By all accounts, he hates her now and has seen her once or twice, out and about, flaunting her new false boobs and eyelashes. He thinks I am so completely different to his ex and he loves the way that I am such a *homely* girl, as he puts it. Hmm, I'm thinking, homely girls are marriage material – right?

"Good, because my mum pesters me all of the time," I say.

"Why don't we go this week sometime?"

I'm taken aback. There's just no stopping him. "I'll see when they are free. Mum only works part time and Dad can come and go as he pleases really."

"Cool. So, back to me moving in then... When do you want it to happen because I'll have to let my landlord know?"

"Err..." I peer at my watch, feigning thoughtfulness. "Let's say... two days ago?"

Ryan sniggers. "OK, I'd better text the landlord now." He pulls his phone from his pocket and places it on the table. "Remind me, when we've finished."

"I will... oh, and Ryan?"

He looks at me expectantly.

I smile. "Welcome to your new home."

"Thank you – when do I get my key, madam?" He laughs. "Seriously, no rush."

"No, it's fine. Just as soon as I've eaten this lush lasagna – you can have Clair's old one."

Ryan peers at me and raises his eyebrows. "Wow – it's real then."

"It most certainly will be."

*** 13 ***

It's official. Ryan has got a key and he's given his landlord notice of his intention to leave (although he has left already, in a sense). For the last two days, we have been going over to his place (a large room in a shared house – it's quite nice actually) to clear out his belongings. He really doesn't have that much in the way of personal belongings... but then there is his sport equipment, that's quite a lot to be honest, and well over half of it is school stuff.

"Where are we going to put all this?" I say when we arrive home with the last of it.

"Err..." Ryan peers at me, apprehensively.

I smirk. "Well, I suppose that, as from today, it's official – you live here. You're my flatmate, so you're sleeping in the spare room, so that's where it can all go."

"Ha ha, very funny. Maybe my *stuff* can go in the spare room."

"But where will Clair and Archie stay?"

"Well, for a start, they aren't coming any time soon and this will all be gone in September. I'm either ditching it or taking it into school."

"OK," I say, slightly relieved. "That's good to know."

We unload the car and then have a quick cup of coffee. We're off to see my mum and dad and both of us are feeling nervous. Mum texted me this morning, she's so excited, and said that Dad will be doing a barbecue this evening. I pleaded with her to make sure that he does not wear any of his silly aprons. Mum assured me that he has a new one and we will like it. Luckily, I have already warned Ryan about my dad's aprons, but Ryan seems to be amused by it and thinks it's pretty cool. Men – huh.

"Are you ready?" Ryan calls out. I'm in the bathroom, putting the finishing touches on some subtle make-up. I open the door and Ryan is standing by the front door. He looks twitchy and jittery. "Wow, you look really nice," he says, eyeing my short, flowery skirt and figure-hugging, white t-shirt.

"Well, you're not whisking me off to bed now – you rampant monster."

He laughs. "Would I ever do anything like that?"

"Yes, you would. Oh, and before we go... I haven't mentioned to Mum or Dad that you've moved in yet."

"O...K... Does that mean you're telling them today?"

"Err... well, maybe if it comes up in conversation."

"It's hardly going to come up in conversation if they don't know, is it?"

"No, I know but..."

"Are you worried what they might say?"

"No... I... well, I don't know why I haven't told them yet."

"So, let's tell them today."

"No," I reply, quickly. "Don't you think they should meet you first?"

Ryan looks at me and smiles. "Well they are meeting me."

"No, I mean, get to know you first?"

"I'm not comfortable meeting them under some pretence that we don't live together."

I peer at Ryan, thoughtfully. "It's not a pretence. Look..." I reach for his hands and hold them. "If they ask anything like, where do you live, then we'll tell them – OK?"

Ryan nods. "OK... It's just... well, you know I hate lying."

"Absolutely – me too. There's no way I would lie to them – or anyone for that matter. I've had my fair share of lies in my time, trust me."

Ryan leans in and kisses my lips. "Me too."

"And it's not lying, it's more a case of... withholding information unless asked."

"Absolutely. Right, let's go." He grabs my hand and pulls me out of the door like, all of a sudden, he can't wait to get to my parent's house.

Once again, Ryan wanted to drive (I think he likes to take the lead but that's fine by me – I can't be bothered with driving). I've directed him to

Mum and Dad's house and we're just pulling into the drive. Mum had insisted that I text her to let her know we were leaving home (I think she's probably nervous too... Dad won't be though) so I am surprised to see that she is not at the front door, or at least, peeping out through the net curtains when we arrive, like she always does. We climb out of the car and Ryan straightens his shirt, runs his fingers through his hair and shakes his shoulders. "Are you OK?" I say, joining him.

"Yes, sure. Just a bit..."

"Nervous?"

"Yes, something like that."

"They won't eat you, you know." I giggle but I suppose it's more of a nervous laugh, to be honest. I can imagine that I would be far more nervous than Ryan is, if I had to meet his parents and I suppose that could happen one day. It would be nice to know a little more about his family, but he doesn't seem to want to tell me anything about them. I'm hoping that, meeting my parents, will spark off a discussion about his at some point.

"I just want to make a good impression," he whispers.

"Trust me, you will. Just by the way you look."

"Thanks." Ryan places an arm around my lower back and we move towards the door.

I open the door and call out. There's something very odd going on because Mum always comes to the door or at least she waits at the window, like I said before (unless I pay them an unexpected visit, which isn't very often because Mum *always* wants to know when I'm coming). I peer down the hallway, into the kitchen and can see dad's bottom sticking out. "Hi Dad... we're here," I call out, puzzled.

Dad stands up, straightening his back with a wince, and smiles. "Come through – we've got a mini crisis going on here."

Ryan follows me down the hallway and into the kitchen. I halt abruptly, the instant I see Mum. She's sitting on a stool with her foot up on the worktop, resting on a tea towel.

"You must be Ryan – nice to meet you," says Dad, offering his hand towards Ryan.

"And you too... err... can I call you, John?"

"What have you done, Mum?" I'm gawping at her little toe on her right foot – it's bleeding and swollen and it's turning a horrible colour too.

"Your only other option is, Dad." My dad laughs and shakes Ryan's hand warmly. "But I'll probably answer to most things."

"Hello... nice to meet you," Ryan says, stiffly, as he shoots a cursory glance at Mum's toe. "Have we arrived at an awkward moment?"

"Hello Ryan, nice to meet you and... yes, you could say that." She peers at Dad with a critical eye and then turns to me. "How many times have I asked your father to get rid of that silly doorstop on the floor – one of these days I'm going to break my neck."

I'm horrified – this is like being in my own worst nightmare, one I've created all by myself.

"It looks broken," says Ryan, wincing as he peers at Mum's toe again.

I know Ryan is just trying to be empathetic, but I wish he'd shut up right now.

"I wouldn't be surprised if it is," says Dad, bending down again to unscrew the metal doorstop from the floor. "They won't do much at the hospital for a broken toe."

"I am *not* going to the hospital," Mum exclaims. "Get me a bandage from the drawer behind you, please, honey."

As I grab a wad of bandage from the drawer, I freeze as I see Ryan open his mouth to speak again.

"Is it the same foot as last time? Sorry, I hope you're not offended but Susie told me about..." Ryan breaks off, his cheeks are beginning to flush. Not half as much as mine though.

Mum is staring at him completely perplexed. Dad looks up at him, from the floor and I am holding my breath as I suddenly feel so sick. "Oh, look, here's the bandage, Mum – let's get it wrapped up," I say, trying to detract from Ryan's words.

"The same foot as last time?" Mum quizzes. "What do you mean, my love?"

Ryan shoots a glance at me and frowns. "I'm sorry," he says, turning back to Mum. "Susie mentioned that you broke three toes a little while ago?"

Dad stands up and peers at me, incredulously. "Are we talking about the same mum here?" He laughs and takes the old doorstop out through the back door.

"Sorry my love, I don't know what you're talking about..." She looks at me, questioningly. "I've never broken a toe before... let alone three." She lets out a short burst of laughter.

I'm done. Oh my God, how am I going to get out of this? I want to shrivel and disappear at this present moment. I can't even look at Ryan. My heart is racing, and it feels like it's become lodged in my throat. I gulp hard and stare down at the bandage in my hand.

"You didn't fall down the stairs recently?" Ryan asks.

Why can't he just shut up, for God's sake? OK, I've been caught out. I'm a liar. He is going to hate me.

"No, my love, I didn't..." Mum looks at Ryan sympathetically and smiles. "I think you might have me mixed up with someone else."

"I'm sorry – I probably have. Please, forgive me." Then he turns and gives me a steely glare while Mum is tending to her toe. I look down at the floor and cannot meet his eye again. I know he's staring fixedly at me – I can feel it. Oh no.

Thankfully, Dad has returned to break Ryan's scowl of doubt. "I've got the barbecue going – fancy a beer in the garden, Ryan?"

"Yes, sure. I'm driving but I could have one, thanks. I hope your toe will be OK, Mrs Satchel." He passes me, and our eyes meet again briefly but there are no words and no warm smile from Ryan. I want to cry. I've deceived him, and he's found out, yet, he is covering up for me and making it look like he's been mistaken. That is so admirable of him, but I fear what might come later. Why, oh why did I say such a stupid thing that night when Kallum had turned up unexpectedly? Why didn't I just tell him the truth like Clair said I should have done? Especially when I know how much he hates lies. God help me.

Mum has bandaged her foot up, securing her little toe to the next one. "Don't you think you should get it checked out, Mum?"

"I'll see how it is tomorrow, honey. Your dad could drive me to the doctors."

"I was thinking more the hospital."

"Oh, good heavens, no. I am not going to sit down at A and E for four hours just for them to tell me there's nothing they can do and to go home and take paracetamol."

I suppose she's got a point because that is probably what would happen. "Are you sure you need it bandaged like that though?" The bandage is covering her whole foot and goes right up her ankle.

"Just while we're in the garden, honey. I don't want to knock it or anything."

I nod and smile at her.

"He seems very nice," she says, indicating, with her eyes, to the garden.

"Yes, he's lovely." As soon as the words have left my mouth I'm devastated. Why did I lie to him?

"That was an odd thing he said..."

"About your toe?"

"Yes," she laughs. "Perhaps it was his mum that fell down the stairs and broke her toes and he's got muddled."

I sigh. "No, Mum. I told him a lie, a few weeks ago. I feel so bad now." I turn and look out to the garden as I hear Ryan laughing with my dad. They are just inside the summer house, peering into Dad's box of aprons no doubt.

"What? Why?" Mum leans in to me and puts a hand on my shoulder. "Honey, you haven't known him long, why would you lie to him? I don't understand."

I take a deep breath and look Mum in the eye. I want to cry but I won't. "I told him you'd broken your toes, falling down the stairs."

Mum stares at me, astonished. "Why on earth would you do that, honey?"

Ryan and Dad are laughing aloud again. I peer out of the window to see Ryan trying on one of my dad's aprons. It warms me, and I have a momentary heart flutter to see them both getting on so well... then the crushing guilt returns, and I look at Mum. "God, I wish I hadn't..."

"Because I've now made you out to be a liar?"

"Yes – it's not your fault though, Mum. I should never had told him such a story, but I panicked."

"Why?"

I proceed to tell Mum why I made up such a stupid story and she listens empathetically while Ryan and Dad are still looking through all his aprons, in the summerhouse. I can see that Dad is wearing a bright red one now and it must be his new one because I certainly haven't seen it before. I cringe at the large white writing on the front of it. *Susie's dad is the best cook in the world.* "So that's it – that's why I said it and now... well, he's going to hate me for lying to him because he hates lies." Mum says nothing, and I watch her eyes darting around as she thinks things through. "And before you say anything, Mum, no, we cannot backtrack and say it was true."

"Oh, I thought it might help if I said I'd forgotten about it – what with the pain in my toe."

I shake my head at her. "No, because it would then become an even bigger lie and involve you and Dad as well. Somehow, I need to redeem myself for this. I don't know how, but I've got to try."

"Is he really going to take it that badly?"

I nod. "We were only saying, before we came out, that neither of us can stand lies."

"Oh dear..." says Mum, rubbing my back. "I'm sure he will forgive you if you just tell him the truth."

I muster up a half-smile. "I do hope so."

"He didn't need to cover-up for you like he did, you know."

"No, I know."

"He made out that it was his mistake – that's very good of him to have done that."

"I know," I sigh, forlornly. It *was* extremely good of him, that's why I'm so upset. He had every good intention not to create a scene or make me look bad, or even crazy, in front of my parents.

"Come on, let's go and join them in the garden, it might not be that bad at the end of the day. It looks like he's getting on very well with your father." Mum hobbles outside and I follow behind her like a little lost sheep, feeling sheepish.

Dad and Ryan have really hit it off. They just seem to have gelled and it's like they have known each other for years. They certainly have a love of aprons in common. Ryan has donned Dad's ridiculous udder apron for the whole evening. At one point, when Ryan was offered another beer, I plucked up the courage to speak up and said that I could drive us home if he wanted another drink. He met my eye briefly and said, thank you, then he gladly took another beer from my dad.

We're still sitting in the garden and it's gone way past ten o'clock. I'm surprised my dad is still awake, to be honest, but he's having such a laugh with Ryan that it has been an immense pleasure to sit back and watch and listen to them both. They seem to bounce off each other with endless jokes and banter. Dad likes Ryan, I can tell that, for sure. And Mum thinks he's utterly adorable and shocked me with her unprecedented words, 'He's a keeper'. Honestly, since when has my mum spoken like that or even heard of the saying?

"It's eleven o'clock," I say, surprised that the time has sped past this evening. "Shall we make a move soon?"

Ryan turns away from my dad and peers at me with squinted eyes. "Is it that time already?"

I nod and give a wavering smile as I realise that he's quite tiddly.

"Make sure you bring him again then," says Dad. "We've had a right old laugh, haven't we mate?"

"Yes, I've really enjoyed the evening, thank you, both of you, and…" Ryan looks down at Mum's bandaged foot, "I hope your toe gets better soon."

"Oh, I'm sure it will." Mum smiles warmly. "It's been a pleasure to meet you Ryan – you're a fine young man."

Ryan beams at her.

"Make sure you look after our Susie, she's a good girl – she makes silly mistakes sometimes… well, a lot of the time actually, but she's a good girl really."

"I will and yes, she's great."

We get up to leave and Mum does the huggy, cheek-kissing stuff before we go, like she's never going to see us again. She does it all the time, but she has the bonus of Ryan to say goodbye to this time.

We jump in Ryan's car and I drive us home in silence. My mind is racing as the atmosphere is heavy with mistrust. I just cannot look at Ryan, sitting next to me, as he hasn't said a single word yet, which does not bode well for the rest of the night – or what's left of it.

Surprisingly, when we arrive back home, I find that he is fast asleep in the passenger seat – no wonder we drove home in silence. I nudge him gently. "Ryan, we're home." That sounds so weird saying that to him. It makes me feel all fluttery inside. "Ryan?"

His eyes open slowly. "Oh, we're home." Sleepily, he climbs out of the car and wobbles to the door. He ended up having about six beers, at least, with my dad. Well, they were the ones I could count anyway – he may have had more. I wouldn't say he's that drunk though – more like very sleepy. I unlock the front door and we go in. "Would you mind if I went straight to bed?" He peers at me through hazy eyes.

"No, of course not. I'll be with you soon."

He pecks me on the cheek and goes straight to the bedroom – no teeth cleaning, nothing. I guess we'll be having that conversation about my lie, tomorrow. I cannot wait. That's a lie in itself.

*** 14 ***

"Good morning," I say, cheerfully, as Ryan enters the kitchen, bleary-eyed, at half past nine. He looks a little worse for wear, so I automatically jump up and make him a coffee. He grunts a 'morning' back to me and sits down with a thud. "Have you got a hangover?"

"A bit," he mumbles.

I continue to make a coffee for him, knowing full well that he is a little grumpy. In normal circumstances, it would be because he's feeling rough, but I know better today. "My mum and dad liked you..." I start.

"They are very nice people."

"You got on so well with my dad. He loved you."

"Yeah, good man."

"Look..." I turn and face him, my heart galloping. "I want to apologise for..."

Ryan peers at me with a glum expression.

"Well..." I clear my throat and take a deep breath. "I'm sorry for..." Ryan's eyes are boring holes in me, I'm sure. "Oh God, look, I'm really sorry, Ryan." I carry his mug of coffee over and sit down sheepishly, unable to meet his eye yet again. "I've really messed up, haven't I?"

He grasps hold of the mug and wraps his hands loosely around it. "Yep."

"I don't know why – I panicked, Ryan – I'm so sorry. Really I am."

"Any others?"

I shoot a glance at him and then lower my gaze back to the table. "Others?"

"Lies."

"Oh, no. That was the only one."

"Why?"

"Why? Do you mean why is it the only one?"

"No, Susie. I mean why lie to me?" He sighs heavily and twists his mug around, on the table. "Let's clear this up now. You know I hate lies. I thought you did too."

"I do... I... I detest them."

"Yet, you're happy to tell them – and in a big way too. You really put me in an awkward position last night."

God, I feel sick. I want to shrivel up under the table until this all goes away but I know it won't and I'm going to have to tell him the truth. "I know, I've been so stupid and I'm utterly sorry. Really, I am." I glance down at my fingernails and choose one to nibble at nervously.

"So, why do it?"

"It wasn't my mum texting that night, when I told you the story. It was... Kallum, my ex. I just panicked and before I knew it, I'd told you some ridiculous story about my mum breaking her toes."

"Why didn't you just tell me the truth?"

"I have no idea. I guess... I was worried that you'd be angry."

"Why would I be angry, Susie?"

I shake my head, desperately. "I don't know –"

"Because that's how your ex would have been – angry. You shouldn't have a preconception of me because of the way you've been treated in the past."

"I know, I'm sorry."

"You need to believe in me, Susie. We're stronger than that. Believe in us."

"I do – I really do."

"Then no more lies?"

"Definitely – no more, ever. I promise." Ryan reaches across the table and takes my hand in his. His palm is hot from holding the mug of coffee and it comforts me, so much so that an unexpected tear falls from my eye.

"Don't cry," he says, softly. "Tell me why he was texting you."

"He wanted to meet up... for a chat." Am I still lying? I don't think so. Surely, I'm just not giving any additional information, like the fact that Kallum left the front door, literally minutes before Ryan turned up that night.

"He still cares about you then?"

"I don't know. I doubt it."

"He must do if he wanted to meet you. I doubt he wanted to just pass the time of day with you."

I shrug and roll my bottom lip. "Well, whatever he wanted, I said no."

"OK, and do you feel that that was the right thing to do?"

I meet Ryan's eye, questioningly. "Yes, why do you say that?"

"No reason – I'm just trying to see the whole picture. I mean, if you decide that you do want to rekindle your relationship with him, I'd like to know about it – in advance. You owe me that at least."

"Oh God, no way. That was well and truly over last Christmas." I pause and look at Ryan through watery eyes. "You are all I'm interested in and I was so foolish to tell you such a stupid lie. I should have just come out with it and told you – I'm so sorry."

Ryan nods and squeezes my hand. "Be open and honest with me, Susie. That's all I ask. I'm a big boy. I can handle ex-boyfriends who may want you back – after all, forewarned is forearmed, as they say."

"I will, I promise... and thank you."

"Thank you for what?"

"For covering for me last night. You didn't have to do that, but you did. Not many people would. That made me realise that you are so different to what I've been used to in the past."

"I became an expert at covering-up with my ex-girlfriend. Unfortunately, it got to a point where I couldn't take her lies anymore and told her so. That's when she cleared off. I struggle to trust people and that's why I detest lies now, no matter how big or small." Ryan looks at me and smiles. "But, for the record, yours was small – in fact, a pinprick in the universe, so let's forget it ever happened and you can give me a cuddle."

I smile back and another tear falls. This man is so incredibly special, so I need to get as far away as possible from my baggage of deception and the constant dark cloud I seem to live under. In hindsight, even that *facebook* message, which had tormented me for so long, was probably not so terrible. Yet, I went to great lengths to cover up my drunken mistake and will have to live with that dreadful secret of what I did, forever. I hope I can... even more so now. I love Ryan Bagshaw – he is the best thing that has ever happened to me.

I crouch down beside him, and he wraps his arms around me. "And... I've got to say that I've never heard such a ludicrous lie in my life – your mum broke three toes while falling down the stairs – where the hell did that come from in that pretty, little head of yours? I had to have a giggle about it, to myself, last night." He hugs me tighter and laughs into my hair. "Susie Satchel, you are a one-off. I've never met anyone like you."

***

The school holidays have ended so quickly and so much has changed during the time. I'm going back to work today (thank goodness, it's an inset day) but there won't be any children at school and the day will consist of a morning's training and then the new-team planning and preparations for the afternoon. Boundless joy. And of course, I'll be working with Sultry Sarah for the next year... even more boundless joy. I suppose, on the upside, she may be able to give me some make-up tips, she wears enough of it. Perhaps I should not be starting the new academic year off with negative thoughts, but I can't help it – I don't want to go back to school (I'm saying that with a screwed-up face and a crying voice)!

I enter the school apprehensively. I haven't seen anyone for six weeks and it feels like I'm starting a new job. Everyone is meeting in the hall, so I wander down there, hoping I'll bump into Jade before I arrive at the hall's double doors – I need a little moral support this morning.

"Morning, Miss Satchel," A voice comes from behind me. "Did you have a good holiday?"

I turn to see Juicy Jane, literally flowing down the corridor towards me, wearing a bright yellow, flowery maxi dress. She has a deep bronze tan and her hair has lightened considerably. I'm unsure whether her hair has turned a brassy colour from the sun or if she has dyed it. Whatever it is, she looks a picture of health and sun-kissed beauty. "Yes, I did thank you. Did you?"

"Amazing, incredible – insane, in fact. I'm ready for the new term now though. Hectic, heavenly holidays do take their toll, you know. I'm looking forward to a decent night's sleep and getting into a routine again." She looks me up and down, like she normally does. "What have you been up to? It doesn't look like you went abroad."

"No, I went to Devon for a week though."

"Devon? Who goes to Devon?" She breaks off and peers at me. "Only kidding, I'm sure it was very nice. Who did you go with? Your parents?"

"No..." I pause briefly, "my boyfriend."

"Oh. You have a boyfriend? I didn't know." She gives a forced smile. "What his name?"

"Err..."

"Are you thinking up a name or have you forgotten?" She laughs aloud as we reach the hall doors and pulls one side open. Then she saunters off, into the hall, flicking her bronze locks back as she goes, before I can answer her.

The hall is already filled with people and there are only a few chairs left at the tables. I quickly scan each table, hoping I might see Jade, and there be a seat free next to her, or at least on her table. Sadly, there isn't. Jade is sitting right at the back with most of the other TAs and there are no free chairs. She waves at me and I smile back.

"Come and sit with us," Jane calls out from a table at the front. She's sitting next to Sarah, my beloved new teacher – not.

Reluctantly, I walk over and perch on a seat at the end of the table, next to Sarah.

"I was just telling Sarah that you can't remember your boyfriend's name," Jane whispers, before she giggles into her hand and nudges Sarah with her elbow.

I glare at her, my top lip curling disdainfully. "Of course, I do. You didn't give me a chance to answer."

"Ignore her," says Sarah. "She's still in cloud-cuckoo-land at the moment."

"I'll try to," I say, attempting to conceal the sneer forming on my face. I look straight ahead to the front of the hall as Mr Reynolds walks in, wearing bright red tracksuit bottoms and a white polo shirt. He's tanned too and his unnaturally white teeth gleam as he smiles.

"Welcome back," he says, projecting his voice across the hall. "I do hope you have all had plenty of time to rest up. We have a busy time ahead of us." A babble of voices rings out as Mr Reynolds stands at the front, hands on hips, nodding his head and grinning.

"Aren't you wondering why I'm in cloud-cuckoo-land, as Sarah put it?" Jane is leaning right across Sarah as she whispers to me. "And what's your boyfriend's name then?"

"OK, ladies and gents, listen up. This morning we are going to be looking at our school with a growth mindset. Who would like to explain what I mean by that?"

The hush around the room is profound. Sarah nudges me and indicates to Mr Reynolds. I meet her eye with a menacing glare. "Did you have something you wanted to say?" Sarah whispers. I shake my head, furiously, at her.

"Ah, Miss Satchel," I hear Mr Reynolds' voice rip through my ears. "Do you have something you want to say?"

"Err..." I gulp back the rising fear in me. "No..."

He peers at me inquisitively. "Don't be shy, Miss Satchel. Miss Chambers seems to think you have an innovative idea."

I shoot a sideways glance at Sarah who is beaming and nodding her head. "No... I... I've forgotten what it was now."

Jane lets out a giggle and then raises a hand to shield her mouth as she whispers, "You're very forgetful today, Susie. Nothing new there then."

I turn and sneer at her. What is wrong with these two girls? They are consumed with making me look like a numbskull. I hate them both immensely.

*** 15 ***

"I actually hate them far more than immensely. I'm not kidding."

Ryan strokes my hair with one hand while his other wraps me in a tight embrace. "I don't doubt that for one minute. What is up with them? They seem intent on ruining your credibility at school." He releases his arm from my waist and looks down at me. "Do you want me to have a word with them?"

"No, that would make things worse..." I break off, thoughtfully. "And, although I eventually told them my boyfriend's name was Ryan, I didn't say which Ryan. Jane was gloating when she asked me what you did for a living, but luckily, she got distracted before I could answer."

"Were you going to tell her I was a teacher?" Ryan is smiling at me.

"No, I thought she might guess and I don't want either of them knowing anything about my private life – not yet anyway."

"So, what would you have said if she hadn't been distracted?"

I giggle and meet Ryan's eye. "I was going to say that you were a dustbin man."

Ryan's eyes open wide. "Why a dustbin man?"

"It would have given them something to sneer about, wouldn't it?"

"Dustbin men probably get well paid and, Susie?"

"Yes?"

"You can't lie, remember?"

"I know." I look down and remember how he hates lies. "It would have been a joke rather than a lie, don't you think?"

"Hmm, I'm not sure. By all means, avoid the questions if you can, but don't let them have the satisfaction of calling you a liar when they do find out."

"You're right."

"So, how was the rest of your day?"

"Well, once Sarah was away from Jane, this afternoon, she was quite reasonable with me. I made up some resources while she did some paperwork, for tomorrow. Then we went through the week's planning and she actually said she was looking forward to working with me this year. Honestly, I nearly fell off my chair." Ryan laughs and pulls away from me, turning to make a coffee. "So, how has your day been?" I add.

"It was OK... I hate the first day back. Everyone is so miserable, even though we had no kids there. Training was boring, and I did practically nothing this afternoon, apart from clock-watching, as I'd done all the work before the end of term."

"A nice, easy day then."

"No, a boring day. So boring that I almost fell asleep. So boring that I was more bored than a bored thing on a boring day."

"Did you see Amber?" I ask, trying to steer Ryan away from the boring day.

"Yes, she didn't speak to me though."

"Oh well, nothing lost there."

"Exactly, I'd rather she didn't talk to me either, she's really gone weird over the last few months." Ryan finishes making two coffees and brings them to the table. "It's like she's got some stupid little secret and she sniggers every time I walk past her. I'm sure she's lost it."

Oh God. She does have a little secret but why she would think it would affect Ryan, I don't know... unless she has another... Unless she knows about us – no, she can't know. Can she?

"And I didn't tell you about Rachel either. Went right out of my mind when we were doing all the holiday stuff."

"Oh?" I'm intrigued. That's the first time he has mentioned his sister since we've been together. He's very odd about his family. I know he's got his sister, and a brother, and a Mum and Dad but he never talks about them. Even when I ask about them, he changes the subject or says something like, 'oh, I don't see them a great deal – they're always so busy.'

"Yes, she left, end of term. She's got another job now. She can't seem to stay in any one place for long. It's not even a promotion job either."

"Well, perhaps she wasn't happy and wanted to move on."

"Or, it could be something to do with this fella she's been talking to online. He lives somewhere in Sussex and that's where her new job is."

"Oh gosh, so maybe she's seeing him then."

"I think so."

"Well that's nice. I hope it works out for her. I liked your sister."

"She liked you too... I can't think why..." He smirks and kisses me on the nose. "Anyway, I'm sure she'll be so much happier in Sussex."

"Why do you say that? I mean, I get the 'fella' bit but what if it doesn't work out?"

"Whether it does or not, I just think she will be happier living over there."

I peer at Ryan questioningly. "Why do you think that?"

He shrugs. "Our dad gives her a hard time sometimes – she'll be away from him now."

"What do you mean?" I'm intrigued. This is the first time that Ryan has really mentioned one of his parents.

"He's just a pain sometimes. Nothing more." He picks up his mug of coffee and stands up. "Right, what shall I cook for our tea, I'm starving."

He's changed the subject again. He does this all the time, whenever there is the slightest hint that he may have to talk about his family. What is it with him... or them?

"How about a pasta bake?" Ryan is now poised with a pasta packet mix in one hand and the pasta dish in the other. It makes me giggle but I know the 'family' conversation has ended as abruptly as any other time.

How was school honey? Are things OK with Ryan? Did you sort out the little lie problem? Me and your dad thought he was very charming. You must come over again soon xxxx

All sorted, Mum. Yes, we will, and school was OK. No kids today (training day) but they'll be back tomorrow so it'll be all go! We'll come around soon – promise xx

***

Three weeks have flown by already and we're almost half way through the first half-term. I can't believe how quickly it has gone. At home, Ryan and I have a cosy little set-up where he does most of the cooking (when he hasn't got to work late) and I do the washing, ironing and cleaning. At the weekends, we share all the chores. It works well and if anyone could see us, they would think we were a right little pair of newlyweds. In my dreams...

We're flaked out in the living room, snuggled together, watching some rubbish on the TV when my phone tinkles. I drag myself out of Ryan's embrace and reach for it on the coffee table. Ryan hasn't stirred and continues to remain fixed on the television screen. I say that we're watching some rubbish on the TV, but it has certainly caught Ryan's attention – it's a repeat programme about the changes in the American Mafia from the past to the present. Boundless joy – not. Half-heartedly, I unlock my phone and see a message notification.

I've got a little boy – 7lbs 4oz – born last Thursday. Called him Taylor x

I'm stunned. Ryan hasn't taken his eyes off the TV screen, let alone blink, he's so engrossed. I peer at him, wondering whether I should tell him the news, but I don't think he's even aware that my phone went off. I read the message again, searching for some clue as to why I have even received it. I should reply but I'm unsure of what to say. I look over at Ryan again but he's in another world – mafia world. My thumb is poised over the tiny keyboard in my phone. I want to reply but should I ask for Ryan's approval? Of course not. I'm not doing anything wrong. I'm not lying, am I? I haven't been asked anything. *Wonderful news but why would you want to share that with me?*

We could share him if you wanted to x

Whether I've been asked anything by Ryan, or not, I need to share this with him (not Kallum's son, obviously). Oh my God. "Ryan?"

"Hmm?" he replies, without taking his eyes from the TV.

"I've had this weird message from..." I can see that he isn't paying any attention to what I'm saying. "Ryan?"

"Yeah?" He's still staring at the TV screen intently.

I'm holding the phone out with an outstretched arm. "I've had a message..." Ryan reaches for the TV remote and turns the volume up slightly. "Ryan?" I say, with an irritated tone.

"Hang on," he says, holding a finger up in the air as if it's the pause button to my mouth. "I just want to hear this bit..."

I huff and peer down at my phone again. *Are you insane? What do you mean by that exactly?* I send the message and turn back to peer at Ryan. He's totally oblivious.

Sorry, Susie, I should explain myself. I'm a one-parent family now – just me and little Taylor. You'd love him! He's so tiny but he has big brown eyes and loads of dark hair sticking up all over the place.

Sorry, I didn't mean to sound rude. I just wasn't getting the 'share him' bit. And why are you a one-parent family? What's happened to Tania? And congratulations but you and me will never be together again – sorry (if that's what you mean by sharing him).

I glance over at Ryan and he still hasn't peeled his eyes away from the TV screen. I could be having an affair right under his nose and he wouldn't have a clue.

Sorry Susie, I probably didn't mean that bit – had a few too many drinks. I'm out celebrating with some friends and I've had a belly-full. Taylor is being well looked after by my mum tonight. Tania gave him up at birth. She didn't want anything to do with him. She's an absolute bitch and has nothing to do with her family now either (they wouldn't want anything to do with her anyway). She's now under the doctor's care because she has been taking drugs and been acting really weird. Taylor has been cleared and is free of any drugs in his system. We separated a couple of months ago and it was arranged that she would give birth to the baby and I would become the legal guardian. She has been seeing someone else for months too. And yes, before you say anything, I know exactly how you felt now with regards to two-timing. That's why I came around to see you. I wanted to at least try and amend things, if nothing else. Having Taylor has made me realise what huge mistakes I've made in the past. Including, leaving you on Christmas day.

I'm totally stunned. I stare at my phone's screen in the same way that Ryan is compelled to stare at the TV screen. This is like a movie, surely, it's not real. "Ryan?" I say, giving him a gentle nudge.

"Hmm?"

"I've had a message from... Kallum."

Ryan nods his head. "That's nice."

I'm taken aback. "Ryan," I say more forcefully.

"Yes?"

"My ex, Kallum."

"Yes?"

I want to scream. I'm in-between, the love of my life who can't tear himself away from the mafia for more than a nanosecond and my unfaithful ex-boyfriend who wants to share another woman's baby with me. Aargh! I get up from the sofa, brush past Ryan's knees and head for the kitchen, irked by the lack of response from my current boyfriend and abundant response from my previous boyfriend. *Well, I am so sorry to hear your news Kallum. It's terrible, but thankfully you are going to look after your son and I'm sure you'll do a decent job. Unfortunately, it's too late to be sorry now, although, I do wish you well with your baby. Like I said to you before, I've moved on with my life and I'm very happy now. All the best for the future, kind regards, Susie.*

I wish you well too. Sorry for contacting you. I'm going home now as I can't be too hungover for the morning. Parenting is a full-time commitment. All the best, Kallum.

I put the kettle on and gaze out of the back-door window, dumbstruck by the typed conversation I've just had. Then I hear dramatic music coming from the living room and realise the programme is finishing. A moment later, Ryan appears at the kitchen door. "Sorry babe, I was totally engrossed."

"I could see that," I say, turning to make drinks.

"I'm sorry." I feel Ryan's hands slip around my waist and his head rest on my back. "What were you saying?"

"I had a text from Kallum."

"Asking you out again?"

"No, asking if I'd like to share his baby with him, actually."

Ryan pulls me around and peers at me, perplexed. "What do you mean by that?"

"Exactly that. I can share his baby with him, if I'd like to." I smirk before turning back to finish the drinks.

"Is he crazy?"

"Nope."

"What the hell…" Ryan pulls his hands away from my waist. "What the hell is going on?"

"I would have told you if you'd been able to tear your eyes away from the TV screen."

"I know, I'm sorry. I… I'm interested in that kind of stuff. It was coming to the end – I'm sorry."

I turn back around, pass a coffee to him and grin. "If you're going to listen to me, I will explain, or you can simply read the message thread." I hand my phone over and we return to the living room. See, no lies. No covering anything up. It's all in the open. It feels good to live like this. Kallum could certainly learn a thing or two from us.

*** 16 ***

Winter is drawing in. The days are getting shorter quickly and school is just as manic as ever. We had the half-term holiday week, a couple of weeks ago, but I didn't get to spend much of the time with Ryan as he had so many things to do, at or for his school. That's where being a teaching assistant has its good points – I don't have to go to school in the holidays, unless I really want to. And I don't ever want to.

I visited my parents, during the time off, and Mum quizzed me about why her and Dad hadn't seen Ryan again. I had to reassure Mum that we were indeed, still together, and also, tell her that Ryan had moved into my flat to help cover living costs. I then had to explain that Ryan wasn't using the spare room as his bedroom because we are a couple and couples usually share a bedroom. I think my dear old mum got it in the end. So, now they know, and Mum has decided, two weeks later, via a text message, that we should go around for Sunday dinner to celebrate our cohabiting. Hence, tomorrow, we are going to Mum's for a roast. It's Saturday morning and I haven't told Ryan the news yet but I'm sure he'll be delighted to see my dad again. He often asks when we are going to see them again but, what with one thing or another, we just haven't had the time or, when we've had the time, we haven't had the inclination.

As for school, things have been going quite well in my new class, with my new teacher. I can't believe how different Sarah can be when she's not with Jane. I'm starting to think that Jane is the ringleader because I could almost stretch myself to say that Sarah can be quite nice. I know that's a stark contrast to my previous thoughts about her, but I mean it. She *can* be nice. And I have got to give her credit and say that she is a very good teacher too. I've got to know her a little better and have discovered that she still lives at home with her mum and her younger sister. There doesn't seem to be a father on the scene (or at least, not one that she has mentioned) and from what I can gather, she doesn't have a boyfriend either, which surprises me because she is very attractive.

So, life really hasn't been too bad of late and if anything, things are great in my world. Ryan is amazing – he works hard, he plays hard and he loves hard, in the gentlest way imaginable. He's attentive, mindful and studious – well, unless he's watching a programme about the mafia, then he's mindless. He's generous, considerate and humorous. He's everything I could ever want, and more. I'm so lucky to have him.

"What time will you be finished at football tomorrow?" Ryan has just got up and come wandering into the kitchen with a tatty head and sleepy eyes. He's had a tough week at school with several late nights, so a Saturday morning lie-in has been well-deserved.

"Why do you ask?" he questions, flicking the kettle on and reaching for a cereal bowl at the same time.

"We've been invited out for Sunday dinner."

His sleepy eyes open wider, with interest. "Oh?"

"Mum thinks we should celebrate our cohabiting. She's doing a roast for four o'clock. I said you would be home by then."

Ryan smiles. "Yes, definitely. It will be nice to see them again. I look forward to it. It's been too long. I'm happy to meet you there if you want to go over earlier."

I nod. "Yes, that would be nice. I could do with a proper catch-up with Mum. I'll go over about twelve."

"OK," he says as he pours a generous portion of frosted flakes into the bowl and begins to munch on them before the kettle boils. He always manages to eat half of his cereal before he has added milk and says that he likes to eat his breakfast that way. Since being a child, he's always had half of it without milk, the other half with. "And while I think of it..." He swallows his mouthful. "...we should talk about Christmas."

"Oh?" I feel a little flutter in my chest. He's not leaving me for Christmas, is he? I hope he's not going away anywhere. I need to be with him. I need this Christmas to be normal after the last one. I'm panicking. Why am I panicking? "Why?" I ask, tentatively.

Ryan shakes his head and rolls his eyes. "My mum has contacted me..."

"Oh," I cut in. "Your mum?" How long have we been together? I'm gobsmacked – this is the first time he has mentioned anyone in his family without being prompted or questioned but even then, he always clamps up and changes the subject quickly, like I've said before. His childhood and family have all been avoided and so vague. I have got to admit that I am feeling irrationally fearful at this moment.

Ryan peers at me with a look that I haven't seen before. I'm sure his eyes are looking as worried and fearful as mine. "Yes, she wants us all to get together on Boxing day."

"All?"

"Me, Rachel, my brother... and our partners."

"O...K..." I go over to Ryan, just as the kettle boils, and give him a hug. I can see that he is struggling with this. I don't know why he is, but I know he is. "Is that a problem?"

He shakes his head, as if he's just come out of a daydream. "No... no, of course not. I suppose you're going to meet them eventually."

"Well, I've met Rachel already. She was lovely."

Ryan nods. "Yes, I know."

"So, I'm sure it'll be fine."

He nods again, unconvincingly. "I... I've never told you much about my family."

"No, you haven't. To be honest, I've always felt like..." Oh gosh, I might as well come out with it now. "Well, I've always had the impression that you didn't really want to talk about your parents at all... or your brother."

Ryan sighs heavily. "No, you're right. It's been kind of awkward."

"So, do you want to talk about them now?" I place a hand on his back and rub it gently.

"I'll make coffee first. I suppose, if you're going to meet them, you probably want to know about them first."

"That would be nice."

"Trust me, it won't be nice, Susie. Nice is not a word that is suitable to describe my dad or my brother."

I gulp hard. This is why he's never talked about them. He doesn't get on with them. There's obviously some kind of rift in the family. I'm intrigued but slightly nervous for some reason. Now, I'm going to discover who Ryan Bagshaw really is.

Ryan finished his cereal while I quickly put the washing on. It's a bright, sunny day, although it's cold, and there's just enough of a breeze to blow our clothes dry. I think that we could be talking about his family for a while, once Ryan is dressed, so we have decided to get some chores done first, especially as we'll both be out for most of the day tomorrow. That way, we can sit in the comfort of the living room and he can tell me all about his family. I'm sure I'm making it out to be a bigger deal than it really is, by asking Ryan not to say any more until my jobs are done and I'm able to give him my full attention, but that's what I did and that's how it is now. So, I'm currently racing around the flat, tidying up as fast as I can while Ryan gathers his paperwork from the dining table and stacks it into one neat pile.

We're done. It's been a whole lot of fun, as it turned into a game of tag. Only Ryan can make chores so much fun. Now, we're in the living room and the Saturday afternoon football is on the TV, but purely as background noise, according to Ryan. "I could have told you all this earlier. It needn't have waited until all the jobs were done," he says.

"But I wanted to listen properly – you know, I didn't want to be distracted by the list of chores."

Ryan looks down at the carpet. "Your insistence on me waiting to tell you seems to have made a bigger deal of it now though."

"But I'm interested in your family – it's the one thing I know nothing about and I would say it's the main part of your background."

Ryan shrugs and turns the corners of his mouth down. "I don't have much to say about them really."

I nod sympathetically. "That's OK. Tell me what you want to tell me. I promise, I'll ask no questions." I reach for his hand, knowing full well that the light-hearted fun we'd had, playing tag earlier, had instantly evaporated the moment we sat down together.

"My mum's OK, in some ways..."

"OK," I say, reassuringly. A question is already screaming out in my head, but I don't want to push it.

"It wouldn't be so bad if you were meeting her on her own." He turns and meets my eye, a troubled look in his own eyes.

Argh – another question. I give him a wavering smile but say nothing.

"My dad... well, he's a mean man."

I peer at him, not knowing quite what sort of facial expression to use as my face twists and turns from a look of dismay, to pity, to surprise. Questions, questions – I need to bite my lip to contain them.

"And my brother's not much better." Ryan looks down at the carpet again, as if he's searching for words down there. "I haven't seen him for four... maybe nearly five years."

"Oh?" I mutter, trying to sound like I'm not phased at all. Why? Why? Why? Gosh, he's dragging this out and I want to scream questions at him.

"We had a fight..."

Who did? You and your brother? You and your dad? You, your brother and your dad? You, your brother, your dad and your mum? A fight? A real one? Am I just being extremely impatient or is Ryan dragging this out? It's driving me crazy already. "O...K..." I say, squinting my eyes and frowning.

"Everyone got involved one way or another. It was a complete mess."

So, everyone had a fight? Oh God, this is bloody painful – why can't he just spit it out? It's killing me, trying to contain the gazillion questions I have now.

"And that's why I don't see them much anymore." Ryan shrugs and flops back on the sofa.

Is that it? Is that all he's going to say? I said I wouldn't ask but I'm sorry – I've got to. "What... what kind of fight?"

"A proper fight."

"Who?"

"Everyone."

"Who's everyone, Ryan?"

He peers at me, his eyebrows knitted together with frustration. Trust me, it's me who should be more frustrated. "I thought you said you wouldn't ask questions," he mumbles.

I sigh. "You haven't exactly told me anything – apart from you had a fight."

"That's all there is. We had a big family fight – that's why I don't see them much."

Argh! I want to shake him, honestly, I do. Why can't he just explain everything? He's a teacher, a communicator, a speaker. Why can't he just tell me? "Ryan?"

"Yes?"

"You haven't really told me anything. I mean, I could tell you that I had a fight with my mum and dad. You would be shocked by that until I explained that it was over a new school blazer that I had to wear when I was eleven years old. And then, if I told you it was a proper fight, you'd be very surprised."

"Yes, I would."

"So, you've only told me the bare minimum and I'm sitting here feeling a bit shocked as my imagination concocts all these crazy scenarios of how or why you had a fight and just how much of a fight it was. Do you see what I mean?"

Ryan nods and smiles sheepishly. "Yes, I know."

"Incidentally, I did have a bit of a fight with my parents because I refused to wear the blazer until they pinned me down and put it on me."

"OK," says Ryan, resignedly, "I get what you mean so I'll explain."

I slump back and join him in the comfy softness of the cushions. My hands are clasped together tightly. I don't know who I feel anxious for, me or him?

"My dad is a bit like a mafia kingpin – the godfather – "

"Oh my God, really? Is that why you watched...?"

"No, he's not actually part of the mafia but he acts like he is. And yes, I know what you were going to say... that programme I was watching, it did remind me of my dad."

"OK," I say, hesitantly. This is obviously a bit more serious than I thought and I now get why he was obsessed with the TV that night.

"So, my dad is the head of the family, in a big way. We all grew up, living in fear of his wrath. Even my mum was terrified of him. When I was a kid..." Ryan shifts uncomfortably. "I used to lie in bed awake, listening to him shouting at her and on some occasions, hitting her."

"Oh, my goodness, I'm so sorry." I place a hand over my mouth.

"She covered up for him all the time. She told us she'd tripped up or bumped her head on a cupboard, but I always knew that wasn't the case. When I was a little older, I asked her why she put up with him hitting her, but she denied it and grounded me for a month for saying such a thing."

"How awful... for you, I mean... well, and your mum."

"It all came out, one Christmas, five years ago. My brother, Rob, was a drug addict and I suspected him of being a dealer as well. I accused him of supplying drugs to teenage kids. He went crazy and attacked me..." Ryan breaks off and looks at me, his big brown eyes filled with sadness. "When I got the better of him, my dad stepped in and beat both of us until we were unable to move, while my mum and Rachel looked on, screaming and crying. My mum insisted that me and Rob were at fault and got what we deserved. Rachel was the only one who would talk to me for three years after that. Then my mum contacted me and said that I, along with Rob, was forgiven – hard to believe right?"

"Oh God, I'm so sorry, Ryan. I would never have imagined that this was why you didn't like to talk about your family."

"Mum has asked that we all have a reunion this year as her and dad are not getting any younger and, apparently, Rob is a changed man and now has a nice girlfriend. Mum said he's clean and she also said that my dad is calm and fulfilled with his new venture in life."

"Oh?" I say, "and what's that?"

"He owns several businesses and properties now and, like he has always done, he has his fingers in many a pie, as they say. He's always been the same – he gets involved in all sorts of deals. I used to think that he was like this big drug baron, but Mum swears he's never been anything of the sort and has succeeded in life through pure hard work alone..." Ryan breaks off again and gazes out of the window. "I've never thought that he doesn't work hard to get what he wants but I wouldn't mind betting that he's used a little brute-force too."

"Sounds intimidating."

"He *is* intimidating." Ryan looks at me before taking my hand in his. "But I don't want you to feel threatened by him in any way. I knew you'd meet them one day, but I didn't want you to judge them by my story. Sadly, it's too late for that, now that I've told you everything."

"I won't judge them at all. It's none of my business what has gone on with your family in the past. I'm just sorry that you've had such a tough time. I had no idea."

"Oh, don't worry. I'm so over it. I've said, yes, to Mum, about Boxing Day, but it's purely for Rachel's sake. I wouldn't entertain going now that Rob is back there, if it wasn't for Rachel."

"Does he live there?"

"Yes, with his girlfriend, apparently. They are planning to get their own place but are staying with my parents temporarily."

"What's his girlfriend's name?" I know this is all very serious at the moment, but I've suddenly twigged on and I might burst out laughing if her name begins with an 'R'.

Ryan shrugs. "No idea – I haven't asked, and I don't really care." He sighs heavily. "I know I've got to make the effort to let the past lie. Rachel said we both have to."

I peer at him puzzled. "When I bumped into you in the shop last Christmas, you were buying a hamper for your parents. Things must have been OK then."

"That was the first time I'd seen them since... the fight. It was a peace offering, instigated by Rachel. Rob wasn't there – I didn't have to deal with him then."

"Oh, I see. So, your problem lies more with Rob than your parents."

"I suppose so."

"So, if we meet up and it all goes well for you and your brother, then things could be back to normal?"

"I don't ever want things to go back to normal – they've got to get better. Money can't buy love."

"What do you mean by that?"

"Oh, I don't know. It's just a saying, right?"

"Yes, but why would you say that?"

Ryan shrugs. "I don't know really... maybe I shouldn't have."

Wow, this is all so complicated. Ryan still seems a bit cagey about it all but when he pulled himself up from the sofa and offered to make another drink, I got the distinct impression that the conversation was over for the time being. I hear about families like his – usually on the *Jeremy Kyle* show – but would never have guessed that there was one so close to home. I think I've been truly blessed to have the parents I've had. I've always imagined that teacher-types come from good homes – how wrong was I?

*** 17 ***

"Honey, it's been so long." Mum wraps her arms around me like she hasn't seen me for months and months, years in fact. Ryan is standing behind me at the door, looking awkward as Mum lets me go and then gives him a big hug. "It's so lovely to see you again. Is she looking after you well?" Ryan nods and smiles. "Come in, come in... it's been so long." She eyes me with a frown.

"It hasn't been that long, Mum," I say, tutting and shaking my head. "I saw you a few weeks ago."

"Nine," she interrupts.

"Nine weeks?"

"Yes." We follow her into the house and remove our coats. "Nine weeks – I don't think I've ever not seen you for nine weeks." She gives Ryan a silly, exaggerated wink and continues. "This young man must be keeping you very busy." Ryan blushes a little and gives an awkward smile.

"You were away for three of those weeks, Mum. So, it's only six really."

"You can't count those as not being weeks."

"Yes, I can."

"What's all this arguing about?" Dad appears at the end of the hallway, wearing one of his aprons. He smiles at Ryan. "Good to see you again mate."

"You too," says Ryan, edging away from us like he can't wait to get away.

"It's a shame your football was cancelled this morning," says Dad, shaking Ryan's hand as they meet. "It's stopped raining now."

"The pitch was waterlogged anyway – whether the rain continued or not, we couldn't have played."

"Shame – nice you could come earlier though."

"Come through to the lounge, your dad's just putting the kettle on – aren't you, John?" says Mum, guiding us through the living room door. "I'll show you the holiday photos – we've downloaded them on to the television screen. How clever are we?"

I give a little helpless grin to Ryan as we sit on the sofa. I know what's coming as I've been here before. I shouldn't really moan about it as I'm just as bad. I remember being obsessed with the view from our balcony window, in Devon. Luckily, I had warned Ryan that this would happen as soon as we arrived, but I also reassured him that, from my own experience, it wouldn't take any longer than an hour and a half – maximum. I do believe that the record, to date, is 434 photographs of anything and everything that moves – or even doesn't move – having been eternally captured, by my mum, on their holiday. Obviously, this occurrence includes a running commentary too. Both Ryan and I, sincerely hope that Mum hasn't managed to break this record on their two-week cruise, followed by a week in a caravan with their friends.

Mum has smashed the record. No, let me rephrase that – she has annihilated it. By photograph number 516 my dear old dad was desperate – understandable as he's seen them once already. At number 562, it looked like Ryan's sanity was irretrievable and by number 611, I was close to tears. It has got to be said that Mum did whizz through them quickly though. She didn't linger upon any one photo for more than a few seconds, which was a huge relief. So, although she has well and truly defeated her record, in the sense of time comparison, it only took one hour and 56 minutes to complete the torturous event. Pretty good going, I would say. I don't think I would ever have to go on a cruise now as I've seen all there is to see, and Mum's fine-tuned elucidation left us feeling completely informed about cruise holidays, right down to ship-related terminology. We discovered: where the ships take you, what it's like on board a ship, what the cabins are like, what the other passengers are like, who's who, what you can eat, the countries you might visit, what the inside of a bathroom looks like, what the towels look like and countless other things.

I caught Dad raising his eyebrows or rolling his eyes at Ryan, from time to time. Yet, he remained steadfast for the sake of my mum who was enjoying the thrill of the show far more than anyone else and surprisingly oblivious to the desperate, pleading looks which were going on behind her back. Thankfully, it's now over and we can move on to a more natural way of life by moving across the room to the dining table and having a normal conversation while Dad dishes up his slow-cooked stew and herb dumplings (not a roast in the end).

We're just finishing our meal now but have been subjected to further torment by Mum. I'm sure she must have been running the sequence of photos through her head again as we ate our dinner because she kept prompting us to remember this photo and that photo and then she added some extra details or useless bits of information to the respective picture. Ryan was very polite throughout the whole meal and feigned an interest in Mum's stories, while myself and Dad tried not to get drawn back in to the conversation. I have got to say that it was very difficult to not get pulled back in to the reminiscing when Mum used our names though.

"So..." says Mum, placing her knife and fork across her plate and wiping her mouth with a red napkin, "what are your plans for Christmas?"

I freeze, wondering what she's going to say next.

"It's going to be extremely difficult this yea..."

I stretch my leg out, underneath the table, and tap her on the leg.

"Oh," she says, eyeing me and then Ryan. "Who's kicking me under the table?" She lets out a giggle and peers at Ryan. "Was that you?"

Ryan shakes his head. "No... I..."

"Sorry Mum – I didn't mean to. Shall we clear this lot up while Dad and Ryan go and make themselves comfortable?"

"There's no rush, honey. Let's talk about Christmas – you know I like to get it planned – you know I like to see you at Christmas. It will be hard this... Oh!" Mum jumps and looks straight at me. "Are you kicking me again?"

"No, not me."

She peers at Ryan and giggles. "Was that you?"

"No, I can assure you it wasn't." Ryan glances at me, his cheeks reddening.

"Come on Mum, we'll discuss Christmas in the kitchen."

"Won't you be spending it with Ryan though? Surely, he'll want to discuss the plans."

I sigh and give mum a steely glare, trying to send a telepathic message to her to not mention a certain person.

"It's going to be hard for all of us," says Mum, looking directly at Ryan. "Our neighbours..." She breaks off and frowns at me because I have gently tapped her leg, several times this time. "Anyway, we'll clear this up and make a nice cup of tea and then we can discuss Christmas." She gives Ryan a wavering smile before standing up and starting to clear the table. "Please, go and make yourself comfy in the living room."

I grab some plates, give Ryan a reassuring smile, eye my Dad with a wide-eyed, say-nothing look and start to head off to the kitchen, praying that Mum is close behind me. Out of the corner of my eye, I see Ryan get up and go into the living room with Dad. Phew – that was close. I know my dad won't strike up a conversation with Ryan about the terrible events of last Christmas – he'd much rather have a laugh and a joke before the inevitable nap.

"What on earth were you doing? What's wrong, honey?" Mum is whispering as she places a pile of plates on the side. "Are you still going to be together at Christmas? Is everything OK"

"Of course, it is, Mum. Yes, I do hope we will still be together. It's just... well, I haven't told Ryan anything about Jett."

"OK, but don't you think he should know?"

"Does he need to know?" I peer over my shoulder, checking that we are not being overheard. "I haven't told him about Jett at all."

"So, what does that matter?"

"Well, I don't want him to know about him. He knows about Kallum and that's all."

Mum eyes me, thoughtfully. "There's no harm in letting him know what happened. There shouldn't be a problem with him knowing that the neighbours lost their grandson on New Year's Eve – why can't he know about that?"

I shrug and shake my head. "I suppose that bit doesn't matter."

"And it shouldn't matter that you grew up with Jett. Why should it?"

I shrug again. "I suppose that bit doesn't matter either."

"So, what's the problem, honey?" Mum places a hand on my shoulder and gives me a reassuring squeeze.

"I don't want it coming out that I was with him, you know what I mean..."

"But you can't hide away from that – you *were* with him when he died that night. God rest the poor man's soul." Mum peers up to the ceiling and places her hands together as if she's praying. She's so melodramatic sometimes. Don't get me wrong, it is so very sad that Jett had to die but Mum doesn't believe in all that going to heaven or praying to God stuff, so I have no idea why she is doing it.

"No, I mean... *with* him, you know, *seeing* him," I add, for clarity.

Mum rolls her eyes. "Oh, I see what you mean now, honey."

I tut and roll my own eyes. "He knows that I ended the relationship with Kallum, on Christmas day, but he has no idea about Jett and certainly doesn't know that I had two boyfriends in one week. Do you see what I mean, Mum?"

"Oh gosh, I had never thought about it like that. I see what you mean, honey. That doesn't look favourable, does it?"

"That's exactly my point and we *had* discussed this before, I'm sure."

"I don't remember that."

"Hmm... I think I mentioned how bad it all looked after Jett's death."

"OK," says Mum, peering puzzled. "So, what shall we say? And what do you want to do about Christmas?"

"Let's make a cuppa and I'll talk to Ryan to see if he's happy to come here for Christmas day – I assume that's what you're offering."

Mum tuts. "Of course, it is... and Boxing Day too, if you would like to."

"Ah, we can't do both because Ryan's parents have invited us to theirs on Boxing Day already."

"Fair enough – talk to Ryan then. In the meantime, get the posh cups out and I'll make a nice pot of tea."

"So," says Mum, placing a tray, laden with a teapot, sugar bowl and milk jug, on the coffee table. "I hear that you'll be going to your parents' for Boxing Day." She smiles at Ryan as she offers him a filled cup and saucer.

"Yes, and Susie has just mentioned about your invite for Christmas Day, which we will gladly accept."

I let out a giggle as Ryan's formal tone tickles me. He turns and frowns. "It's nothing – sorry," I say, guiltily.

"I don't think we will be doing a New Year's Eve party this year, what with..." Mum breaks off and glances at me.

"Because of Jett, you mean?" Only a few minutes ago it looked like Dad would be snoring within seconds, but he seems to have perked up since Mum brought the tea tray in. I wish he was asleep, to be honest, especially now that he has mentioned Jett. "We definitely won't be having one – how could we? That would be very disrespectful after what happened."

Ryan has perked up too and looks interested in what Dad is saying. He glances from Mum to Dad and back again but says nothing. Dad has noticed Ryan's interest and shakes his head. "The neighbours – that way," he says, tilting his head and rolling his eyes towards the house next door. "They lost their grandson, Jett, last New Year's Eve. Terrible wasn't it, Susie?"

I give a feeble nod while glaring at my dad to try and shut him up.

"A car accident – drunk driver – killed him outright."

Ryan draws in a sharp whistling breath through pursed lips. "He was drinking and driving on New Year's Eve?"

"Oh no," says Dad, shaking his head. "Someone else killed him."

"Dad," I interrupt, "can we change the subject now and talk about something a little less morbid?" I discreetly give him another glare. "Obviously there won't be a New Year's Eve party and obviously, Doreen and Malcolm will not be celebrating that time of year ever again."

Ryan turns his head and looks at me questioningly.

"Doreen and Malcolm – they live next door. Jett was their grandson."

"Oh, I see," says Ryan, nodding. "A terrible thing to happen."

"Yes, it was," I say, reaching for my cup of tea. "Anyway, have you made any cakes, Mum?"

"Oh, good heavens, yes, I have."

"I thought you might have done, like you usually do. Let's not keep them sitting in the cake tin until next year, like the last batch you made, eh?"

Mum laughs and leaves the room while mumbling under her breath, "Now, where did I put them?"

I've managed to steer the subject of conversation away from Jett and now there's the bonus of a football match starting on the TV which both Dad and Ryan are interested in. Result. What Ryan doesn't know won't hurt and it certainly cannot be classed as lying. Not one little bit.

*** 18 ***

I got away with the 'Jett' thing because Ryan hasn't mentioned my parent's neighbour's tragic event once. Since then, I've messaged Mum and told her to explain it all to Dad so that he understands why I don't want the subject brought up again. Mum replied a little while ago with a cheerful, *Entendemos senora. That's what your father said xx*

I had to look up the Spanish bit to see what it meant. *Good, thanks Mum, but why the Spanish? x*

We've decided to learn the language, ready for our next cruise. Lots of people speak Spanish you know xx

Another cruise? You didn't mention it x

Not until next year but we really enjoyed the last one xx

Can't say I'd noticed... from the photos! X

Very funny. Well, I do hope you won't be leaving it 9 weeks before we'll see you and Ryan again xx

Mum, if I left it another 9 weeks, we'd be almost into February and I'm still not convinced it was that long x

Oh yes. Silly me. And yes, it was! Hope we'll get to see you again before Christmas then, honey. Love you lots xx

Love you too, Mum. Might do – it depends on how busy we are buying your presents x

Vouchers are fine xx

I always buy you vouchers x

You bought us hampers last year xx

I look at my phone and laugh. Where is all this backward and forwarding of text messages going? I have got things to do. Writing out a Christmas present list, being the first of my jobs. *Yes, but I had bought you* vouchers every other year so... *you'll have to wait and see what Santa decides to bring you this year... x*

How exciting, honey xx

***

There are just three weeks left at school and me and Ryan are like two small kids – we are so excited about spending our first Christmas together. Honestly, if anyone could see us, at home in the flat, they would think that we are demented. When we brought all the new decorations (Ryan insisted that we have new ones to help blow the web of memories away from the old set that I had) we somehow, ended up with a silly little free gift of three tiny, wooden, Christmas mice (God only knows what you are supposed to do with them). One of them is so small that we decided not to put it in the trunk of the Christmas tree, with the others but since it arrived in our home, it has travelled around the flat, popping up in random places with little messages attached to its tail. Obviously, it is Ryan who is doing this, but it is quite funny to go to the toilet and find the little mouse looking at me, from the top of the toilet roll, with a message saying, *Christmas is cancelled because you told Santa you'd been good this year and he died laughing.* Another one said, *If I dress up as Santa this Christmas Eve, would you let me empty my sack in your socks?* which I found in my underwear drawer. And the best one said, *If one night, you get kidnapped by a big fat man with a long beard, who throws you into a sack, don't panic, I told Santa that all I want for Christmas is you,* which brought a tear to my eye, I can tell you. I found it in my lunch box one day, at school. Talking of lunch boxes, I used to get my lunches lovingly-made by Clair and without saying anything to Ryan, he seems to have taken over the job with about as much love as Clair showed, which is very nice. I think I'm probably spoilt far more than I deserve but then I do wash and iron Ryan's clothes so maybe the lovingly-made packed lunches are warranted.

The flat looks and smells so Christmassy – especially since I bought a 'festive pine' air freshener for the living room. Anyone would think that we had a real Christmas tree rather than the huge, six-foot artificial one which

Ryan bought, as the room smells so strongly of pine needles. The tree is so big that we had to take an armchair out of the living room, just to fit it in. Ryan likes a big Christmas tree and briefly mentioned his childhood and the massive ten-foot tree they had – how big is his parent's living room, I want to know?

We're off to the town today to do some Christmas shopping. Ryan is so organised and has a list of things to buy for his family. He's even buying gifts for his brother and his girlfriend. I questioned how he knew what to get Rob's new girlfriend and he said that he would buy something standard for a young woman. He also said that I would have a better idea of what to get a woman we've never met. Yeah, right – like I would have a clue. She could be a butch rugby player for all we know. I hardly think she would appreciate a floral scented gift set if she likes to wallow around in muddy fields – or maybe she would.

"Do you know anything in the slightest about Rob's girlfriend?" I ask, as we leave the flat dressed like we're off to the Antarctic. To be fair, it is very cold today and the sky is that kind of orangey colour that usually brings snow. I hope it does snow to be honest, as long as it lays, and we can get a couple of snow-days off school.

"Nothing," says Ryan, tugging at his scarf to cover his ears and mouth. "Her name is Ammy if that's any help."

"Ammy? Or did you say Annie?" I link arms with Ryan and we begin to walk towards the town.

"Ammy."

"Annie?" I say, frowning as I struggle to hear Ryan's muffled voice.

He removes the scarf from his mouth and repeats. "Ammy... I think."

I watch the stream of warm breath roll out from his mouth. "That's a strange name – are you sure it's not Annie?"

Ryan removes his gloves, as we're walking along, and pulls his phone from his pocket. He thumbs through his messages. "There, see, Ammy."

I peer over the phone's screen. "Oh, OK. Odd name." As I scan to the end of the message, I see a question. "Have you replied to that?"

"Not yet, I only got it this morning. I was going to ask you what you thought about it."

I shrug my padded shoulders. "I don't mind. It's up to you." Ryan slips his phone back in his pocket and I link arms with him again.

"It will save taxis and a hotel."

"OK," I say, cheerfully. "Let's do it... I trust we'll be allowed to share a room?" I eye him cheekily.

"Let's hope so... but worst-case scenario, if not, you'll get your own room, so don't worry."

"And what about you?"

"I'd have my own room too."

I tug on Ryan's arm and he comes to a halt. "Your whole family are going – how many rooms have they got?"

"Nine."

"Nine," I exclaim. "As in... nine bedrooms?"

Ryan nods and smiles before pulling me back into a slow walk. "Yep."

"They have a big house then?"

"Yes, they do."

"Why didn't you tell me this before?"

"You never asked," he replies, nonchalantly.

"I'd hardly ask you what size their house is, would I?"

"And I'd hardly say, 'Come and meet my parents, they have a big house', would I?" Ryan laughs and shakes his head at me despairingly. "Come on, we'll never get into town at this rate – you're worse than a snail with a sore foot."

***

Ammy, who could be anything from a rugby player to a beauty pageant queen, has got what Ryan called a 'safe' present for Christmas. Ryan couldn't even guess what kind of woman his brother would tend to be attracted to.

"She, he, it could be a transvestite for all I know. I wouldn't put anything past my brother. You'll see what I mean when you meet him," Ryan said as we bought the rather extravagant present.

Personally, I think he spent far too much on a gift for someone he's never met but he insisted that it was the only thing suitable as an all-rounder. I would say that he couldn't be bothered to look anywhere else and simply bought the first thing that jumped out at him – which also happened to cost £25. OK, so it is a lovely gift, but the poor girl might not like chocolate or prosecco or matt black presentation boxes with luxurious white ribbon to adorn the top. She might be a *Boots* gift-set kind of girl – who knows? Anyway, what's done is done and to be fair, we have managed to tick off a considerable amount from the Christmas shopping list. Result, I suppose. Even if it was a little costly, compared to my usual standards. But then, I am now beginning to wonder just what Ryan's standards are. It seems that he comes from an affluent, albeit contentious and imperious family unit. They live in a stupidly big house, which is probably more of a mansion than a house and they have several businesses on the go.

It appears that our upbringings are worlds apart yet, apart from Ryan's position as a subject managing teacher, we are so similar in our likes and dislikes. It's kind of cute when I think about the little quirky ways that we both have and the silliness that we like to share... which includes the latest addition to our family, the tiny Christmas mouse, dressed in its dinky black boots and red Santa coat and hat. Aah, bless.

We arrived home half an hour ago, laden with bags filled with gifts, tired, aching feet and an overwhelming desire to flake out on the sofa, which is where I've stayed since. Ryan dragged himself up ten minutes ago and I can hear him walking backwards and forwards along the hallway, going from one room to another. "What are you doing?" I call out, nonchalantly. I'm rooted to the sofa with not one ounce of inclination to get up.

"Nothing much – just putting stuff away."

"Leave it. We'll do it later."

"No, it's OK – almost done."

I hear him go into the kitchen and turn the kettle on. I feel so lazy, but then, we have been out shopping for nearly six hours today. Reluctantly, I drag myself up and hobble into the kitchen. I suppose I should help to make us a drink, at the least.

As I enter the kitchen, Ryan is standing with his back to the cooker, looking rather suspicious. "What are you up to?" I say, playfully.

"Nothing…" He has a smirk on his face and appears to be hiding something behind him.

"Mr Bagshaw, you are up to something – what is it?"

"Nothing at all. I was just making coffee. Go and sit back down and I'll bring it through in a minute."

I eye him curiously but willingly heed his instruction. "OK, I'm going – just behave yourself."

"I will," he replies, "I promise."

I return to the living room and gladly slump back on to the sofa. I've had enough for today and can see a take-away being on the menu tonight. Ryan seems to have far more energy than me, but I imagine that it's because he is getting up to mischief with that little mouse again – I just know it. He does make me laugh and since that little mouse came along there's been such a fun, magical, Christmassy atmosphere in the flat. Ryan loves that mouse – who would have thought that such a tiny little wooden toy could give him so much pleasure.

The Chinese meal has arrived, and I've gone to all the effort of removing two plates from the cupboard. I'm dishing up while Ryan finishes in the shower. I reach for two wine glasses from the glass display cabinet… and there it is. The mouse is hanging precariously, upside down, from its Blu Tack bottom with a small note attached. I knew that was what he was up to earlier. He's obsessed. I laugh to myself and carefully remove it, along with two glasses. The note says, *Men can do their Xmas shopping for 25 relatives, in 25 minutes on Xmas eve. Count yourself lucky that I'm pacing myself for you. Xx* I smile and shake my head despairingly, he's so funny. I remove the note from the mouse's tail and carry it through to the living room, where the Christmas tree stands in all its sparkling glory. Ryan was the one who decorated it with new silver and red baubles which he bought, along with all the other decorations. I find a pen and a post-it note and after a moment's thought, scribble a message, *I like your balls – they're well hung.* I attach it to a red bauble and smile to myself again. This Christmas is going to be the best ever. I can feel it.

*** 19 ***

"Are you coming to the Christmas party this year, Susie?" It's the last day of school and Sarah has been exceptionally nice. She grins at me. "At least you won't have to dress up as a turkey..."

"Huh," I huff. "Who is the poor victim this year?"

"Jane tried to get the new teacher at Baghurst to wear it but he's wiser than she thought and sussed out her plan. Either that or someone else told him. So, no one will be wearing it... unless you really want to wear it again." She gives a little giggle.

"I'm not going this year."

"Oh?" Sarah's soft features harden, and she peers at me questioningly. "Why not?"

"I have other plans..."

"Oh, please don't tell me you're going out on a dustbin men's Christmas do."

I shake my head. "No." Gosh, I'd forgotten that I did eventually tell her that my boyfriend is a dustbin man.

"Why aren't you going then?"

"No particular reason, I just didn't fancy it this year." The truth is, me and Ryan had a discussion about it and decided that neither of us would go as we still haven't told anyone about us. We didn't want to go to the Christmas do and either have to announce it there or pretend that we weren't a couple all night. It's my fault really – I'm not ready to let people know at work and Ryan says that he understands but I'm not sure he does. The truth of the matter is that I do not want his colleague, Amber, to know. I don't trust her, I don't like her, and she knows too much. I haven't figured out how I'm going to get around it because I think Ryan wants to start telling people soon but for now, I'd rather it was kept quiet. I'll deal with the Amber issue at some point later. I'm guessing I might have to kill her or lock her away somewhere forever – joke. Ryan said that she has cut her hours since returning in September, so hopefully, she's either pregnant, thinking of leaving or ill (hopefully not the later, I'm not that cruel).

"Oh, that's boring. Please come..."

"No, I really don't want to this year – maybe I will next year."

"You're going to miss all the fun then."

"I know."

"No, I mean, the real fun. Jane wants to bag, Mr Bagshaw – she's going all out to get him this year."

"He's not go..." I break off, realising what I'm just about to say. "I mean, is he not with someone?"

"Young, free and single still, according to Amber, but she's not interested anymore as she has a new boyfriend."

"Oh, OK." I want to get away from this conversation. "Maybe he does have someone but keeps it private."

"What do you mean? Like... a boyfriend? Is that what you think?"

"No, not at all. Anyway, I really must get going. Have a wonderful Christmas, Sarah, and don't get too drunk at the do tomorrow."

She gives me a half-smile and rolls her eyes. "Trust me I *will* be getting drunk and if Jane doesn't succeed in bagging in the Bagshaw department – I'll be having him."

I give a faltering smile before leaving the classroom and head out of school as quickly as I can, with a conceited grin. Mr Bagshaw has already, well and truly, been bagged and he is all mine and when the day comes to tell them, I'm sure they will fall off their chairs. That's if they are sitting on chairs at the time, obviously.

"You are very popular at my school," I say, as we sit down for our evening meal. Ryan has just got home rather late, because he wanted to get things finished at school, so that he didn't have to bring any work home with him over Christmas. He is determined to have a school-less Christmas break, and so he should, he works hard enough.

"Aren't I always?" he gives me a cheeky grin.

"Yes, I'm sure you are but you have new admirers now... or maybe they were undeclared old supporters."

"Oh?"

"Jane is set on 'bagging' you tomorrow night, at the work's do and if she fails, Sarah is going to bed you." I'm surprised to see Ryan shaking his head and laughing into his dinner – I thought he might have been shocked.

"Those two have always been the same." He laughs again. "They just weren't ever as full-on as Amber was."

"Really?" I'm the one who is shocked now. "I didn't know..."

"They were much subtler about it, but once Amber started her overzealous objective, they backed off quite a lot."

"You've never said anything..."

"You've never asked." Ryan laughs again before shoving a forkful of food into his mouth. He swallows before adding. "They're going to be disappointed tomorrow then."

"Hmm," I say, swallowing my mouthful. "Have you ever been interested in either of them? After all, they are beautiful girls."

"Outside, not in. They could never love anyone else but themselves. I like them as colleagues but that's it. They are, most definitely, not my type."

I smile warmly and feel reassured. Ryan Bagshaw is mine, one hundred percent, and no fancy filly will ever take him away from me.

***

Talk about, shop-till-you-drop, we have done nothing else these last few days. It surprises me, because we won't be at home much over Christmas, hence, we don't need a lot of food. It's been quite amusing to watch Ryan scuttle off down the road, after telling me not to look where he's going and to meet him in the coffee shop in half an hour because he wants to get my presents. Honestly, we're both so excited about Christmas, it's ridiculous. However, I am starting to feel quite nervous about meeting his parents and his brother. I still hardly know anything about them as Ryan still doesn't like to talk about them much, even though we did have that afternoon session where he revealed quite a lot, which must have been very hard for him to do. Still, I refuse to let the trip hang over me like a black cloud and spoil Christmas day, which we are spending with my parents. I'm probably overthinking things and it will all turn out to be absolutely fine... well, as long as there is no fighting. That's a joke. Maybe I shouldn't joke about it. I'll shut up now.

"We should have a drink this evening," Ryan says, as he places the last wrapped present under the brightly lit tree.

I smile and nod. I'm so content I can't even be bothered to reply. I've just curled up on the sofa, in my pyjamas, on Christmas Eve. The atmosphere in the room is magical. The tree lights are gently flickering, creating thousands of tiny light reflections, which bounce off the 'well hung' baubles. There's a Christmassy program on the TV, a festive pine fragrance swirling around the room, two stockings hanging from hooks on the back of the door (OK, I couldn't make that bit sound romantic and festive, we don't have a fireplace) and a handsome, kind and loving man poking about under the Christmas tree. What more could a girl ask for (OK, maybe a fireplace but I can live without one)?

"There's a bottle of wine on the side in the kitchen. Would you get it while I finish up here?"

"Sure," I say and gladly float out of the room with a permanent smile etched on my face.

I giggle to myself as I pick up the mulled wine. The little mouse is sitting on the very top with a new message, *This Xmas, let's drink mulled wine and talk shit.* I roar with laughter – it's the funniest one yet. Wow, I am one lucky lady to be spending the holidays with a man I love so dearly. "Absolutely," I call out. "I'll warm it up and we can talk hot-shit."

Suddenly, Ryan is standing behind me.

"What?" I say, eyeing him curiously. "Cold-shit? What kind of shit do you want to talk?" I giggle and wrap my arms around his neck before kissing his warm lips.

He kisses me back and just for a moment, I wonder if we won't be talking any shit or drinking mulled wine before he whisks me off to the bedroom (in fact, it doesn't necessarily have to be the bedroom come to think of it). "I need you to look after this until the morning." He hands me a large, plain brown envelope.

"What is it?" I can feel that there is something hard and flat inside and what feels like it might be a card.

"Keep it under your pillow and open it in the morning." He kisses me again and then pulls away. "Come on, let's get this wine warmed then we really can talk shit."

I stare at the A4 size envelope, confused. "What is it?" I ask again, before giving it a little shake.

"Go and put it under your pillow – you can open it first thing."

My tummy flutters and turns over with excitement as I head off to the bedroom, trying to peer through the envelope and shaking it to no avail – I have absolutely no idea what is inside, apart from it being hard, flat and a rectangle shape. I tuck it securely under the middle of my pillow and pat it down as if, somehow, it's going to disappear overnight. I lift the pillow and peep at the envelope again and wonder what on earth it could be. There's no name on the front, it looks like an envelope from my stationery drawer and there is Sellotape holding the back flap down. My mind suddenly recalls a moment like this from last Christmas which makes me angry to think about. I thought Kallum had bought me an engagement ring and I remember the state of euphoria that I was in as I opened the little box. I tut to myself – why have I just thought about that? I don't for one-minute think that Ryan would have done anything like that. It would be the last thing on my mind, unlike last year when I was totally desperate to belong, to be someone, to be betrothed. Things are so different now. My relationship with Ryan is not a needy one, it's more of a loving friendship and unity. I don't need a ring to know that it is going to last and I'm a little annoyed at myself for the memory flash that I have just allowed to creep into my head. Go away.

***

I'm awake and as I open my eyes the room is still dark. I turn and look at the clock – it's only a quarter to five. I smile to myself and stare across the room to the faint glow coming through the curtains from the street lamp across the road. It's Christmas.

I'm lying next to the love of my life and after one too many mulled wines last night, a delicious, meaningful love-making session on the living room carpet and lots of cuddles, we talked silly shit, which ended up being quite hilarious. Ryan was playing with the tiny mouse and it developed a little high-pitched voice of its own, which was hysterical. "'Twas the night before Christmas and all through the house... everyone was on their phone," Ryan squeaked, as he held the little rodent between his fingers and moved it up and down in rhythm with his words. I had the giggles for the rest of the evening, especially when Ryan went all serious, with a stern look on his face and squeaked, "Remember the *true* meaning of Christmas..." I peered at him and for just a moment, wondered if he was actually religious and about to preach the word of God.

"Yes, go on..." I said, unsure of what he was going to say next.

"You know, the birth of Santa and the coming of the reindeers."

I laughed so much I gave myself a headache.

I smile to myself again and turn over. A little more sleep wouldn't go amiss. Honestly, I was like the *Princess and the Pea* last night, tossing and turning, wondering and guessing what might be in the envelope under my head. I just couldn't sleep for ages and kept on clock-watching. I think another hour would be good and then six o'clock will be quite an acceptable time to get up on Christmas day. Gosh, I can't wait.

"Happy Christmas babe..."

I come to and open my sleepy eyes. It's daylight and Ryan is crouching down beside the bed with a mug of tea in one hand and a plate of hot buttered crumpets in the other. I smile at him and mumble a 'Happy Christmas' back as I pull myself up.

"Breakfast in bed, madam."

I plump the pillows up behind me and take the mug from him. I peer over at the clock and am surprised to see that it's almost seven thirty. "I can't believe I've slept so long... I was going to get up at five because I was awake then, but I decided to go back to sleep."

Ryan sits on the edge of the bed and holds on to the plate. "You can open that envelope now."

I take a quick sip of the tea and place the mug on the bedside table. Then I grab the envelope from behind me. "I should have given you something to open, first thing," I say, excitedly, "but if I'd made you put it under your pillow, you wouldn't have slept all night because all your presents are big and bulky."

Ryan laughs and leans over to kiss me. "It doesn't matter... I hope you'll like it..."

I peer deeply, into his eyes, turning the envelope around to open it. "Thank you," I say, tearing the corner. "I'm sure I will." There's a large Christmas card inside, saying, 'To the One I Love'. As I open it, another, slightly smaller brown envelope falls into my lap. "Thank you, I love it."

Ryan smiles. "Go on then – open the other one."

My heart is galloping now. Oh God, what if I don't like it? I'll have to pretend – just like last year, with Kallum and the stupid keyring. Oh dear, why am I back to that again? Ryan has turned this envelope into such a significant thing that I hope to God it won't be reduced to an anticlimax. I open the other envelope and another, smaller one is inside... along with a folded sheet of paper...

I look up at Ryan. "What is this?"

"It is what you think it is..."

"For me?" I scan the sheet of paper disbelievingly. I think I know what is in the smallest envelope now.

"For you babe – happy Christmas. I love you, wholeheartedly."

Wow. And I mean a big wow!

*** 20 ***

I am seriously struggling to eat the buttered crumpets. Ryan has gone off to the bathroom for a shower, even though I showered him with kisses, hugs and copious amounts of tears – in fact, so many eye-droplets fell that I couldn't have a coherent conversation with him. OK, fair point, he prefers to shower in water, rather than salty tears and saliva kisses – I get it. So, anyway, I'm still sitting in bed and I'm trying to swallow each mouthful of crumpet with a gulp, but it's difficult because I am so emotional. Don't get me wrong, I love crumpets... in fact, I'd go as far as saying, I love crumpets as much as I hate Brussels sprouts. There you go – it's Christmas day and I've mustered up the courage to mention those nasty little brain-like, green, mutant-cabbages. Yuk! I hate them with a passion. I hate the smell of them, the look of them and as for the taste... well, who in their right mind could possibly like the taste of them? Guinea-pigs maybe. Anyway, once again, I've gone off on a tangent, like I always do. So, getting back to the fact that I am a bit emotional at the moment, I think a more apt definition of my feelings would be that I want to run out of the flat, barefoot in my pyjamas, whooping and cheering at the top of my voice as I hop, skip and dance down the road. I have so many questions to ask Ryan, once I can compose myself (and once he's out of the shower), like how, where and why? I'm just a tad overwhelmed. That's the understatement of the year (what's left of it).

I hear Ryan come out of the bathroom and I just about manage to swallow the last bit of crumpet as he walks into the bedroom. He looks so sexy with his wet hair sticking up in spikes and droplets of water speckled over his muscular chest and broad shoulders. I want to drag him back into bed and ravish him, even if he is soggy, but I know that we don't have much time this morning, what with opening the other presents (my gifts to him pale in comparison to what I have just received) and getting ready to go to my parent's. And our time will be taken up even more so now, since I opened the envelope. Gosh, I still can't quite believe it. How?

"Are you getting dressed before we go out?"

"How far is it?" I ask, swinging my legs over the side of the bed and pushing my feet into my slippers.

"Three houses down, that's all." Ryan slips on a pair of jeans and a t-shirt. "I'll put a shirt on later, when we go to your parent's," he adds, as he catches me eyeing him admiringly. "Or we can do other presents first – it's up to you." He laughs at me. "Come on, you look like a dazed rabbit in the headlights."

I *am* a dazed rabbit – seriously. "We'll do the other presents first then," I say, as I decide that I can just about contain my excitement for a little while longer. However, the insignificant little presents I have bought for Ryan could never live up to the one he has bought for me – not for at least 50 years which is great because it means he'll have to live with me for a considerable length of time.

I pick up the empty envelopes, the document and the key and head into the living room where Ryan has put the Christmas lights on already. It really feels like Christmas today. Yet again, there's a magical atmosphere all around and it's Ryan who has created it. There's a pile of presents on the coffee table and the little mouse is sitting right on the top with a new message attached to its tail. I peel it off, open it up and read it. *What do angry rodents send each other at Xmas? Cross-mouse cards!* I giggle as Ryan walks in. "You are crazy," I say, before giggling some more. I'm so happy at this moment that I think I want to cry again. What a stark comparison, the reason for my tears are this year, compared to those of the last Christmas day.

"And you're not?"

"We're both crazy... you a little bit more than me though. I can't ever thank you enough for what you have done." A tear wells in my eye again.

"Don't start that again or we'll never get out the front door today. Gratitude accepted, now let's get on with the rest of Christmas."

I wrap my arms around him and kiss his cheek as he sits down. "We should keep the mouse out all year – mice are not just for Christmas, you know." We are both giggling now. It's silly, I know, but that's just how we roll. Now, we're laughing so much that I can see it taking rather a long time to get these presents unwrapped, go outside and check out my almost brand new – like, only two years old, it's that new – metallic silver *Beetle Cabriolet* (I've wanted a *Beetle* forever but never dreamed of owning a newish one – it must have cost him a small fortune, but I don't like to ask, not at the moment anyway), cry a lot more, and then get ready to go to Mum and Dad's for dinner.

Ryan loved all his big and bulky, yet thoughtful presents. I loved mine too. Especially the engraved heart locket on a chain which he pointed out was white gold. The engraving says, *381 Susie* which I puzzled over for several minutes while I was admiring it. According to Ryan, the numbers mean, three words, eight letters, one meaning. It still took a few more minutes for me to work that out, but now I know. *I love you Susie.* He is the best. This Christmas is the best and I am hurriedly getting dressed right now, so that we can go down the road and have a look at *my* new car!

Oh, my giddy aunt (I still don't have one of those... or maybe I do, who knows. I should ask Ryan if he has a giddy aunt then maybe I will own one, one day, if we were ever to marry). It's astounding. Is it mine? Really? The log book says it's mine. Oh my God. I want to drive it to my mum and dad's – they'll be amazed. I want to drive along the road with the roof open...

"What do you think then?" Ryan asks, as he leans over and peers in. "No, wait, don't answer that. I think I know and I don't want you to start crying again." He climbs into the passenger seat, next to me. "Happy Christmas babe." He kisses my cheek. "You deserve to have nice things."

'Nice things'? He classes this as being 'nice'? A 'thing'? This is far more than a 'nice thing'. I've never been so spoilt in all my life – it's crazy. The interior is spotless and smells of lemons. It's the most exquisite 'nice thing' you ever did see. And it's mine. Nice. "How...?" I look across to Ryan, blinking away yet more tears.

"How? Do you mean, how did I get it?"

I nod, unable to speak as a lump swells in my throat.

"I got it three weeks ago..." he breaks off and grins at me. "Trust me, it was hard work rushing home every lunch break to check the mail, until the log book arrived."

"Really?" I say, aghast. He's done all of that for me? Of course, the log book is in my name, so it would have been addressed to me. I can't believe he's been so sneaky (sneaky – who am I to talk, from past experiences?).

"Yes, really. Fancy a spin?"

"Can we have the roof down? I want to feel the wind in my hair, ride through country lanes, cruise along coastal roads, spin around the..."

"Susie?"

"Yes?" My imagination has run away with me and I am living the dream.

"It's winter – the temperature, there," he points a finger at the dashboard, "says minus two. Let's keep the roof up or you'll have more than wind in your hair – you'll end up looking like the snow queen, speeding on a motorbike."

I laugh aloud, although I want to cry again. I love this man so much, it almost hurts. And to think, this time last year, I thought I loved Kallum – I can see now that that was seriously a joke. I now know what real love is.

OK, so we just spent 20 minutes poodling around the local area while I got used to the feel of the car – maybe not living the dream but it was great though. There were no rattles, vibrations, humming or knocking sounds (unlike my dear old banger) and it drove like a dream on the deserted roads. I love it.

We've just arrived back home and now we need to get ready to go to Mum and Dad's. "Whose car are we going in?" Ryan asks, as he makes a quick coffee.

I peer at him, amazed by his silly question. "That's a silly question – obviously, we'll be going in Bella..."

"Bella?"

"Yes, Bella the Beetle." I giggle. "That's her name."

"Oh, it's a girl then?"

"Yes, of course she's a girl – she wouldn't have a name like, Bella, if she was a boy, would she?" I wrap my arms around Ryan's back as he prepares two mugs of coffee. "Thank you again, Ryan. I can't believe you would have done that for me."

"I'd do anything for you, babe."

"But it must have cost a fortune... how?"

"I haven't mentioned it before, but I have some money... savings."

"Oh, OK." I can see that he feels awkward as I turn to stand beside him.

"But, should you be spending your hard-earned savings on me?"

"I can't think of anyone else I'd like to spend it on," he says.

"What about yourself?" I suggest.

"I do sometimes... that's how I got my car, a few years back." Ryan makes the drinks and carries them over to the table. I follow, and we sit down. "Look, I haven't said anything before, but I have a fair wad of savings. Enough for the deposit on a house, in fact. When I met you, I was looking around for a house but couldn't quite make my mind up where I wanted to live, what sort of house I wanted or how big. That's why I was living in a shared house."

I'm listening intently and astonished by this revelation. "When you say, enough for a deposit on a house... that means you must have at least ten grand."

Ryan smiles at me. "Thirty-five... well, around thirty-five left now, give or take a few hundred."

My mouth drops open and I snap it shut quickly. "Thirty-five thousand? Pounds? Left?"

Ryan nods before picking up his mug of coffee and sipping at it.

"Thirty-five thousand pounds?" I whisper, like the neighbours might hear through the walls. "How have you got so much money?" I pick my own coffee up but am unable to drink any as I stare at Ryan incredulously.

He smiles again. "Inheritance. My grandparents left each of us, fifty thousand."

I put my coffee back on the table with a thud. "Fifty? Each? Thousand?"

"I haven't told you before because... well... I didn't want..."

"You didn't want a false, money-orientated relationship or a trail of gold-diggers," I cut in.

"Something like that, yes."

"Oh my God, Ryan, I can't believe it."

"It's not easy having that kind of money, I can tell you."

I laugh. "You must be worry-free though."

"Not really... I don't spend it, if I can help it, as I want to use it as a deposit." He peers down at his mug and turns it around and around on the table. "But now... I only want to buy a house with you..."

*** 21 ***

What a crazy Christmas this is turning out to be. Not only does Ryan want to buy a house with me but he wants me to choose it. He wants me to choose the furniture that we'd have in it too. He wants me to keep my flat and rent it out, as a surety for the future, should anything go wrong. He anticipates that nothing will go wrong – he loves me and wants to be with me forever and he feels that I want the same thing. That's a no-brainer. He wants me to be on the deeds to the house, the mortgage – the whole kit and caboodle – it's total madness. He'll be asking me to marry him next. Am I dreaming? How can this all happen this Christmas day when, last year, I was kicking my turkey across the garden and crying over my ruined glass-heeled boots. Stark contrast is putting it mildly. Worlds apart is probably more fitting.

As I've driven us to my parent's house, in *my* new car, I've mulled over the morning's course of events. So far, Christmas day has gone from 'nice' to absolutely unbelievable and it is barely afternoon.

I pull into the drive and the front door opens instantly. Mum appears with a new Christmas headband, I notice, and a new snowman jumper. The tiny Santas sticking up from her headband wobble erratically as she totters down the drive, frowning curiously at the car. "Honey... what?" she says as I climb out of the driver's seat. "Happy Christmas, honey." She wraps her arms around me and hugs me like there's no tomorrow. "What's this?"

"My Christmas present from, Ryan."

"Are you serious?"

Ryan steps out of the passenger side. "Merry Christmas, Sharon."

"And to you, Ryan." Mum indicates to the car. "And, what is this?"

Ryan grins. "Well, we couldn't have her driving around in the old heap anymore."

"My goodness – what a present, honey. You must be in shock."

I nod. "I am, Mum. It's amazing. This is a crazy Christmas."

"And so it should be, after last year, honey," she whispers in my ear as she hugs me again.

Ryan grabs the Santa sack from the back seat and we follow Mum into the house. "John? John? Leave the dinner for a moment and come outside quickly, honey. You should see what Susie got for Christmas."

Dad is the chef, as always, and has rustled up an amazing dinner for us. We're seated at the dining table as dad brings the final plate in and sits down. "Now then," he says, eyeing Ryan with a glint in his eye. "Who'll be having a drink? Are you both drinking – you can always stay the night."

I shake my head. "No, we can't stay. We're leaving early in the morning. Ryan's parents live right out in the sticks somewhere. I'll be driving tomorrow, under his direction." I look across to Ryan. "Go ahead – have a drink if you want to, I don't mind at all. I'm more than happy to drive anyone anywhere now." I grin smugly.

"In that case," Ryan starts, "I'd love a drink, thank you."

"Beer?"

"Yes, please."

Once again, I am quite amused by how well my dad and Ryan get on together. We've finished our delicious Christmas dinner and Dad and Ryan have finished four pints of beer between them. They have joked and laughed and had us all in hysterics with their banter and comical outlook on life which are so similar it's scary.

We've just finished exchanging presents and Mum and Dad are very pleased with their gifts, which I have to say, are not vouchers for the second year running. It did cross my mind to buy them a hamper again, like last year, but then I don't want them to think that hampers have replaced vouchers – it's all too easy. I surprised myself this year by buying Dad a new apron (I would have never dreamt that I would do it – I hate his cheesy aprons) which he was absolutely thrilled with. The apron has the wording, 'The Grillfather' on it which is printed in a font like *The Godfather* film. Ryan loved it and bought one for his dad too and did say that he hoped his dad would find it funny (I'm dreading meeting his parents tomorrow, to be honest). I also bought a barbecue utensil set for Dad as Mum told me he needed a new one. As for my dear old mum, she wanted a new Christmas jumper (I'm sure she gets a new one every year and must have hundreds stashed away somewhere... well, maybe not hundreds because that would make her hundreds of years old, but you know what I mean). So, I bought her a cute wintery scene one and a bottle of her favourite perfume.

As we're all settling down to watch the Queen's speech (Dad's cue to have a nap and I wouldn't be surprised if Ryan joined him) there's a tapping at the door. Mum looks up and tuts before dragging herself up from the chair. "It'll be Doreen and Malcolm. They said they might pop in to see you. Sorry honey, I forgot to mention it."

I freeze and hold my breath for a moment. Why? Not now, please.

The living room door opens and Malcolm totters in. He's lost a bit of weight since I last saw him. "Susie, it's good to see you again. How have you been my love?"

Politely, I stand up and greet him with a peck on the cheek. "I've been good thanks, Malcolm."

Ryan rises to his feet and politely shakes Malcolm's hand. "Hello, my name is Ryan, nice to meet you and... a merry Christmas to you."

Malcolm nods and smiles at Ryan and goes to sit down, acknowledging Dad on his way past.

"Susie..." I turn to see Doreen standing in the doorway, shaking her head. "Darling, I..." she breaks off and reaches out for my hands as she steps into the living room. "Oh, dear Lord... I..." Her eyes fill up and then she dramatically pulls me towards her and wraps her arms around my neck tightly. "Oh, Susie, Susie, Susie..."

"Hello Doreen," I splutter, as I'm being strangled by her overacted embrace. "It's nice to see you again."

Doreen lets go of me and slumps down into the nearest armchair. She looks up at me and shakes her head again. "I'm sorry dear... I thought it would be OK but..." She shudders into full-on crying and I'm left speechless, looking from her to Mum and back again, not knowing what to say.

"Can I get you two a drink?" says Mum, trying to distract from Doreen's apparent meltdown.

"It's that time of year... I'm so sorry... I didn't want to drag it all up again... especially for you Susie... it must be so hard for you." Doreen sniffs into a handkerchief which she pulled from her sleeve. "Is this your new man?"

Ryan smiles weakly. "Hello, nice to meet you," he says, awkwardly. "I was very sorry to hear about your..."

Oh God, why did they have to come around and why does Doreen have to make such a scene?

"Susie told you, did she?" Doreen blows her nose hard.

Ryan nods and pulls a sad face.

"It must be so hard for Susie too," she mutters. "Young love ripped apart so violently."

"Sorry?" says Ryan, looking perplexed.

I turn to Mum and eye her desperately. "I'll help you make tea," I say. "Ryan do you want to help us?"

"Sure."

"Come on then." I grab his hand and pull him out of the living room, closely followed by Mum.

"What was that all about?" Ryan whispers, once we're in the kitchen.

Mum is busily preparing her posh teacups and saucers behind us, trying to avoid any questioning.

"Why's it so hard for you and what does she mean by young love being ripped apart?"

"Oh... she gets confused... dear old Doreen. Jett was in love... I do believe... when he, err... you know, died. It must have been a terrible thing..." I splutter, unconvincingly.

"Ah, I see," says Ryan, nodding his head, sympathetically. "It must be extremely hard for them – their first Christmas without him."

"Yes, Doreen thinks it's hard for me too because I grew up with him but..." I shrug, nonchalantly, "well... yes, it was bad, what happened to him but... well... yes... it's sad." I catch a glimpse of Mum eyeing me from the other side of the room. "Sadder for them I guess... you know... being their only grandson and all that."

Ryan nods again. "Yes, sure, it must be." He sighs and walks over to Mum. "Let me help you with that."

I'm literally sweating with fear. I'm compelled to lie over and over again. I can't stop myself. How the hell did I get myself into this pathetic predicament – oh wait – of course, it was through constant lying. I'll worry myself to death, I'm sure. God, I hate myself sometimes. I really don't deserve Ryan.

"Shall we go for an impromptu walk?" I ask Ryan.

"What now?"

"Yes, why not. It'll help our dinner go down and then by the time we return we'll be ready for tea."

"But..."

I cut in. "Doreen and Malcolm will be busy talking to Mum and Dad – won't they Mum?"

"Err... yes honey. You go if you want to. Leave us oldies to natter."

"But I thought they popped in to see you..."

"Oh," says Mum, feigning a laugh, "they'll come up with any excuse to pop round. They would have come around whether Susie was here or not."

"Well, if you're sure," says Ryan, "I could do with some fresh air after that big meal and the beers – it always makes me tired, eating and drinking in the afternoon." He sniggers to himself, "I guess that's why we have the Queen's speech at three o'clock – it's like an adult version of a lullaby."

Mum giggles and shakes her head at him. "I'm absolutely sure – now, off you both go. I'll tell Doreen and Malcolm you've gone out for some fresh air, they won't mind at all. Doreen will use any excuse to have a cry on someone's shoulder."

"Thanks Mum," I say, taken aback by her unusually cold comment which is very unlike her. Kissing her on the cheek, I whisper in her ear, "You're a saviour."

Mum tuts and continues to make the tea as I grab Ryan's hand and pull him towards the coat hooks by the front door. We're escaping... although, Ryan does not realise it's an escape.

If I'm perfectly honest, this is slightly reminiscent of last year, except it was Boxing day when I walked towards the park, in an arm link with Jett. Ryan hasn't said anything since we left five minutes ago. He has buried his face, right up to the top of his nose, inside the high collar of his padded jacket. "Are you OK?" I say, watching my breath escape in front of me and swirl upwards.

"Yes, sure. You?"

I nod and give him a faltering smile.

"Did you tell me that this, Jett, had a car crash?" Ryan says in a muffled voice from deep down in his jacket.

"Did I? Err... I mean... did I tell you that?"

"It might have been your dad..." Ryan breaks off, thoughtfully. "Wasn't he drunk or something? Jett, I mean, not your dad." I can tell he's grinning, underneath his coat, by the way his eyes have crinkled.

"Oh, no, the person who hit him was drunk, I do believe." God, why are we still talking about this? "Let's go to Grimly park and sit on the swings," I say, joyfully, steering Ryan across the road.

"Must have been one hell of a crash."

"Hmm..." I mutter, nonchalantly, "I guess so... I'm not really sure..." I peer at him and give a faint smile before taking a deep breath and turning upbeat. "Come on, let's go and have some childish fun on Christmas day, it's just down there," I say, pulling him along faster. I need a distraction. I want to get off this subject as quickly as possible as I hate lying, and the more Ryan asks about Jett, the more I'm lying.

I unlink arms with him and rush ahead, through the entrance to the park, and towards the swings. "Come on," I call out, before jumping on to the moulded seat and pushing myself back as far as I can push. "Whee..."

Ryan joins me and takes the swing next to mine.

"Woohoo..." I shout. I want to act like a child – free, happy and devoid of worry. I wish I could be like a child. "Come on – I bet I can go higher than you."

***

I am frozen right through to my bones. I'm sure I could snap myself into pieces if I tried. We've just arrived back at Mum and Dad's and Doreen and Malcolm are still here. By the look of Malcolm, sprawled out on the reclining chair with his slippers on, it looks like they're here for the night. That's fine by me as long as... well, you know what I'm going to say.

"Did you have a nice walk, you two?" asks Doreen, directing her gaze towards Ryan.

"Yes, we did thanks – very cold out there though."

Doreen nods. "I do apologise about earlier, my dear, we weren't introduced properly."

"Oh, that's no problem, really."

"No, it is," says Doreen, "I was quite rude, please forgive me."

"Apology accepted and it's very nice to meet you."

Doreen takes Ryan's hand in hers and smiles. "You're a very nice young man... you know... you remind me a little of..."

Oh God, here we go again. "Anyone for a game of Monopoly?" I call out as loud as is acceptable within the confines of a house. "Mum? Come on – we're playing a game." Phew!

Doreen is always up for a game of Monopoly and has quite a competitive streak in her old veins. Let's hope this steers her thoughts away from Jett.

I've decided that either, Mum and Dad will have to move to a new house, or Doreen and Malcolm will have to move, or Ryan and I will have to spend Christmas times in the Bahamas from now on – just to avoid the Jett-anniversary each year. I don't mean to sound cold and callous (I am so not like that), but I need to move on with my life and unfortunately, Jett doesn't fit into it anymore. Anyway, just for the record, if I had to choose how Christmases should be spent in the future – I'm liking the Bahamas idea.

*** 22 ***

Doreen and Malcolm ended up staying for the buffet tea. Luckily, between me and Mum, we managed to keep the atmosphere light and jovial and when Doreen won the game of Monopoly, she was happy and smug for the rest of the evening. We gave her lots of jobs to do, preparing the buffet, and she merrily did them without shedding another tear or mentioning poor Jett's demise. Please don't get me wrong here – I do understand how her, and Malcolm, must be feeling because, I too, have had some passing thoughts about Jett and how sad it all was, but we're not even at the anniversary of his death yet. That's to come next week, on New Year's Eve. Gosh, thinking about that night now makes me shudder. The violence of it and the utter disbelief. He was a good, loving man who, just like Doreen said, was ripped away from a blossoming relationship. It was all so cruel. I'm sure that when the day comes, I will be extremely remorseful as I'm still here, alive, and in a new, loving relationship which makes Jett's death even more poignant.

We've arrived home now, expertly driven by *Moi*, in my beautiful new car and poor Ryan is a little rugged around the edges as he had quite a few beers with Dad, during the course of the evening. I know he's going to want to climb into bed at any minute, but I insist that he stays up long enough to have a cup of tea with me. "Come on, just a quick one," I say, flicking the kettle on and grabbing two mugs all at once. "So, we're taking my car tomorrow – yes?"

Ryan nods and smiles at me. "Yes, if you want to."

"I do want to. You can be the navigator – I don't have a clue where I'm going."

"Sure." Ryan has buried his head in his hands now.

"Headache?" I ask, knowing how rough he looks.

"Yep, I'll take a couple of pain killers with the tea... then I'm off to bed."

"What should I wear tomorrow?"

Ryan peers at me with a frown. "Whatever you want babe."

"Jeans?"

"Yes, you don't have to dress to impress."

"OK, and... what do I call them?"

"Who?"

"Your parents, obviously."

"Oh," says Ryan, rubbing his forehead. "Err... just call them, Mr and Mrs Bagshaw – they'll soon let you know if they want you to call them something else."

"What about calling them by their first names, like you do with my mum and dad?"

Ryan perks up and looks at me, a little startled, like I've just asked him what his mother's bra size is. "Err... no, I wouldn't... they might say that you can but... well, I'd wait until they give you permission. Honestly babe, don't worry about it – just call them Mr and Mrs Bagshaw. They'll be happy with that."

I nod an OK and finish making the teas. It all sounds very formal – I am extremely nervous about meeting them, to be honest. You know what it's like when you build up an image of someone, just from what you have learnt about them and then when you do meet them, they're nothing like what you imagined. I am sincerely hoping the latter is true because my images of Ryan's parents are not for the faint-hearted. I envisage Mr Bagshaw as being this big tyrant type of guy who maybe wears a trilby hat and a long black coat. He'll have shifty, narrow eyes that could turn your blood cold and thin, unkind lips from where course, cruel words can sprout from. As for his mum, I imagine her to be a cowardly, small-framed woman with big, please-don't-hurt-me eyes and the odd misplaced bruise or cut about her body. I also picture her wearing the best cut dresses, lots of make-up and cascading brown locks tumbling down her back. I feel she could be mutton dressed as lamb, as the old saying goes. I hope to God they are nothing like what I imagine but in less than 12 hours, I will find out. What's the worst that can happen?

***

We're off. It's almost seven o'clock and only just starting to break dawn on this dull, damp morning. We're expecting the roads to be quiet at this time and particularly as it's Boxing Day and most people will still be in bed with a mince pie overdose. Ryan said that it will take us a couple of hours to get there, get settled in and have a breakfast.

"It seems odd that we're going to your parent's house for breakfast," I say, as I follow the Satnav's instructions. Funnily enough, although I've known all along that we were going there early and would have breakfast when we arrive, Ryan and I haven't actually talked about any of it. Once again, it has been one of those things that he doesn't really want to get into a conversation about with me. Now, I'm determined to have that conversation with him because the situation is imminent, and I have a right to my questions being answered.

"What's odd about it?"

"Well..." I break off and wonder what is odd about it. To be honest, the whole thing is odd if you ask me. The fact that Ryan never wants to talk about them is odd. I wonder if he is ashamed of them. He should know me better – if he has a dodgy family, it makes no difference to us because I would love him all the same. "Well, I just wondered why we need to be there so early. Is it just so that we can have breakfast with your family? Before we have dinner with them?"

Ryan begins to laugh and shakes his head.

"What's so funny?" I say, shooting a sideways glance.

"I don't think I made things clear, did I?"

"You haven't made anything clear, Ryan. I've had the impression, all along, that you didn't want to talk about it too much."

"No, they aren't my favourite thing to talk about, I have to be honest."

"So, that's why I'm wondering, because... because you don't explain anything and leave me having to guess what's going on."

Ryan's face drops, and I can see it dawning on him. He has been so terribly vague about anything to do with his family and I think he suddenly understands how I feel now. "Sorry babe, I should have said before but sometimes I think things through in my head and then I think I've told you when I haven't."

"You sound just like me..."

"We're very alike in a lot of ways." He places a hand on my knee and squeezes it. "I'm sorry – my head is always filled with so much school crap that I forget stuff. Important stuff."

"OK, fair enough, I do get it. Let's start again. So, why do we have to be there so early?"

"Well, we don't... I just thought it would be nice if we did."

"Why?"

"Because we can have a nice breakfast – it will be brought straight to our room, and then I can take you for a walk around the grounds."

"In our room? I thought you meant have breakfast with your family."

"Oh God, no. We won't see them until the dinner is served."

"You are making it sound like they live in a mansion and have servants."

"They do and there's a little breakfast table in our room where we can eat, right by the double doors, which lead out to a balcony, overlooking the drive and gardens at the front. Breakfast will be brought to our room by..." Ryan breaks off, thoughtfully. "I think Harriet is still there, so yes, she will bring breakfast for us."

Oh my God, this is something else. Why has he not told me all this before? "Why haven't you told me any of this before?"

He shrugs. "I thought it would be a pleasant surprise."

"Surprise? I'm flabbergasted," I say, as the satnav interrupts me and directs me to turn at the next junction.

"I knew you would be, babe. I deliberately wanted to surprise you."

"Are you and your family millionaires?"

Ryan laughs. "Wish we were... but no, not at all. It's the family home which we've owned for over a hundred years. My grandparents lived there as well, before they died. They left a vast sum of money to be shared between us all, which is why I have all the money I have got. So, there you go, you know it all now."

"So, your grandparents were the rich ones?"

"They certainly started some of the businesses and my dad was their only child, so he got the lot."

Honestly, I don't know how I'm still managing to concentrate and drive because I am truly stunned by this revelation. This is like a fairytale romance, isn't it? I thought it was only in books and movies that a woman meets a man, falls in love with him, only to find out later that he comes from an affluent background and is totally loaded. Not that money means anything to me really – I certainly am not the type to be influenced by money and definitely would not be interested in a man just because he's got money, but I can't help feeling that I have landed the biggest catch ever. Is that contradictory of me?

"Is that a problem? You've gone all quiet on me," Ryan says, which brings me back from my daydreaming. How is it that I can drive along, in a daydream, and be able to know where I'm going, read road signs and avoid any collisions when I don't remember having driven anywhere for the last few minutes, yet, we've travelled another few miles?

"Oh... err, no. It's not a problem at all – sorry, I was miles away."

"Already there, having breakfast, were you?"

I smile. "Yes, something like that."

"Wish we were," says Ryan, "I'm starving."

"I'm sticking to the speed limits, so you'll have to be patient."

"Absolutely, I wouldn't dream of making you speed up. You take it easy – I can't guarantee my tummy won't start roaring though."

"Don't worry because mine might join you," I say, with a giggle. I can see that a gurgling tummy and a perplexed brain are the way forward here. I think I'm going to have to take Ryan's family and his childhood home as I find them. Accept and cogitate later.

*** 23 ***

We've arrived in the middle of nowhere, literally. Where is this place? I know the last sign, a few miles back in the last village of Shedford said, Aberford 14 miles which is the next village along. This place is nowhere, I'm sure. We've pulled into a layby which has a narrow, winding dirt track leading off at one end. I'm sure no one would know it was there if they didn't know it was there – you know what I mean.

"OK," says Ryan, excitedly. "You're going up that track – follow it to the end and we'll be there."

There are so many tall bushes and trees around that I cannot see anything at all and can only take Ryan's word for it that this is the right way (obviously, he would know where his own parents live) because the little woman inside the satnav would have had us sitting in a cow field by now, if I'd listened to her.

I head off along the track and it snakes from left to right, going on and on. "Are you sure we're going the right way?" I say, turning the steering wheel hard to the right and then hard to the left.

Ryan laughs. "I think so, I did live here for... hmm... it must have been at least 19 years."

"Blimey," I say as we continue to get further away from the main road. "I guess you didn't walk to school then?"

"I went to boarding school."

I shoot an astonished glance at Ryan. "Did you really?" Do I even know this man? I mean, talk about being vague about his family, it seems he's been vague about a lot of things. Or is it that I have simply never asked the right questions? Whatever it is, it's certainly not dull being with him.

"Yes, really. That's one thing I will give my parents – they made sure that we had a good education."

"Well, yes, I get that because you and Rachel have become teachers but what went wrong with your bro... Oh my God! Are you serious?"

It's ridiculous. Honestly. I've never seen anything like it. Am I dreaming? "What the hell..." I utter, before my jaw drops. From out of nowhere, this scene has appeared in front of me. It's like the trees and bushes parted, making way for this spectacular scenery before my eyes. "Oh my God, Ryan..."

Ryan says nothing and just sits with his hands clasped together in his lap. He's watching me, obviously amused by my stupefied expression.

I pull the handbrake on and stare out of the windscreen. I cannot believe what I am seeing. This belongs to his parents? How can that be? OK, I admit that I was expecting a little mansion-type thing, but this is way beyond that. It's totally insane. "Can I..." I can't take my eyes off the magnificent setting. It's so beautiful that I feel overwhelmed with emotion. Oh dear, am I going to cry? Over an iron gate? Seriously?

Yes, I am.

"Why are you crying?" Ryan places a hand on my leg. "Babe... why?"

"It's... it's so beautiful. I can't believe it, Ryan."

"I knew you wouldn't. I didn't want to tell you too much before because I wanted you to see it without knowing anything."

"Gosh, so, I've reacted how you expected?"

"Absolutely."

"I did think it would be like a mansion, when you told me how many bedrooms it had but... nothing like this." I turn to smile at Ryan. "Are you sure we haven't just driven to America because I had no idea that we had places like this in England, where real people live."

He laughs at me and leans in to kiss my cheek. "I'll get the gates opened."

The gates – huh. This place would have to have these ornate iron gates and high, white stone walls to protect everyone in it from being kidnapped and held to ransom for millions of pounds – that's the type of place it is – honestly.

Ahead of us, at the end of a white stone drive, stands a magnificent, white building – I'm not kidding you, it resembles the White House in all its glory. The drive is lined with an array of green bushes in every hue imaginable, large ferns and trees. On both sides of the drive, and across the grounds as far as I can see, are shaped borders filled with plants of varying heights and spreads. There is so much colour, it astonishes me, in the middle of winter. How can it look like spring or summer here with an array of colourful plants and bushes? Are they real or is someone in the family extremely green-fingered and knows a dandelion from a daffodil? The lawns are immaculate and sweep up and around the impressive building in the distance. I'm in awe of this magnificent estate in front of me and can only stare, fixedly, as Ryan gets out of the car. He walks towards the gate and presses a buzzer. He tilts his head upwards and peers at a small screen. A moment later, I hear him speak to someone. "Jethro, is that you?" I hear him say.

I can just make out a faint sound coming from the intercom but can't quite work out what the man's voice says. Then, with a click and a clunk, the huge iron gates open slowly. Ryan jumps back in the car and kisses me on the cheek again. "Come on, let's go. I've got so much to show you this morning."

I move slowly, along the drive, admiring the view on both sides. As we approach the house, I see the drive splits into two and veers off to the left and right. "Go left," says Ryan, indicating with his hand. "The road goes around in a circle, underneath the porte-cochère."

"The what?" I ask with a giggle, as I turn to the left.

"The porch – there – go under it."

I sweep up the drive and arrive underneath a magnificent structure with enormous white pillars, where I come to a halt. It's like a palace, honestly. To my left is a decorative, towering double-door and just to the right of these, I notice a plaque on the wall which says, *Bagshaw House – Welcome*. "The house is named after you?" I say in a breath.

"Well, not me personally." Ryan lets out a short laugh. "Come on, let's get our bags from the boot."

"Are we leaving the car here?"

"No, Jethro will take it to the garages."

"You said that in its plural form..."

"Yes, they house all the cars." Ryan winks at me before climbing out of the car.

I follow him out, stretch my legs and back out and peer up at the porch. "When you say all the cars, you mean your family's cars, right?"

"Yes, my dad has a few old ones as well."

OK, this is getting increasingly like that American program, *MTV Cribs*. "Have you ever watched that American program, *Cribs?*" I ask, taking my overnight bag from Ryan and setting it down on the ground.

"Yes, I have... and yes, it is."

"Ha ha, you knew what I was going to sa..." The giant doors swing open behind me and an elderly, small man appears, wearing a black suit, a white shirt and a narrow black tie. He has a pair of black rimmed glasses, hanging from a cord around his neck and his balding head glistens in the wintery sunshine which beams down through a domed skylight in the porch's roof.

"Young Ryan, Sir, it's good to see you again. It must be a year since..." He takes Ryan's hand and shakes it warmly. "And this must be your good lady, Miss Satchel."

I smile and extend a hand to shake but the man takes my fingers gently in his hand and bows his head in front of me. "It's an honour to meet you, Miss Satchel."

"Please, call me Susie," I say, warming to this charming, dear old man, instantly.

"This is Jethro," says Ryan, grinning at me. "He will take your car to the garage."

"Oh, OK," I say, "thank you."

"No need to thank me Miss... Susie, it's my job."

"Well, thank you anyway." I hand the keys to Jethro and he takes them with a gracious nod of his head.

"Shall I take your bags up to your room?"

Ryan shakes his head, "No, it's fine, thank you, Jethro."

"Your room is ready, and I do believe your breakfast will be served at nine-fifteen sharp. I wish you both a merry Christmas and shall be on my way."

As I watch my car drive away and disappear around the back of the building, I get a giddy rush of excitement flutter through me. This is like a dream. "He is a lovely man," I say, picking my bag up and linking an arm through Ryan's.

"Old Jethro has been with the family for years... since I was a kid, in fact. He has served as our lifelong butler – I wouldn't like to guess how old he is now though."

"Does he live here?"

"Yes, he's got an apartment in one of the outbuildings."

"Well... of course he would have. An apartment? In *one* of the *outbuildings?* What is this place, Ryan? It's like a millionaire's mansion."

He laughs and shrugs. "I suppose it is a bit."

"A bit? I can't believe you have never told me."

"What's there to tell? I did mention that it had nine bedrooms. That must have been a clue."

"Yes, but..." I break off as Ryan pulls me towards the double-doors and pushes them open. They glide open without a sound and once again, I am taken aback by the scene in front of me as we step inside. Everything is white. Gloss white. The flooring, the walls, the ornate pillars in the corners, everything is pure, brilliant white. The entrance hall has an airy feel because of the expansive domed skylight way above and floor-to-ceiling windows at the far end which are the backdrop to an exquisite, glass, spiral staircase. I take a breath and blow it out slowly. "Oh my God, Ryan," I whisper, cutting through the silence. "It's just..."

"White." Ryan looks at me and smiles. "Very white."

"Whiter than white," I reply in a small voice. "It's incredible. It's incredibly white." I scan the hall again and note the numerous, closed doors on either side, the white leather sofas and illuminated coffee tables, situated underneath the sweeping, spiral staircase and the rows of small, white downlights, glistening in the high ceiling above. I'd be the happiest girl in the world if this were the only room in the house and the place we would be staying – let alone anywhere else in this magnificent place. "It's so quiet – where is everyone?" I whisper.

"In their rooms I expect. Come on, I'll take you to ours then we'll have some breakfast before I show you around."

154

I hold on to Ryan's arm tightly, for fear of either slipping or scuffing the perfectly polished white floor. "Are you sure I shouldn't have bought a posh dress with me? Won't it be dinner jackets and the sort?"

"No, don't worry, babe. Jeans and a nice top will be just fine."

"But..." I whisper, as we reach the staircase. "Blimey," I add, eyeing the thick glass steps leading upwards and around. "Oh my God..."

The stairs go up and up, around and around, ending at the top with another dome skylight, much bigger than the one in the entrance hall. The windows, at the back, which I thought went from the floor to the ceiling, do indeed go from floor to ceiling but not the ground floor ceiling. I have never seen such an expansive window, which goes up and up, lighting the whole staircase, up to the roof it seems.

"Nice, isn't it?"

"Nice? Nice? You use that word so modestly. You said I deserved to have a 'nice' present for Christmas. You say this is, 'nice'..."

"Well, don't you think it is?"

"Oh my God, Ryan, it is so much more than, 'nice'."

He nods at me agreeably. "Come on – we're at the top."

I hold on to the sleek, black glass bannister (yes, it's the first bit of black I've seen but it's so small that it's pretty nondescript in comparison to the main structure) and begin to ascend the stairs. My brain is telling me not to go up each step, as my eyes can't see any solid flooring beneath my feet. It's quite scary to climb the stairs when you can see straight through them. I grip the bannister tighter and tighter as we go higher and higher.

As we pass the first floor, I can see that the hallway is very similar to the main entrance hall with doors on either side. Everything is white and at the end is another set of white sofas and illuminated coffee tables – the only difference being that they are at the opposite end. The second floor is exactly the same. "Do your parents like white?" I whisper, as we go past the second floor.

"I guess so," says Ryan, looking down at me with a smirk. "It's not all white though – wait until you see our room."

*** 24 ***

'Our *room*', he said. Is he having a joke with me? Or did he mean, 'wait until you see our apartment'? I haven't asked yet, because I'm speechless, but I wonder if he would describe this as 'nice' too. As we reached the third floor, our 'room' as he calls it, was the second door on the right. When Ryan opened the door, I thought, 'cool, we have a miniature hallway, just like the other floors, only this one is inside our 'room'. It's so miniature that there is only one sofa in it – huh – only one. But, silly me, that was just the entrance to our 'room'. When Ryan opened the next door, well, I don't know how I am still upright, to be honest. That's where I am right now – standing in the inner doorway, clinging on to the frame and peering out at our 'room'. I thought that rooms had just one door, a window and some furniture in them. This is no room, I can tell you. It's a grand, opulent suite, fit for royalty.

"This is our lounge," says Ryan, pulling me in, "and through there..." He points to an open door. "... is the bedroom. And that's the bathroom and dressing room," he says, spinning on his heels and indicating to the other side of the lounge.

I drop my holdall on the floor and peer around the 'room'. In front of me, two large doors open on to an oval shaped balcony which is big enough to fit my car on. We're overlooking the front and I can see the sweeping drive going all the way down to the iron gates. I walk over to the doors and take in the view. There are fields and woodland as far as I can see. It's truly remarkable. As I turn back around, I peer at the plush, white and pale grey three-piece suite, the pearl-white piano standing alone in one corner, the already prepared, breakfast table with four elegant, high-backed chairs, the fifty-inch TV screen, fixed to the wall and the intricately detailed chess pieces, sitting on a chequered glass board.

"What do you think then?" Ryan asks, his voice breaking into my overwhelmed mind.

"I don't know what to say... I don't know who you are... what is this place?"

"Babe," He approaches me and puts his arms around me. "I'm still me, Ryan, your partner – remember?"

"Of course, I do," I say, hugging him back. "But... you never told me..."

"Sit down – I want to talk to you. Let's get things straight."

He offers me the sofa behind me and I sit down, tentatively. He kneels in front of me. "Babe, this is not something I have ever boasted about to anyone. The last thing I would have wanted was to get hitched up to someone who was only with me for my money..." He breaks off and gazes into my eyes, looking straight past me. "I mean... my ex, for example – there was no way she was ever going to know. Do you know what I mean?"

I nod. "Yes, I do know. I'm sorry, I've just been so taken aback by all of this – and the car. It's all so unreal."

"I know... and I'm sorry to have surprised you like this."

"No, please, don't be sorry. You have your reasons and I totally get it. Really I do."

He kisses my lips tenderly, before pulling me back up. "Come on, I'll show you around the room and then it should be time for breakfast."

If I thought the lounge was amazing, then maybe I should have reserved judgement until I'd seen the rest because there's a possibility that I could run out of luxurious words to use, to describe it all. The bedroom not only has a Queen size bed and beautifully crafted, white bedside cabinets but it also has a chaise lounge, a dressing table and mirror, a beautiful, pale grey suede ottoman and another, fifty inches at least, wall mounted television. As for the bathroom and 'dressing room' – I mean, who has a 'dressing room'? They too, are rooms to be admired in great depth. Honestly, my phone is going to run out of battery soon as I can't get enough photos of the place, from every angle conceivable, and every photo I have taken has not done the place any justice whatsoever.

As I am admiring the view once again and Ryan is sitting on the sofa playing with the TV's remote control, there's a gentle knock on the door. I freeze and turn to peer at Ryan. He smiles at me, knowingly. "It's our breakfast," he glances at his watch, "bang on time."

"Oh, good," I whisper, "I'm starving."

Ryan goes to the door and opens it. A middle-aged lady is standing behind a trolley, which is laden with plates, bowls, cups and saucers, a stainless-steel tea pot and a coffee pot. "Good morning, Master Bagshaw and may I take this opportunity to wish you and your lady a very merry Christmas."

"Thank you, Harriet. It's good to see you – how have you been?"

"Very well, thank you sir. Would you like me to...?"

"No, no. I'll take it, thank you."

Harriet bows her head. "Give me a call when you have finished."

"Thank you, I will."

Harriet turns to leave.

"Oh, and Harriet?"

She turns back around. "Yes, sir?"

"We wish you a very happy Christmas too. I trust you will be getting off early?"

She smiles warmly. "In time for tea."

"Good, good – and thank you again."

Harriet gives a small, courteous nod and walks away before Ryan pulls the trolley into the room. "We've got everything here," he says with an excitable tone in his voice. "I'm starving too. Come on, let's devour this lot and then I'll show you the rest of the house and the grounds.

By 9-50am we are both sitting at the breakfast table, staring at the rest of the food – there is so much of it. I could have had a full English breakfast, a continental breakfast, a bog-standard, cereal and toast breakfast, a vegetarian breakfast or a slimmer's breakfast. And then there was the endless array of fruit. In the end, I chose a small bowl of cereal, two slices of toast with marmalade, a pork and herb sausage and a small spoonful of scrambled egg, a croissant and a low-fat muesli bar – just so that I could say that I had a bit of everything. I think Ryan's thoughts were the same because he ate similar things to me, except he also had bacon and hash browns with his sausage and egg. Now, neither of us can move. We're sitting back in our chairs, patting and rubbing our extended tummies. "What time did you say we would be eating the meal later?" I ask, hoping the answer might be, tomorrow.

"Not until four so don't worry. This was designed to keep you full for the day."

"Thank goodness for that." I give a little laugh, stand up and try to stretch my torso upwards, hoping to relieve the fullness, but it doesn't work. "The staff are lovely here, aren't they? Very respectful."

"They are great but... I always hate it when they feel like they have to treat me like aristocracy."

"But you are, aren't you?"

Ryan shrugs. "I don't consider myself to be."

"Why?"

"I don't know, I never have done. My brother speaks to the house staff like they are second class citizens and not worth him wasting his breath on. I think it's terrible."

I suddenly remember that I will be meeting his brother and his girlfriend later today and a chill runs down my back. I am not looking forward to it. In fact, the only person I am looking forward to seeing is, Rachel – she's nice and I'm hoping her boyfriend will be nice too. "Where is your brother's room?"

"Directly below us, funnily enough, so no bouncing about on the bed later."

I gasp, "I wouldn't dream of it, Master Bagshaw."

"Oi – don't you start that."

I laugh and step around the table to hug him. "Let's go for that walk – I need the exercise, in preparation for the dinner, if breakfast is anything to go by."

"OK, I'll call Harriet and then we'll be off."

I don't know why, but I sort of expected Ryan to call Harriet from the door. I should have known that there would be a telephone in the room with a direct, 'Room Service' number. This place is just like a hotel.

We have just arrived back in the entrance hall, donning coats, ready to go outside, but Ryan wants to quickly take me around the ground floor. There are six doors, three on each side and Ryan pulls me by the hand, over to the first one on the right. "Follow me," he says, opening the door, "It's like a maze in here – you could get lost." He peers over his shoulder and smirks at me as I grip his hand tightly.

We've walked into what Ryan calls the, kitchen/breakfast/family room. It has the same gloss white and light grey theme as the rest of the house – or what I have seen so far. It's a huge, round kitchen with an oval marble breakfast bar in the middle which has eight white leather bar stools around it. The kitchen cupboards go from floor to ceiling and the units are all slightly curved to give the kitchen it's round effect. It's quite incredible and looks so clean that I'm sure it's never been used. Ryan looks at me and smiles, before he pulls me through the kitchen to another room. "This is the private lounge," he says, eyeing me for a response.

Once again, I am taken aback. You would think that I wouldn't be shocked by this place by now, but this room is... "The private one?" I gasp.

"Yes, we have a bar lounge too – I'll show you that one in a minute."

"A bar lounge..."

Ryan nods and guides me towards the massive curved window, which again, is floor to ceiling. Outside is a huge marbled patio with pillars supporting a roof above. It overlooks beautifully landscaped gardens in the forefront, with fountains and sculptures dotted about, and tree lined paths and other buildings in the background. "Is all this yours?" I say, gesturing to the land I can see in front of me.

"Yes, we have about 4.7 acres, I think."

I have no idea how big an acre is, but I know I can see a lot of ground.

"Here – watch this," says Ryan, placing his hand on a square plate, fixed to the wall.

Suddenly, there is a mechanical sound and then a faint humming noise as the mass of glass begins to move, sliding to the right and disappearing into the wall at the far end. A few moments later, the window has gone and the 'private lounge' has become a part of the patio and garden outside. "Wow," I say, as I shake my head disbelievingly. "That is something else."

"It's cool, isn't it? It's the latest improvement to the house. We used to have triple French doors here, but Dad discovered these things and got one installed. It took a year to get it made and have it fitted but was well worth the wait."

"I should say so. I've never seen anything like it..." I break off and look at Ryan, puzzled. "Can I ask you something?"

"Yes, what is it?"

"When I first met you, you lived in a shared house. Why would you live in a place like that when you have this?"

"Like I said before, I have been looking for a place but couldn't make my mind up what I wanted. I also wanted to experience normal life – you know, do what normal people would do. I don't want all that fancy lifestyle and certainly not given to me on a plate. Rachel's the same as me – we wanted to earn our place in life..." Ryan peers out across the gardens, thoughtfully. "Unlike, Rob, he's more than happy to be given everything on a plate."

I nod in acknowledgement. I can see that there is still a rift between Ryan and his brother and wonder how this afternoon's meal will go. "So, your gold-digger of an ex-girlfriend never realised that she had her very own rich man right under her nose."

"No, she didn't and I'm glad she never knew."

"Why have you shown me?"

"There has always been something different about you, Susie. Right from the start, I could see that you were a hard-working woman, scraping together enough money to pay a mortgage and bills and expecting nothing from anyone. You're not influenced by money, you're not swayed by grandeur and you're not a glory hunter. You accept life as it is, see the good in everyone and have a warm, kind heart..." He breaks off and smiles at me. "Is that enough?"

I let out a tiny laugh and look down at the floor, abashed.

"I want to share everything I have with you and I know that all sounds crazy when we haven't been together for much more than six months, but it just feels right. I can tell." Ryan raises his hand to the square plate on the wall and taps it. The window begins to close again which is a relief as it has got very cold in the room, even though the hazy morning sun is pouring in and illuminating the whiteness to a blinding degree. "Come on, I'll show you the rest," he says, taking my hand in his and pulling me across the room and back out to the entrance hall.

The next room is the 'bar lounge', just as Ryan had said earlier. The clue was in the word, 'bar', although I didn't pick up on this before. It has only become apparent to me since Ryan pressed another square plate on the wall and a huge bar area swung out from a false wall. I can tell you, I was completely shocked as it appeared from nowhere.

"Mum and Dad use this room a lot, when they have guests over... We'll probably start off in here this afternoon," says Ryan.

As the bar comes to a halt, I scan the bottles of alcohol, hanging upside down in two rows of twenty or more. "There's a lot of drink there," I say, after staring agog for a few minutes.

"Yes, whatever drink you can think of, it will be there. Dad makes cocktails as well but steer clear of them unless you want to be wrecked within an hour."

"It might help calm my nerves," I reply.

"Are you nervous?"

"I was a little bit, before we arrived, but now..." I catch sight of the Baileys and instantly have a desire to down a few glasses, to help the said nerves. "Now I'm really, ultra-nervous – this is all way out of my league."

Ryan pulls me into him and wraps his arms around me. "No, it's not out of your league, Susie. They are not in *your* league. Trust me, you will see."

Oh God, that hasn't helped matters but I'm not going to tell Ryan that. I need to have a mindset of, what will be will be. Que Sera, Sera and all that jazz.

*** 25 ***

I've now seen the drawing room, the living room, the study and the dining room. I've also seen the rooms below floor level – the secondary kitchen, the gymnasium, sauna and steam rooms and the cinema room. Huh – I can't tell you how silly this place is. Silly is probably not the correct terminology to describe such a commodious, magnificent family home but I'm sorry, it is silly.

The final door opens and I'm looking at a full-size swimming pool with floor to ceiling windows running along its entire length (I bet they open too but Ryan hasn't shown them off) which look out over the lower gardens. Obviously, this place would have an indoor swimming pool with a picturesque view as you're swimming along and obviously, there would be lower and upper and no doubt, middle-y gardens to feast your eyes on while you're doing it. I don't mean to sound sarcastic but it's all becoming too much.

"These windows open but it takes forever so I won't open them," says Ryan, standing beside me with his hands in his pockets. Huh – see? I said they probably opened. Of course, they would.

"That's OK – I believe you." I smirk and wink an eye, playfully. "Where next?"

"Outside? I'll show you the outbuildings and the pool."

"The pool?" I say, inquisitively. "Isn't this the pool?"

Ryan laughs. "It's not *the* pool – this is the small, indoor one."

Oh dear, of course it is. This pool will be the teeny tiny one and the other pool will be the monstrous one. Ryan is an expert in understating everything, like, 'nice' for instance. Silly, silly me. OK, I know I'm making a bit of a joke about all this now but it's seriously beyond my scope of imagination. This Christmas is an absolute stark contrast to last year and if anyone had told me last year where I'd be this year, I would have laughed my head off at them.

Ryan was right, the indoor pool *is* smaller, teeny tiny in fact, so I was right too. The outdoor one is monstrous, just as I had suspected, and it is surrounded by exotic plants and palm trees, creating a Mediterranean feel. How these things survive in our freezing winters, I don't know. Apparently, Ryan said it's in the mulching. I didn't ask about 'mulching' and didn't want to appear to be a non-mulcher who knows nothing about mulching or mulchy people who do mulchy stuff, so I accepted his know-how at face value and that's good enough for me.

We're now walking towards several buildings, which are set out in a row, along a pavement of white stone which contrasts beautifully with the black tarmac road. It looks like they have their very own street, in their back garden as I notice the decorative streetlamps along the way and door numbers on three of the buildings. "Gosh, you've got your own little street in your back garden," I say, looking up and down in awe.

"It does look like a street, doesn't it?" Ryan grins at me. "These are the apartments for the staff and a guesthouse. Number 3 is for guests..."

"Why wouldn't guests stay in the house, like we are?"

"They do sometimes but some guests bring their own guests who like to stay in the guest house – you know, have their own bit of space and not be tied in to the main house."

"So, how many apartments are there?"

"Four," says Ryan, pointing to numbers 1 and 2. "Two up and two down but there's only Jethro living there now – he lives at number 1, on the ground floor..." he pauses, thoughtfully, "I think Dad wants to turn number 2 into an office block now."

"Really?"

"Yes, he wants to bring the businesses and his workers closer to home."

"Why would he want to do that?" I ask.

Ryan shrugs. "I don't know – that's just Dad's way of doing things."

"Fair enough," I say, shrugging too.

We've walked along the mini street to the end building which is as big as the other three put together, except it has no number on it. The road continues to the end of the building and then sweeps around the side. We reach a door and Ryan leans over and whispers, "Zero, three, six, nine."

I look at the combination lock, he's pointing to.

"Go on, open it. Punch the numbers in and turn the lever."

I do as he says, and the door clicks. I push it open.

"There's yours," says Ryan, pointing into the huge garage space. "Over there."

I'm not kidding you, it's like a mini car park in here. There are ten cars, neatly parked in rows of four with empty parking bays for another six and there's enough room for each car to manoeuvre and drive out of the doors, over at the back, easily. My car is right at the back and closest to the doors.

"If you want to go out for a spin," Ryan starts, "just use that code on the back doors and they will open up as well. They close automatically after three minutes if there's nothing in the way – it's the same code as the iron gate at the front but that one closes as soon as your back end is out."

"Ah, so I can make my escape easily then," I kid.

Ryan laughs and nods. "Yes, if you need to. Or you might want to go back to that village we came through and have a look around, it's very quaint."

"When would we get time to go and have a look around there?"

"We could go this evening if you wanted to. You might get bored..."

"What about your family?"

"Oh no, they wouldn't want to go..."

"No," I say, trying not to laugh, "I mean, won't we be spending time with them this evening?"

Ryan frowns and shakes his head. "No... they'll retire after dinner."

"What? All of them?"

He shrugs. "I expect so. We always have done before. We kind of do our own things after dinner."

"Won't they make the effort to get to know me and Rachel's boyfriend?"

"I doubt it – they're not that sociable. The fact that they've invited you is a big step forward."

Oh my God, now I am terrified of meeting them. I feel like I'm going to be having dinner with the Queen, it's that scary.

"So, anyway, if you want to make that escape later, the doors and gate will all close safely behind you, so you don't need to worry about leaving the place open," Ryan says, hurriedly, and I get the impression he's trying to change the subject.

"But what if there were two cars going out?" I ask, not wanting to return to the subject of his weird parents.

"The doors all have sensors to detect whether there's one or more cars leaving."

"It's all very clever stuff then."

"Yes, it is, anyway, while we're here, come and have a quick look at my dad's cars – he's got a couple of vintage ones."

Really? Do I have to do this? I'm not being ungrateful but old cars are really not my thing. I certainly wouldn't spend time looking them over. "OK," I say, feigning interest. "Show me."

***

The cars were OK, I suppose. They looked old but sparkly new, if you know what I mean. What I do mean is, they are all well-kept and maintained cars but I'm sorry, at the end of the day, a car is just a car to me (except my new one, of course).

We are back in our 'room' as Ryan still calls it and I'm rummaging through my clothes, wondering if the jeans, peplum, red top and stiletto shoes are appropriate. Ryan insists that they are, but I just don't get it. Surely his family would dress for dinner. How could they live in a house like this and not dress for dinner or live any sort of lavish, well-presented lifestyle? According to Ryan, they don't. He says that they are very plain people but I'm sure that even plain people would dress for dinner.

I'm holding the stilettos in my hands and wondering whether they will be suitable for walking on the beautiful glossy floors – not that I'm worried about sliding about anywhere, it's more a case of, would I chip or scuff the flooring? I don't have much choice really because my only other shoes are the comfy ones I drove here in. They would not look good with nice jeans and my new top. I wish Ryan had told me a little bit more about this house before we came.

Ryan is having a soak in the bath at the moment, he waited patiently for me to have mine first. We could have done the 'together' thing, as the bath is so big, but we would have been doing a lot of splashing about and then Ryan would have wanted a nap afterwards, so I said he had to let me have one on my own. And besides, I'm far too nervous to be thinking about or taking part in any shenanigans before I've met his parents. Right now, I feel guilty just for being Ryan's girlfriend, let alone anything else.

I put my shoes on the floor and peer at my reflection as a foul stench begins to fill the room. The unmistakable smell of Brussels sprouts is penetrating our privacy and it turns my stomach. Yuk. I've just realised that the second kitchen is directly underneath us and I expect that the cooks are busily preparing our meal. My tummy turns over again but this time it's not because of the smell but the impending meeting. God help me. Ryan has given me enough information to make an informed judgement on these people before I've met them and already, I don't think I am going to like them. They sound a bit weird, or is it just me?

Ryan appears, dripping wet and wrapped in a soft, white towel, tied around his waist. I don't know what it is about him being wet, but he always manages to look like some Hollywood heartthrob and it makes me fancy him stupidly – not that I don't fancy him the rest of the time, but I want to touch him all over when he's wet. I need to keep composed though as there's no way I'm going to dinner with an after-sex flush on my cheeks. "Can you smell the dinner cooking?"

He nods and sniffs his nose in the air. "Smells good – it will be good. It's coming up through the dumb waiter."

"Sorry?"

"The smell – it's wafting up here through the dumb waiter."

"Who's he?" I ask. "Why is he dumb?"

Ryan bursts out laughing and shakes his head at me. "Let me get dressed and I'll show you."

OK, well I didn't know what a dumb waiter was, did I? Would any normal person know? We're standing at the end of our hallway and behind one of the sofas is a large hatch, concealed behind a door in the wall. It's a lift and used to transport trolleys of food. Apparently, it wouldn't have been so big in the old days and would have been used for food trays but now it has been made bigger to accommodate trolleys. "It's how our breakfast trolley came up this morning," says Ryan, with a giggle, obviously still amused by my lack of knowledge in these things. "How else would they have got the trolley up here?"

"I don't know, I hadn't thought about it."

"Well, now you know." He smirks at me. "We've got ten minutes before pre-dinner drinks, are you ready?"

"I just want to check my hair and make-up but yes, pretty much ready."

"Come on then, dumb waiter lesson over."

As we head back down the hall to our 'room' we hear a man's voice coming up the spiral staircase from the floor below. Ryan stops in his tracks and listens.

"Who's that?" I whisper.

"My brother, Rob." Ryan takes my hand and pulls me back into our room.

"Are you OK?" I ask as Ryan closes the door behind us, softly.

"Yes, why do you ask?"

"You seem a bit sca... worried, that's all."

"I'm not worried... or scared. I'm probably as nervous as you are about seeing everyone though... especially Rob."

***

We've made it all the way down the staircase, passing two floors, without seeing a soul. I would have much preferred meeting Ryan's family in dribs and drabs rather than having to walk into a room filled with people I don't know. Still, there's nothing I can do about it now and I will just have to brave it. We've arrived outside the bar lounge and I can hear voices inside. I hold my breath as Ryan opens the door and we step inside...

There are just two men and Rachel, sitting alongside the bar drinking and chatting, while Jethro is at the other end, looking busy. I desperately need a drink to calm my nerves. I smile at Rachel as she turns her head to look and she gives me a little reassuring wiggly wave of her fingers.

"Ryan, Susie, it's so good to see you both. Come and have a drink with us," she says, rising to her feet. She is wearing a full-length, black skirt and a sparkly jumper. I wish I had worn a skirt now. "This is, Jacob," she adds, indicating to the tall (I can tell he's tall by his long legs), slim man, seated next to her. He stands (tall – I knew it) and shakes Ryan's hand. Then he shakes mine and smiles.

"Pleased to meet you both," he says, pushing his glasses back up his nose. "I don't know about you but I'm as nervous as hell, meeting everyone today."

"I know what you mean," I reply, warming to him straight away. At least I'm not on my own now.

The other man turns around on his bar stool slowly, and grins. He's wearing jeans and a shirt, like Ryan and Jacob, which puts me at ease about the dress code a little. He has a familiar look about him. You know that feeling you get when you're sure that you've seen someone before but can't quite place them. He's that type with the chiselled, Hollywood jawline, the kind of guy who would fit right into a blockbuster movie. The sort that you think you know because he might resemble your favourite megastar. He nods at me with a deadpan expression but says nothing, then he looks at Ryan. "Good to see you again, brother – it's been a long time."

Ryan extends a hand to shake, but Rob has jumped off his stool already and is leaning over the bar, calling to Jethro, who is at the other end, polishing glasses. "Jethro, let's get some more drinks up here," he shouts. "Ammy will be here in a minute and she'll need to down a few." He laughs in a way which is unsettling, and I grip hold of Ryan's hand tightly as Jethro takes our orders.

Rachel is as lovely as the first time I met her. I can see us getting along very well which is a comfort because I feel like I need some allies. Her boyfriend is also nice but appears to be far more nervous than me. He's not the most attractive of men and certainly not the type that I would imagine

Rachel being with. She is very pretty and just like her brothers, seems to have been blessed with the attractive gene, it must run in the family.

Rob is particularly handsome; however, his persona is not, from what I've seen and heard of him so far. There is something about him which I do not like, and I've spent more time wondering where I know him from than I have talking to him. He just sits on his stool and watches us all with a shifty look in his eye. I'm wondering if that is why Jacob is feeling so uncomfortable, the poor man is like an antelope being stalked by the lion.

I've practically knocked my first drink back and the warming sensation, from the brandy and lovage (brandy and lovage – look at me. My usual would be anything but, but this is a posh place so I'm having a posh drink... or two... or maybe even three) is calming my nerves. Ryan looks at my glass. "Do you want another?"

"Dutch courage?" says Rob, eyeing my glass and then raising his eyes to meet mine with a smirk.

I smile politely. "Yes, something like that."

"Then get them down your neck – you'll need them." He laughs and gives Ryan a friendly thump on the arm. "Ammy will soon catch up when she gets here, have no doubt about that."

"Isn't she here yet?" Ryan asks. "I thought she lived..."

"Yes, we do both live here – temporary of course. We're in transition, you know. Ammy spends her weekends here but works away during the week. She's looking for a new job, closer to home and hopes she will get one a-sap."

Ryan smiles waveringly and then gives Jethro a nod for more drinks.

"She's upstairs, putting all that shit on her face – excuse my language," he says, peering at me and waving a finger around my face.

Instantly, my face burns red with embarrassment, tinged with a hint of anger. Who does he think he is? How dare he point at my face when he's talking about putting 'shit' on her face? I turn to Rachel and Jacob and give them a faltering, awkward smile. Oh my God, I'm a sensitive being – get me out of here.

Rachel rolls her perfectly, natural eyes. I hadn't noticed before, but I don't think she wears a scrap of make-up which is now making me feel completely upset and self-conscious about my own. "Ignore him, hun. He's just jealous because he's not as good looking as us girls."

Rob raises one eyebrow and looks at Rachel with contempt. "Sweet sister, you will never be in my league." He then swivels his stool and turns towards the bar. "Ah, Jethro, good man. Let's have another round of drinks – don't want you getting bored, do we?"

I already feel sorry for Ammy, unless of course, she is arrogant and insolent, just like her boyfriend. Then they would be a good match and one to stay well clear of. Which, I imagine, is going to be incredibly difficult once we are all seated at the grand dining table in the other room. I hope to God that Ryan's parents aren't as egotistic as Rob is. I dislike the man considerably already.

Ryan and Rob have been talking in muted tones while myself, Rachel and Jacob have been making polite conversation about school-related things. We're on our third drink already but there has been no sign of Rob's girlfriend yet.

Out of the corner of my eye, I see Rob pull his mobile phone from his pocket and peer at the screen. He smiles at the phone and then looks over to me with a smirk. "Ammy is on her way down now, ladies and gents. Ryan – be prepared to be astounded."

Ryan shoots him a quizzical glance and looks at me with a frown.

Oh my God, why would he announce the arrival of his girlfriend? Who does he think he... or even she, is? How dare he be so conceited, saying that Ryan will be astounded. How dare he say things like that in front of me. I'm sorry but, who *does* he think he is? And who *does* he think she is, Miss frigging-world? How dare he.

The handle clicks as it turns down and the door slowly opens. She's standing there, side-on with one leg bent slightly at the knee, like a model would pose. Her long hair is sweeping over her shoulders and falling down her back in a sea of gorgeous blonde waves. She's beautiful. She's wearing a black mini skirt, which accentuates her long, slim legs and a low-cut blouse. She scans the room and smiles before she meets my eye…

We stare at each other with widening eyes as the realisation dawns. Transfixed, I am speechless. I can see that her horrified expression has rendered her speechless too. I sense that Ryan is speechless beside me as well...

Oh my God...

No... no, no, no.

*** 26 ***

No... no...

It can't be...

How?

Oh my God, now it is becoming clear. Now, I think I know who...

Oh no, please... That means...

Sickness rises in my throat as my mind turns into a scrambled mush. No one has moved. No one has spoken. There's an electrical charge fizzing around in the air, waiting to ignite and explode me into a trillion pieces. I shoot a sideways glance at Ryan who is hypnotised, his jaw hanging slightly. I can't even bring myself to look over at Rob. The nanoseconds turn into a lifetime as I gulp back the lump in my throat, silently. This can't be real...

"Ammy, you look gorgeous. Doesn't she folks?" says Rob, cutting through the atmosphere with his supercilious voice.

Ammy glares at him and turns her attention back to me. Then she scowls at Ryan. "What is *she* doing here?"

"What are *you* doing here?" Ryan retorts.

I've never heard Ryan speak in this tone of voice and it has stunned me. I shake my head disdainfully. Ammy indeed. Her name is not flipping, Ammy. Or maybe she likes to be called that. Bloody, Ammy, what a stupid flipping name. I want to leave. Now. This is my worst nightmare come true.

"I'm living here... for a while."

"What the hell," says Ryan, thrusting his hands into his trouser pockets and shuffling his feet agitatedly. I can hear the exasperation rising in his voice.

"Why didn't you say –" I begin, defensively.

"Why didn't you?" Ammy cuts in.

"I..." I don't know what to say. My mind is unscrambling everything, and the comprehension of this whole situation is setting in. It makes me want to retch. It makes me want to run. To hide. To scream. To cry.

"Well?" Ammy prompts me. "Why didn't you say anything? Or you, Ryan?" She gives Ryan a piercing scowl filled with contempt.

"It was none of your business," I jump in, before Ryan can open his mouth.

"And mine was none of your business," she bites back, a vicious sneer on her made-up face.

Rob lets out a laugh and walks over to meet Ammy. "Come on, beautiful, let's get you a drink and we can all talk about this."

I turn around to the bar, not looking at Ryan at all, and grab my drink. I knock it back in one mouthful and give Jethro a desperate nod to refill it before he serves Ammy. I need another drink. I need the whole bottle of brandy. I need to be numb. The worst is to come. I now know exactly who Ryan's parents are...

Everyone has calmed down a little, apart from me, and the drinks are aplenty. I'm sure Ammy, or Amber as I would much prefer to call her, has caught up with the rest of us by downing two double vodkas in about four minutes flat.

Yes, it's Amber – Ammy is too much of a sweet name to be hers. She's not Ammy at all, she's Amber the stirring, stalking freak who works with Ryan in the PE department at his school. I now know why Rob looked familiar because I met him earlier in the year while on a caravan holiday with my mum and dad. I also met Ryan's parents (unbeknown to me) and things didn't go too well – on my part at least. Right at this moment, I would really like to leave but I know I can't do that, for Ryan's sake. Maybe I will get away with it and the meal will run smoothly but I'm doubtful because Amber was not pleased to see me here, with Ryan. Only time will tell now, whether the day will end well or go completely tits-up. Why do these things always have to happen to me? Perhaps a liar always gets their just deserts, as they say.

"Mr and Mrs Bagshaw request your company in the dining room," announces Jethro, eyeing everyone with a quizzical look. He has obviously sensed that something has gone adrift. He shoots a glance at me and smiles warmly, which comforts me. At least I have one friend in the room. I'm not even sure at this moment if Ryan is going to remain a friend, especially if Amber has anything to do with it. I've caught her eyeing me with a steely glare, through narrowed eyes, once or twice and I'm on edge as we begin to make our way out of the bar lounge, clutching our refilled glasses.

The dining table has been decorated with a magnificent centerpiece of holly, baubles, tinsel and glittering, curly strands of ribbon – it's beautiful. I draw my eyes away from it and bravely look up as we shuffle into the room. Ryan's parents are standing at the end of the table with drinks in their hands. They look smart but casual and instantly, I recognise them from that evening at the caravan. I didn't like Ryan's dad, Reg, the first time I met him, and I certainly don't now, after what Ryan has told me about him. As for Ryan's mum, Gracie, she has the same red-rimmed glasses and a round, smiley face as before but her delicate charm has an undertone of betrayal now. I thought she was sweet before and I felt sorry for her, living under the wrath of Reg, but how could she back her husband up when he was, or maybe still is, abusive to her and her kids?

"Welcome," Reg's voice booms around the dining room. "Merry Christmas to you all. Be seated."

I grab the chair closest to me and pull it out. I am desperate to sit down, to be swallowed up by the height of the table decorations or at least slide down my chair and slip under the table where, hopefully, I won't be noticed.

"I think you'll find that's mine... if you can read correctly." Amber has stepped up behind me and she's pointing to the name card on the table.

Oh great – we've got to sit where our name card is. "So sorry, Am...my," I say, sarcastically. "Here, I've pulled the chair out for you..." I lean into her and whisper, "you wouldn't want to break a nail, would you?"

"Up here," says Ryan, tugging my hand away. I give a faltering smile to Rachel and Jacob, who are seated at the far end, and let Ryan guide me to my seat... right next to Reg, who is sitting at the head of the table. Gracie has made her way to the other end and sits opposite her husband. Great, I would have much preferred to be sitting at the other end – at least Gracie looks friendly.

"Merry Christmas, Mr Bagshaw," I say, extending a hand towards him.

He looks at my hand, like I've just presented a dead rat to him. "Be seated," he says, avoiding my eye. I peer at Ryan who is making his way to the other side of his dad, but he is also trying to avoid my eye. He has a sheepish expression and I imagine he feels the same way as I do. I hope he does anyway.

A high-pitched chink rings through my ears as Reg taps an empty glass with a knife. "It's good to have my family together again," he starts, as everyone looks up at him expectantly, "with a couple of additions – welcome to the Bagshaw household. Before the meal, as always, I want to say a few words."

The silent stillness in the room is overbearing as Reg eyes each and every one of us singly. When his eyes meet mine, I can't help but lower my gaze to the table – he's terrifying. He has an aura of intolerance about him that everyone seems to be in awe of. He pulls his chair out and sits down. "Heads up," he commands, and I glance around the table, wondering what he means. I note that Jacob is looking up to the crystal chandelier, hanging from the ceiling, in the middle of the room. So is, Rachel... and Gracie... and Rob and Amber and Ryan... I look up with a frown, wondering why they are all staring at the chandelier.

"For what we are about to receive..." Reg continues.

Oh God, they are obviously religious and saying grace before dinner. Why are they looking up though – surely, they should have their heads bowed, in prayer?

"... we must be grateful and thankful to the great universe. We will devour our gift of decent food, leaving nothing unturned. We will show our appreciation by consuming every last mouthful and thank the universe in our hearts and minds at the end. Thank you for bringing additional bodies to the table, so that we may grow in strength and number. We thank you, great universe, for bestowing these things upon us..." he pauses and out of the corner of my eye, I can see him looking around at everyone again. "Ladies and gentlemen, eat your fill until nothing is left... commence."

Everyone has lowered their heads, so I do the same. This is all quite bizarre. I peer across the table to Ryan, who is staring at me with a nervous smile.

"I bet that was a bit of a shock for you, Susie." Rob has just called out. He's seated next to me, but the table is so large that we are all spread out by at least a metre and a half, if not two. And I believe that Rob wanted everyone to hear his words anyway.

"Sorry?" I say, turning to look at him.

"Meeting us... when you knew us already."

I hear Ryan gasp and feel his eyes on me. "What are you talking about?" he says, to Rob.

"Ah," sighs Reg, "we know young Susie here, we've met her before."

Oh, for God's sake.

Ryan looks at me, puzzled. "Susie?"

"I... I didn't know I'd met your parents before. I didn't have a clue that they were your parents."

"When, where?"

"At the caravan park," says Reg. "I was there for the weekend, checking our land, the caravans and the inexperienced staff they've got for me now – they need to get experienced quickly or they're out."

That explains why the staff behind the bar, at the caravan park, looked terrified when he walked in. I remember now.

"You never mentioned that," says Ryan, looking at me curiously.

"I didn't know they were your parents, did I?"

Ryan nods. "Of course, right, I get it now. Small world." Then he frowns. "So, you knew Amber was with Rob?"

"Well," I start, shooting a cursory glance to Amber and then Rob, "again, I didn't know he was your brother, did I?"

"But you knew she had a..." Ryan has lowered his voice and sort of mimed his words to me. I nod to him and he rolls his eyes at me.

Suddenly the dining room door opens, and two young men walk in, pushing trolleys. They set about serving plates of food to everyone in a courteous manner. I'm surprised by this because I would have expected the meal to be a self-serve affair and not a, here's-your-plate-of-food-eat-it kind of thing. As a filled plate is placed carefully, in front of me, I peer at it and think how delicious it all looks... apart from the sprouts. Oh God, there are five of them. Was Reg serious about eating everything, leaving nothing unturned, for the good of the universe? Do I really have to eat these? I give a wavering smile to Ryan and wish I was sitting closer to him, then I could sneakily pass them under the table – I'm sure he likes sprouts.

OK, I'm going to do this. I'm going to eat a sprout – how bad can it be? Everyone else seems to be eating them and they haven't dropped dead or began to choke to death, so they must be reasonably edible. I don't want to be the only one leaving things, 'unturned'.

I peer down the table and see Amber tucking into her meal. She looks up and our eyes meet. She gives me a sneering glare before diverting her gaze, deliberately to Ryan and smiling sickly-sweet at him. I stare down at my plate and push a sprout around in the gravy, hoping it will dissolve into a mushy green liquid (easier to swallow) but sadly it doesn't. I stab the little green monster with my fork and hold it up, my top lip curling disdainfully, as I examine it. I can do this. If I eat just one, it will look better than eating none. I turn to see if Reg is looking at me but thankfully, he's not and is in deep conversation with Ryan, about his caravans.

It's in. Oh my God, it's disgusting. I crunch down on it and the sprouty juices squirt out from it. As I'm desperately chewing it to get rid of it as quickly as I can, I peer around the room. Amber is staring at me again and she is sniggering to herself. She's watching me eat and can obviously see the grimace on my face. Defiantly, I stab another sprout and push it into my mouth. God, this is awful. I smile scornfully, and Amber shakes her head at me like she's amused by my obvious agony.

The first sprout has gone now, and I persevere with the second one, wondering why I didn't eat them along with something else. I guess I want to enjoy my dinner and the only way to do it is by getting rid of the nasty little brain-like things first, that way I can eat the rest, happily.

Two more in. This is like torture but I'm almost there. Once again, I look up and see that Amber is still watching me. I stuff the last sprout into my mouth and smirk at her in a haughty manner.

The waiters have returned with wine and begin to pour a glass for everyone. Then one of them disappears again, only to return with another trolley. Starting at Gracie's end, the waiter goes to each person and asks them if they would like more food. Some do have more, some don't. When he arrives behind Amber, she puts a hand up and says, no thank you, before pointing at me. "Susie would like more Brussels sprouts – she loves them, don't you, Susie?" she bellows across the table. "She can't eat them quick enough – hurry, give her some more."

I glare at her, my mouth still full, and shake my head.

"Go on, Susie, it's OK, they won't mind you eating them all if you love them so much." She looks up towards Reg. "She does love her sprouts – she's addicted to them," she adds, with that same sickly-sweet smile.

Reg peers at my plate. "You've eaten them all – good girl. Have more. Waiter?" He clicks his fingers and the waiter comes scurrying down, pushing the trolley in front of him. "Give this girl more sprouts, she's eaten hers already – we have another sprout lover in the family."

I shake my head at him. "No, no, it's fine, really… thank –"

"You want sprouts – you will have sprouts, young lady," Reg cuts in. "The universe is looking down on you today and you will have everything you desire." He waves a finger at the waiter. "Give her a side plate and fill it." The waiter nods and follows the instructions hurriedly.

I stare in horror as a small side plate is placed next to me and the waiter begins to spoon sprouts on to it. I raise a hand after the second spoonful. "Please, that will be enough, thank you."

"Nonsense girl," says Reg. "The universe is plentiful with sprouts. Give her more."

The waiter adds another large spoonful and I have got to conceal a shiver as the thought of eating all those nasty little things consumes me. "Thank you," I say, holding my hand up again. "That really will be enough." I look to Amber and she is still watching me, in between sniggering into her plate. "Thank you, Ammy," I call out. "I really do *love* Brussels sprouts. Thank you so much – I owe you one." I shoot my most evil glare at her and then smile sarcastically. That's it, I'm going to eat them all, even if it kills me, just to spite the conniving little bitch.

Ryan has ended his conversation with his dad and is peering at me with an amused expression. He frowns at my side plate and then looks back to meet my eye. I shrug at him and smile, before stuffing two sprouts into my mouth and forcing a hamster-style grin. Before I've finished my mouthful, I take a long drink of wine to help swill it down. I really think these sprouts could kill me. A quick count tells me there are seventeen of them left, on the side plate. I'm going to play a countdown game by drinking copious amounts of wine while eating each sprout with a forkful of my main meal. It's the only way. I will beat Amber. I know she's set me up for this. She will pay for this.

Number twelve... five to go. Thirteen...

You know, after a while, your taste buds become immune to the foul taste of Brussels sprouts – I wouldn't go as far as saying that I like them now, not even in the slightest but they're bearable. Reg keeps looking at me and then he looks down at my side plate, then he smiles at me, before nodding his head. I think he admires me for ploughing my way through the sprouts. This could be the way to his heart – result.

Amber is also looking at me, again, and her expression is one of astonishment now. Huh – that will teach her to mess with me. I can deal with anything that she could throw at me. I sneer at her before pushing number fourteen into my mouth.

"This must be an extremely difficult Christmas for you," shouts Amber, across the table. "It's the first anniversary, isn't it? You know, since your beloved, other boyfriend..." She runs her hand, sideways across her neck, in one sharp movement, while sticking her tongue out.

I freeze. Everyone has just watched Amber do her 'death' impression and they are now peering at me, aghast. Number fourteen has slid midway down the back of my throat and I can't swallow it. I try desperately to gulp it down. The sprout is stuck. I panic. I'm choking. Coughing. Spluttering. My eyes begin to water, and my nose starts to run.

Oh my God, I'm going to die with a Brussels sprout stuck in my windpipe. *Susie Satchel died from eating a Brussels sprout*, I can see the headline now. My face turns a hot red and I continue to cough wildly.

"Susie – oh God, Susie." Ryan jumps to his feet but not before his dad has. Reg makes an almighty lunge towards me and – whack! A powerful blow to the middle of my back dislodges the sprout, sending it shooting from my mouth and landing across the table, near Ryan's plate. Reg has hold of my arm and starts to pat me gently.

"Are you OK?" says Ryan, reaching my side. He looks at his dad and then takes over from the patting of my back.

"I..." I can't even talk, I'm coughing so much. Reg pours a glass of wine and hands it to me. Everyone else is watching anxiously. "I..." I still can't get the words out. Ryan begins to rub my back and I shake him off, embarrassed by the whole situation. "I'm... OK..."

"Are you sure?" Ryan asks, concern all over his face.

I nod and calm myself enough to drink more wine as everyone else breathes a sigh of relief and their transfixed expressions return to normal.

"I'm so sorry, Susie..."

Oh God, she's talking to me again... I look across to Amber and glare hatefully at her.

"I didn't mean to upset you by mentioning your God-awful Christmas last year," she adds. "I know it was terribly tragic. I'm so sorry... I just thought... well, because he was number two of the week..."

"Amber," I say, curtly, my voice having returned, "do we really have to discuss this over dinner?"

"No, of course not, Susie, but... well, I'm here if you need to talk about it. It must have been a dreadful thing to witness – I can't imagine what it must have been like for you being right there when it happened. I hope Ryan has been supporting you..."

At this moment in time, I wish to God that I had just choked to death on the Brussels sprout because Ryan is staring at me with a serious frown on his face. I have never seen him look at me, or anyone else for that matter, in such a somber way.

*** 27 ***

The waiters have returned and are clearing away the plates. Luckily, I have managed to get away with not finishing my meal, which included the remaining sprouts. I think I can honestly say that I will never, ever eat a sprout again. Even though Reg has just said to me that it was such a shame that I choked because I looked like I was enjoying my meal and the extra sprouts. I had to nod politely and agree with him but only because he terrifies me and even more so since I felt the force of his hand on my back. I do wonder if he actually enjoyed thumping me like that – maybe I'm just a little over sensitive at the moment. But then, I think anyone would be feeling emotional if their boyfriend was sitting opposite them, giving them an odd, what-the-hell-is-going-on look. I smile weakly at Ryan and his frown deepens.

"Who are you talking about?" Ryan has turned to Amber now. Oh, dear Lord, please swallow me up and spit me out, into the universe to disappear forever.

"Who me?" Amber replies nonchalantly, placing a hand to her chest.

"Yes, you. What are you talking about?"

Amber smirks but avoids my eye. "You know... Susie's tragic Christmas, last year – she must have told you about it, Ryan? Did she tell you?"

Ryan is staring at Amber nonplussed, shaking his head slowly, while his furrowed brow deepens.

Amber lets out a devious little laugh. "She must have told you – you know, the 'two' in one-week thing?"

Luckily for me (Huh – that's a joke – how can anything be classed as 'lucky' for me now?), Gracie, Rachel, Jacob and Rob are in deep conversation with each other, so the only people listening to Amber and Ryan are myself and Reg.

"To be honest," Amber continues, "I felt so sorry for you, Susie. I've never known anyone to have as much bad luck as you had last year." She meets my eye just briefly, before diverting her gaze away. She knows exactly what she's doing, and I can't believe that she can be so downright wicked.

"I don't know what you are talking about – and I don't want to know, Amber. Don't you think that you might be hurting Susie by your vile little comments – not to mention completely embarrassing her?"

"But she did have two boyfriends in one week – didn't you?" Amber is looking directly at me now, her expression, desperate. "One died, didn't he? He was practically in your arms when he passed away – your parents told me everything. That's why you were in such a state."

"I'm not listening to any more of this," I say, standing up and pushing my chair back with the backs of my knees. I peer over to Ryan, tears filling my eyes. "I'm going to our room to freshen up – I'll be back in a minute."

Ryan looks startled but there is also deep disappointment in his eyes. He nods at me. "Do you want me to...?"

"No," I say, sharply. "Stay here."

As I walk towards the dining room door, I feel every pair of eyes boring holes in my back. I have never been so humiliated in my life. I am sickened by Amber's utterly evil attack.

I hear Ryan's raised voice as I leave the room, "What the hell do you think you are doing, Amber?" he says.

"Hang on just a minute..." I hear Rob retort. "Who do you think you're talking to?"

The voices fade a little as I begin to climb the spiral staircase, but I can tell that there is a heated exchange going on in the dining room. I'm distraught, it's all my fault. It sounds like the whole family are involved now.

I reach our room and open the door. My heart is racing. I need to get away. I'm in my *facebook*-message nightmare. It's all become real, and after everything I did to make sure that Ryan didn't find out what really happened last Christmas. I grab my coat and handbag and leave the room as quickly as I entered it. I need to go – get away. I need to think about what I should do next. This could be the end for me and Ryan.

Oh God, what was the number? I sneaked past the dining room and could hear them all arguing, over me. It was awful. Now I've reached the garage and I'm trying to remember the code. Was it... three, six, nine? No, that doesn't work. I tap my head, trying to knock some clarity into it. Three, three, six, nine... Three, six, six, nine... Aargh – what was it? I'm on edge, I need to escape. Ryan said I might need to escape and I really do now...

Zero, three, six, nine. It works. The silence is broken by the door clicking. I open it and rush towards my car. It may not be my car for long – Ryan might want it back when he decides to leave me. For now, though, it's mine. I'm out of here...

Zero, three, six, nine, the double doors open, and I drive out of the garage, steadily heading down the drive towards the gates.

Zero, three, six, nine, the iron gates open slowly. I put the car into first gear and drive out of the gates. I've escaped. I'm free. I need time to think. Away from here...

I drive along the dark, deserted country roads, heading for the quaint village nearby. I have no idea what I will do once I get there but I remember passing a picturesque park with a large pond in the middle, on our way here. I could park up there, gather my thoughts, plan my next step and even venture into the precinct and see if there's a McDonalds, or something like that, open. It's not that I'm hungry in the slightest but a strong cup of coffee would not go amiss. As I'm nearing the village, I wonder how long it will take for Ryan to realise I've left. What will he do? Will he even care now?

I feel terribly weak and weary, all of a sudden, and think it might be a good idea to park up somewhere – just so that I can have a quick nap in the car. I always find that I want to sleep, when I'm in a dire situation, it's as if the act of sleeping will make my terrible situation disappear. It gives me clarity and renewed strength to deal with the dilemmas in my life. Or is it simply a form of escape? Whatever it is, I need it now.

I've arrived and there is a road that leads around the back of the precinct, so I head down that way rather than go to the park. The village is like a ghost town – I don't think I've seen one car or pedestrian anywhere. But then, it is Boxing day so what should I expect?

Once again, I briefly reminisce about this time last year and again, I mull over the stark contrast between my last two Boxing days as I drive along. Suddenly, the road ahead narrows, turns into a single carriageway and then comes to an abrupt end – I didn't even notice a dead-end sign at all, but now I'm here it doesn't matter. This is the perfect little spot to hide away and take a quick nap – I need one desperately and I'm sure that no one will be using the back of the shops for deliveries tonight. I park alongside the kerb, turn the engine off, pull my coat further around me and wind the back of my seat down. I snuggle down and close my eyes… just 20 minutes… that's all I need… then I'll be able to think things through more clearly…

A loud thud on the side window jolts me awake. I blink my eyes and see a man's face peering in through the glass. I blink again, startled by the face staring at me. I rub my eyes as I slowly pull the back of the seat upwards, my heart thumping in my chest. The man is wearing a fluorescent jacket… it has reflective strips running across it… he's also wearing a…

He thuds the window again and I can hear his muffled voice outside. Shit, he's a policeman and there is another one standing behind him. They are both peering inside my car. Oh no, I bet I am parked on double-yellow lines. I didn't even think to check. After all, I didn't notice the dead-end sign, let alone anything else.

I wind the window down and smile, guiltily. "Yes?"

"Good evening, madam."

"Hi," I reply, sleepily. I glance at the clock on the dashboard – I've only been asleep for ten minutes. Damn, why couldn't they come back later or just stick a parking ticket on the windscreen? They could at least let me get a little snooze in.

"How long have you been here, madam?"

"Literally five minutes – honestly… OK, ten maybe. I was just going to move on." I let out a nervous giggle.

"You drove here and parked the car, is that right?" he questions, while sniffing the air.

"Yes," I say, nodding politely.

"Would you step outside the car please, madam?"

"Who? Me?... Why?"

"Step out," says the police officer, sounding far less friendly and polite than he did a moment ago.

"But..." I hesitate and peer at the two men through narrowed eyes. "But, what if you're not real?"

"Excuse me?"

"What if you're trying to trick me and you're not really policemen – I've seen it on the TV you know."

The policeman pulls a wallet from his pocket and shows me his warrant card. "Now, please step out of the car, madam," he repeats.

Reluctantly, I open the door and climb out but as I do so, I misjudge the pavement and stumble, landing in the policeman's arms. "Oh, gosh... I'm so sorry," I say. I'm not kidding you, I want to scream with laughter at the officer because his expression is one of utter amazement.

"Your name please." The other officer has moved closer now.

"Susie – look, I'm really sorry if I've parked on yellow lines but I don't know the area and... I just needed a break from driving..." I shoot a cursory glance at the kerb edge.

"Your full name?"

"I've just said, I'm sorry. Please, come on, Mr officer, it's just a little yellow line or two..."

"Your full name please madam. Do you have your driving license on you?"

I shake my head. I never carry it around with me – perhaps I should. "Look, it is Boxing day. I promise I won't park on any more yellow lines – how about that? Am I even parked on yellow lines?" I scan the road underneath my car but can't see any. "Pleeeease? Can I go?" It seems that the park is calling me now. I should have gone there first.

"Your full name," demands the officer.

"Susie Satchel – as in the bag." I let out a giggle and smile at the policeman.

"Susie Satchel," the officer repeats. "Have you been drinking, Miss Satchel?"

I freeze. Oh God, no. Can they smell it on my breath? Oh no, I never thought about that...

"Susie Satchel, I am arresting you on suspicion of being drunk in charge of a vehicle." He produces a set of handcuffs. "You do not have to say anything but anything you do say..."

"You can't... I... I work in a school... I'm a good person... You can't arrest me." The officer hasn't listened to my protest as he continues to make his arrest statement. "I'm a good person. I don't drink and drive... I just..."

"We will bring your vehicle in here," says the officer, pointing to the small car park behind us. "And I'll bring your keys into the station." He shakes his head at me, despairingly. "As you can see, Miss Satchel, you are parked across the entrance to our car park..."

The officer takes hold of my arm and guides me into the police station through the back door. "I'm a good person," I repeat, hoping that my plea might help this dreadful situation. "I work in a school... with children... and teachers. I'm not a drink-driver... I'm not... I promise. I don't live around here... I didn't know I'd parked in front of your car park – I'm sorry. I'm really, really sorry. Please don't arrest me – I can't be arrested. Please...

"I'm a good person," I repeat, hoping that my plea might help this dreadful situation. "I work in a school... with children... and teachers. I'm not a drink-driver... I'm not... I promise. I don't live around here... I didn't know I'd parked in front of your car park – I'm sorry. I'm really, really sorry. Please don't arrest me – I can't be arrested. Please...

We're in the front of the station now and I've been checked in – it looks like I'm getting a room for the night. The officer standing behind the high counter, leans over and smiles at me sympathetically. "Do you understand why you have been arrested?" I nod. "You have the right to make one phone call. Who do you wish to call?"

"No one," I say, forlornly. Who the hell can I phone? It's Boxing day – my parents do not want to receive a call from me this evening, saying I've been arrested for drinking and driving, or whatever it is they've arrested me for. Ryan probably hates me enough already, so I can't call him either...

Suddenly, my mobile rings. It's in my handbag, which they have taken from me and will hold in a locker while I have the breathalyser test and some other tests done. The officer behind the counter removes my phone from my bag. "You can answer it as your one phone call or you will have to turn your phone off," he says, passing it to me.

As I take the phone, it stops ringing. The notification on the front of the screen says it was Ryan. My heart sinks as I turn the phone off and hand it back to the officer. "I don't want to call anyone," I say, with a lump in my throat. "But thank you anyway."

*** 28 ***

It's official. I am a fully-fledged criminal. I had the breathalyser test, which showed I was two and a half times over the limit. I've had a DNA test, a mug-shot, and my fingerprints done too. I asked why they were doing all the tests when I only needed to have the breathalyser test but apparently, it's routine to build up my criminal file. I really will be a proper criminal when this goes to court – which I've been told it will.

I'm now sitting on the edge of a hard, narrow, makeshift bed where I will have to stay until early morning. I'm inside a cell and there's a hatch in the door – just like in the films. I'm a real criminal, it makes me want to laugh hysterically. I'm sure I must be suffering with some sort of delusionary mental disorder. Across the room, behind a small wall, is a very tiny wash basin and a toilet which I will not be using for fear of someone peering through the hatch and seeing me. Apart from that, the room is completely empty, and the stark, cold stone walls are beginning to bear down on me. My feet are freezing on the stone floor because they took my shoes, how could they do such a thing? They also took my jewelry in case I try to do myself harm – apparently. The last hour has been a mishmash of emotions as I followed orders and instructions while they went through the criminal process with me. I'm now alone and everything is really starting to sink in...

Oh my God, what have I done? What an abominable mess...

I lie down on the bed and try to curl into a ball, hoping that this nightmare might go away, but the bed is too narrow. I lie on my back, on my side, on my front. I cannot sleep. I have no idea what time it is now. Why did Ryan call me? Is he wondering where I am? Of course, he will be wondering where I am. I left all my clothes in the room... what was I thinking? How can I go back there to retrieve them now? Why did I get in my new car when I'd had quite a few drinks this afternoon? I don't think I felt drunk... or was I so drunk that I didn't realise I was drunk? Am I still drunk now? I didn't even notice that I'd parked outside the police station... Is this all real? I should sleep, then maybe I'll wake up and it won't be real...

I can't get comfortable... this bed is awful. How can they expect me to sleep on this? How can they expect me to get comfortable in this nasty, cold cell...?

The hatch lifts and I just catch a glimpse of a pair of eyes looking in. Then it closes again. Are they not going to say anything? Are they not going to ask me if I'm OK? If I would like a cup of tea? Is this how a criminal is treated? Am I really a criminal? Or will the court say I'm not a bad person and this terrible nightmare will end well?

I close my eyes... I want my mum and dad... I can't tell my mum and dad...

What will school say? What will Mr Reynolds say? I can't tell school...

Oh no, what the hell am I going to do?

During a sleepless, fretful night, the realisation of what I have done has become more prominent in my mind... My alcohol addled mind has been clearing, sobering and remembering. I've cried twice but not in a noisy, 'boo-hoo' way but more of a silent, tears falling on to my cheeks way. The policemen have looked in on me regularly, throughout the night, and it now looks like dawn is approaching as the darkness I could see through the narrow window at the very top of the wall, is slowly turning from black to dark blue/grey.

I rise from the back-breaking bed and swing my legs over the side. My body aches all over, my head is thumping, and I am desperate for a cup of tea. Christmas is over, and it has turned into another mess, just like last year. Where do I go from here? What will happen next? I have no idea what the protocol is, now that I have been arrested. I know they can't leave me in here forever to rot away... surely, they can't... can they?

My thoughts are broken by the hollow sound of the cell door being unlocked and then opened. I look up to see a friendly looking police woman standing in the doorway. "You're free to go, Susie," she says, smiling at me. "Come with me and we'll get your things."

I hobble towards the door, my feet and back stiff from the cold and fatigue. They are letting me go? Just like that? Have I got away with it? "What about my car?" I ask, apprehensively.

"It's in the car park and you'll get your keys back as soon as we've finalised the paperwork."

"Will I?" I continue to follow the police woman along the corridor, past several cells which all have their doors firmly closed. Just for a moment, I wonder who could be locked behind those doors. Are they *real* criminals, like murderers, thieves and the like or are they more like me, a foolish victim of the law? The woman turns her head and nods briefly before pulling a door open which leads back out to the reception area where I arrived last night. It's getting lighter by the minute outside and I suddenly have a sense of hope. "Does that mean...?" I daren't ask unless the answer is not what I want to hear. "Does it mean I can...?"

"Drive your car?" The woman finishes the question for me.

I nod and meet her eye, not daring to smile. "Yes."

"I'll return everything to you as soon as we've dealt with the paperwork – including your car keys. Now..." she begins, thumbing through several sheets of paper in a folder. "I need to check your address – a copy of the full court summons will be sent to you in the post."

"Court? Summons?" So, I didn't dream it – it's real.

The woman does not respond except to ask me to read and sign a form that she hands to me. I pretend to read it and sign where she pointed her finger. I don't want to read it – I can't – my eyes are filled with tears. I haven't got away with this, have I?

I take all the sheets of paper from the police woman and stand at the front of the counter, waiting for my bag, jewelry and shoes. I'm trembling as the cold rises from the stone floor, into my feet. I'm confused. I have no idea what I am supposed to do once I have my things.

The woman hands me my belongings and I quickly slip my shoes on, stuffing my jewelry into the side pocket of my bag. Then she hands my keys over. There is a label attached to my keyring with the registration of my car written on it. "You are free to go now," she says, her face expressionless.

I peer at my car keys. "Can I drive my car?"

"Yes," she replies, "at least until you attend court, anyway."

"But..." I'm puzzled as to why I'm allowed to drive it. The officer who did the tests last night told me I was looking at a ban.

"You will be able to drive until the fourth..." the policewoman adds.

Oh God, the fourth of *January* – that's the date on the summons sheet. "Thank you," I say. "Can I go now?"

The woman turns and nods at me with a frown on her face. She's not quite so friendly as I originally thought. Perhaps, in my dire hour of need, when I was stuck inside that cell, a blood-sucking zombie would have looked friendly. I turn around and go out of the main door. It's freezing outside, and the dark blue/grey has turned even lighter. I still have no idea what time it is as I'm not clued-up on sunrise or sunset times. I should have looked for a clock inside. I clutch my handbag to my side, tightly, and head towards the back of the police station, where my car should be.

Guiltily, I turn on the ignition, go into first gear and slowly pull out of the car park. My car's engine is so quiet that I am sure it knows what has happened and is creeping silently out from the police station grounds. My Bella the beetle is on my side and it feels so good to be back inside her. It's like being at home.

I have no idea where I'm going but I need to get away from here. I recall the small gravel parking spaces alongside the park in the middle of the village and decide to head there. If I park up there, I can compose myself without being disturbed (hopefully) and turn my phone back on to see if Ryan left a message at all. I have absolutely no idea what the situation is back at his parent's house and I do not know if I would be welcome back there or if I will, somehow, have to find my way home on my own without my clothing. I just don't know anything anymore.

The stars are disappearing, one by one, as the twilight minutes gradually turn to sunrise. It's going to be a bright winter's day with not a hint of cloud in the sky. I've been sitting in my car watching the stars fade out and the scenery before me, fade in. And all the time, I have clutched my phone, too scared to turn it on because of the knowledge it may hold. It's almost twenty-five past seven now and my car's temperature gauge read minus two before I turned the engine off. The icy breeze outside seems to be seeping into my car now and I give a little shudder as my cold, stiff finger turns my mobile phone on.

I have 13 notifications. Two of those are voicemail and the other 11 are text messages – all from Ryan. I listen to the voicemails first...

"Babe, where are you?"

"Susie, are you OK? When are you coming back, I need to talk to you? We have got to sort this mess out."

Then I go through the text messages, realising that Ryan is worried about me and sounds like he's not that angry with me.

Come back, please xx

Call me xx

Susie, I'm worried, text me xx

It's 10pm now and this is no joke – call me, please xx

Susie, I love you, please get back to me xx

Where are you? Xx

Everyone is worried about you – please get in touch xx

Susie, for God's sake, will you respond? This is getting beyond a joke. Xx

Me and Jethro have been out looking for you – where the hell are you? Xx

Have you gone home? Xx

If I don't hear from you by the morning, I'm calling the police! I am f**king worried, Susie, for God's sake. Please reply, even if it's just to tell me to f**k off. I'm getting really frustrated here. xx

Now he does sound angry. That last message was sent at 2.20am. I need to text him and let him know I'm OK and then we can go from there.

Hi Ryan, I'm so sorry, from Susie xx

Within a minute of the message being sent, my phone rings.

"Hello?" I say in a small, sheepish voice.

"Where the hell are you?" Ryan has that gravelly just-woken-up voice.

"I'm... I'm so sorry, Ryan... I..."

"Are you still here in Shedford?"

"Yes..."

"Then come back here. Please, Susie. We need to talk, don't you think?"

"OK," I say, wondering how the hell I'm going to tell Ryan what has happened."

"How long will you be?"

"About half an hour."

"OK, I'm getting up now – I'll order some breakfast for us. And babe...?"

"Yes?"

"I know about everything and we can talk about it. We can get through this, I'm sure. Amber is mortified at what she has done. She said she drank too many drinks, way too quickly. She was in tears all night. Even Rob apologised."

"OK," I say, feebly.

"Hurry up and get back babe, please."

"I will... goodbye."

"I'll see you soon – bye."

The phone call ends and I look up and out of the windscreen, at the picturesque view in front of me while fighting back the tears. What have I done? Is there something wrong with me? Why are things always such a mess in my life? If Ryan does know everything, he seems to be OK with it. Why have I made the last year of mistakes and tragedy such a bugbear for myself to live with? I'm far too hard on myself. No one is perfect.

*** 29 ***

"Hello Jethro, it's me... Susie."

"Good to hear that you're back safely, Miss Susie, dear. Do come in." His voice is so warm and friendly. It almost puts a smile on my face.

The gates begin to open as I climb back into my car.

As I pull into the garage at the back of the house, I can see Ryan waiting by the other door. He smiles and waves as our eyes meet and then he slowly walks towards my car as I park in the same bay as yesterday. As I turn the engine off, I pause briefly – what a difference a day makes. If only I hadn't left here... If only I'd stayed and faced the situation that was brewing. If only...

Before I get out of the car, I check my bag for the paperwork the police woman gave me, making sure that it is tucked right down at the bottom, out of sight... out of mind. It's not real, it can't be.

"Susie..." Ryan pulls me to him and hugs me tightly. I feel him kiss the top of my head. "Babe, I've been so worried about you." He's still hugging me and rocking us both gently, from side to side. "Are you OK?"

"Yes," I say, from deep within his embrace. And it's true, I am OK. Ryan cuddling me like this is making everything feel better. I want to stay inside his jacket forever.

He pulls away and peers into my eyes. "Where have you been? I was pacing the hall half the night..."

"I..." Oh God, where have I been? This is the point where I choose whether to get into another huge lie or be honest for once and tell him the awful truth… This could be a life-changing moment. I have got to do it – I have got to tell the truth. "I…"

"Come here, you," he says, giving me another tight hug. "I've missed you so much… It has made me realise how…" He pulls away a second time and meets my eye again. "How much you mean to me – how much I love you, babe – how much I can't live without you, whatever you do, whatever you say or don't say, whatever has happened in your past…"

I smile waveringly. "I'm sorry."

"Come on, let's get you back to the room and you can freshen up – you look really tired. Where have you been, babe?"

"I…" He offers his hand and I take it before we walk towards the other door. "I…"

"Go on," he says, looking at me expectantly. "Tell me – I don't care where you've been now that you're back but tell me anyway."

OK, I'm going for it. I've got to. "I… I've been…" I break off and check his expression. "I've been sleeping in my car all night." Oh God, I've done it again. I've just told him the biggest lie ever. There's no turning back now.

"Bloody hell, you must have been frozen. Where?"

"In the village." I hate myself. There must be something wrong with me. I'm a compulsive liar. How have I turned into this? "By that park…"

"Why didn't you answer your phone?"

"I look down at the ground, shamefully. "I'm sorry, I… I turned it off. I was… scared."

"Scared?" Ryan echoes. "Why?"

I shrug, trying to think why I might have been scared. "Because… I was worried that someone might hear my phone go off and… well… you know… there could have been weirdos in the park."

Ryan lets out a short laugh. "Oh God, babe, I am so glad you're back. I'm sure there wouldn't have been any weirdos in the park because…" he laughs again, "they're all here."

That makes me smile momentarily and I hold his hand tighter as we walk through the gardens, back towards the house. I'm hungry, I'm tired and I do need to freshen up – I am such a wretch.

***

Breakfast has just arrived, and I feel so much better after the hot shower and a change of clothes. Ryan is busily setting out the table as I join him there. "Feeling better?" he asks.

"Yes, so much better. I'm really hungry."

"Good, because we have got the works here again, but we could eat even more this morning to see us through until we get home later..." He breaks off and looks at me with a serious expression. "My parents want to see us before we go... and... so does Amber."

"OK," I say, nodding at him. Oh great, Amber. I don't particularly want to see her ever again, but I've got to go with it for Ryan's sake.

"We're meeting in the private lounge for coffee at eleven – is that OK?"

"Yes, fine... I think."

"Trust me babe, you have the upper hand this morning, so you will be fine. Everyone is very disappointed by Amber's actions yesterday. Even Rob had to admit that she shouldn't have said what she did at the table."

I pull a chair out and sit down as my tummy begins to rumble. The smell of the bacon and sausages wafts up my nose and my mouth begins to water. I'm sick with hunger – I think it's hunger, although, the queasy feeling has been with me since I left the police station.

"So," Ryan starts, as he pours a small packet of cereal into a bowl, "about the 'Amber' business..."

I look at him aghast. In my self-pitying state of being a compulsive liar, I really can't handle having to discuss it all with Ryan now. "Yes?" I say, feeling the nausea hit the back of my throat.

"Look, I know everything, babe. I just don't understand why you didn't tell me the truth." He pours milk from the jug, over his cereal as I watch him. My appetite has suddenly disappeared, and a sick guilt overwhelms me.

"I..." I can't bring myself to meet his eye and remain fixed on his cereal bowl. "I... don't know..."

"You were seeing Jett – is that right?"

I nod, ashamed. "Yes... it was only..."

"Were you there, the night he...?" I dart my eyes upwards to see Ryan shaking his head despairingly.

"Yes," I reply. "I'm sorry I didn't tell you."

"It's not that you didn't tell me, Susie..."

"Oh," I say.

"You lied about it. You said you didn't know much about his death... but you were there... why would you do that?"

I hate myself. The problem with telling lies is that you forget what you have said and what you haven't said. And now it's happening all over again. I'm a criminal. Why am I doing this? "I know... I'm sorry, Ryan. You wouldn't believe how sorry I am. I was scared..."

"Scared? Why are you always scared?"

"I don't know," I say, and cannot stop the unexpected flood of tears that spill out on to my cheeks.

"Susie." He drops his spoon, which flips out of the bowl and falls to the floor, and rushes to my side. "Babe, am I some sort of a monster?"

"No." I'm crying uncontrollably as Ryan holds me.

"Then why can't you tell me things? Why can't you tell me the truth?"

"I don't know." I sob.

"What did you think I would do?"

"I don't know..." I bury my head in his shoulder. "I'm... I'm sorry. I'm so sorry."

"Susie, I need to know the truth. All of it."

"I thought... Amber had told you... already," I splutter

"I want to hear it from you, babe. Please..."

I shudder with hopelessness. I want to tell him what happened last night – never mind Amber's bloody revelation. I can't tell him though. I just can't. "I was ashamed..." I cry. "Ashamed of..." I break off. I can't speak. I want to climb into bed and hide under the duvet until this all goes away. I feel sick.

"Why were you ashamed? Of what, Susie? I don't get it. The man died – he was your boyfriend. Why would you be ashamed of that? Tell me." The tension in Ryan's voice is rising. Understandably.

"I need to go to the bathroom," I say, broken-hearted. I need to get away. I can't cope with *myself*, let alone anyone or anything else.

"Susie, come out please," says Ryan, tapping on the bathroom door. "Are you OK in there?" He knocks again. "The breakfast is going cold. Come out and have something to eat – please."

I wipe my eyes and nose for the umpteenth time. Peering in the mirror, I see a bubble-eyed goldfish with a bulbous, red nose staring back at me. What a mess I look. What a mess I *am*. "I'm coming," I mutter, and flush the tissues down the toilet. As I open the door, Ryan is standing outside holding a box of chocolate muesli in his hand.

"Come on, I know you like it," he says, shaking the box in front of me. He smiles and takes my hand, leading me back to the breakfast table. "Eat," he says, pulling the chair out for me.

A tear wells in my eye again but I brush it from my cheek the moment it falls and sit down. "Thank you," I say, taking the box from him.

Ryan sits opposite me, clasps his hands together under his chin and watches me. "Let's get the rest of today out of the way and you can tell me about last Christmas in your own time. I won't badger you – it's up to you, babe."

I nod without looking up at him. "Thank you, I will. I promise."

"And no more cover-ups..."

I pour the cereal into a bowl and reach for the milk jug. I can't look at Ryan, but I nod several times as I pour milk into the bowl.

"We had a huge argument after you left yesterday."

"I can imagine... I did hear you all as I left."

"Yes, Amber had a right go at me for not telling her about you, but I said it was none of her business. I asked her why she hadn't mentioned that she was seeing my brother and she said it was none of my business either. She couldn't seem to understand that there was a difference between our relationships and that hers did have something to do with me."

I shake my head, displeased. "That woman is nothing but trouble. She's a vicious, conniving..."

"Bitch," Ryan cuts in. "I'm not sure how she will be in the future – or Rob, come to mention it. I shot the pair of them down in so many ways. Amber was in tears within an hour of you leaving and I think she is genuinely remorseful now."

"Good," I say, stirring the cereal around with my spoon. "What did your parents say about it all?"

"Mum didn't say much – she never does – especially when it's an argument. Dad had a few words with Amber and totally defended you, saying that she made a mockery of your unfortunate circumstances last year." Ryan lets out a short, nervous laugh. "So, you're in his good books – lucky you."

I muster up a brief smile before eating the cereal, eagerly. I am so hungry, I'm sure most of the nausea is from an empty stomach now. "Who will be in the lounge when we go down there?"

"Ah, I forgot to mention, Rachel and Jaycob send their apologies, but they won't be around – they had to leave early this morning. I sent Rachel a text message when I knew you were safe because she's been worried too – everyone has been worried. You've made quite an impression, Susie."

"Huh – I expect they all pity me, that's all."

"No... well, yes, a little, but only because you have had a terrible time in the past through no fault of your own. You never asked to be dumped on Christmas day by a two-timing rat, you never asked to fall for another man the very next day and you certainly did not deserve to be involved in a terrible accident, only a week later... and neither did he..." Ryan breaks off and stares at me empathetically. "I get it Susie – I understand how you fell for him. I get that you had deep-rooted feelings for Jett before anything else happened and I imagine that is how and why it all happened so quickly. The fact that Amber would merrily criticise you and disapprove so openly and publicly is absolutely disgusting and she can see that now."

Oh God, he is so understanding and reasonable but... I just can't bring myself to tell him what else has happened now. I should but I cannot. He hasn't even mentioned the fact that I left here in my car while under the influence of alcohol. I don't think it has even crossed his mind. Just like it didn't cross my mind last night.

"She wants to apologise – although I don't think it's enough to redeem what she has done. I actually hate her for it, Susie."

"You shouldn't hate her. She is a colleague of yours – you have got to work with her. Don't hate her."

"Not for much longer..."

"What do you mean?" I ask, cramming another mouthful of cereal in.

"She's leaving. She's handing her notice in when we go back to school – she'll be gone by the February half term."

I'm surprised by this but also relieved to hear it. I can't think of anything better than getting her out of my life... except, thinking about it, she won't ever be out of my life all the time she is with Rob. God help me if they should decide to get married and Ryan and I get married – we would become sisters-in-law. What a nightmarish situation that would be. However, Amber has done the damage now. There's nothing else she could torment me over... unless... she ever found out about last night...

No way, she couldn't, no one will ever find out about that – not even my parents. That's how it's got to be.

Ryan is having a quick shower before we go down to say goodbye to everyone. As I'm packing up my things, I decide to have a quick look at the charge sheet which the police woman gave me this morning. I'm hoping that the ink will have faded away and there's nothing on it, no 4th January court date...

Oh my God, the ink is still there, but worse still, is the name of the magistrates' court where I must attend. It's here – in this county. It's not a court at home. Oh my God – how the hell am I going to come back here on the 4th of January. And, it has just dawned on me that the 4th of January is the day we go back to school – it's an inset day. I had the 5th in my mind because that's when the kids return but the staff have got to go back on the 4th for training. The familiar rush of nausea hits the back of my throat again and I'm desperate to stop the rising tension in my stomach for fear of my breakfast spewing out and landing in my lap. Oh God, no...

I hear Ryan come out of the bathroom and quickly stuff the paperwork back into my bag. I feel a flush on my cheeks and the queasiness remains stuck in my throat.

"Are you OK babe?" Ryan asks, placing a hand on top of my head. "You look unwell."

"I'm OK," I lie. "I think I ate too much breakfast, too quickly."

"Hungry work sleeping in a freezing cold car all night."

I nod at him. "Hmm... silly really."

"No, it's not silly – I'm just relieved that you didn't drive all the way home without me."

"Talking about that..." I say, "do you want to drive back today? I've got a bit of a headache." To be honest, I'm far too nervous to drive home – I mean, what if I got stopped for something and the police officer says, 'I know who you are, you're the woman who got arrested last night'. After all, can't they just tap in to some sort of central database where they can see all the criminals around the country. Oh God, I won't be able to go anywhere – they will all know who I am. It's really dawning now, and I'm doomed.

"Yes, sure, no problem. You can get your head down and hopefully you'll feel better by the time we get home." He rubs the top of my head and smiles. "I'm taking you out for a meal tonight."

"Why?"

"No reason... just because I love you..."

*** 30 ***

"Susie, I can't tell you how sorry I am. I... I was drunk. I acted so cruelly, and I sincerely hope that you might forgive me one day. We got off on the wrong start last Christmas, when I was drunk in the toilets. I am truly sorry for upsetting you yesterday. I should never have done it."

I'm wondering what last Christmas has got to do with anything when she takes a deep breath and sighs. I thought I was being helpful when she was throwing-up in the toilets at the Christmas party. It wasn't my fault that Jane and Sarah chose to wind her up with the 'stuff the turkey' thing.

She peers at me expectantly with a wavering smile and pathetic puppy-dog eyes. "I was so out of order. Will you please accept my apology?"

She is standing directly in front of me, clasping her hands together and twitching from one foot to the other. Rob is right behind her, straining his neck to look past her at me with a sympathetic glint in his eyes. He gives me a short, faltering smile. Ryan is standing beside me, holding my hand which he squeezes gently to reassure me.

Over on the sofas are Reg and Gracie. They look relaxed as they sit right back in the deep cushions. On the coffee table in front of them lies a long tray filled with coffee pots, mugs, cream, sugar and posh little shortbread biscuits.

"Thank you," I say, to Amber.

"Thank you?" she questions. "Do you accept my apology or not?" Already, I can hear a shortness in a voice. I'm sure she's not sorry at all. This is all a front so that she will look good in front of Reg and Gracie.

"Yes," I say, forcing the word out with a sarcastic smile. I'd much rather punch her on the nose but I'm not a violent person at all. "Yes, thank you, Amber."

"Good," she replies, nodding her head triumphantly. "Now we can start from scratch, can't we?"

"Absolutely," I say. "From scratch." Does that mean I can scratch her eyes out, impale them on to pipe cleaners and poke them into the top of her head? Then we could start all over again? Except of course, she would be the laughing stock with deely bopper eyes. I grin to myself and peer at the top of her head – if only.

"What?" she says, brushing a hand over her hair.

"Nothing," I reply. "It's nothing, really."

"Shall we sit," says Rob, gesturing to the sofas, "now that that is sorted out?"

Ryan pulls at my hand and we join his parents.

"We were all worried about you last night, Susie." Reg eyes me with a hint of disdain.

"I am so sorry about that, Mr Bagshaw... and Mrs Bagshaw. I was very foolish and let my emotions carry me away without any regard for anyone else. I apologise, sincerely." That was a pretty good statement, even if I do say so myself. I peer at Reg and Gracie, dolefully, hoping they will forgive me.

"You're back and safe – that's the main thing. Come and have some coffee before your journey home."

At this point, I'm sorry if I'm sounding finicky but wouldn't any normal person have said, 'please, call me by my first name – you don't have to call me Mr... or Mrs...' by now? I'm really uncomfortable with all this formal nonsense. Especially when Ryan's parents aren't exactly dressed to act formal – pyjamas just don't cut it.

"We'll be nipping into town today," Amber starts as she sits on one of the armchairs looking pretty. "Anything you need while we're out, Mum? Or you, Dad?"

Mum? Dad? She calls Reg and Gracie, Mum and Dad? Who the hell does she think she is? Blimey, she can't have been with Rob for more than nine or ten months at the most, yet she calls them Mum and Dad and she lives here. How has she managed to wangle her way into their lives so quickly?

Both Reg and Gracie shake their heads at her. "No thank you, Ammie, dear," says Gracie. It's one of the few times I've heard her speak. She's one of those quiet, watcher types. To be honest, I can understand now why Ryan doesn't ever want to talk about his family much. They are a bit weird and adding Amber into the mix has simply made it weirder.

"So," says Reg, wiping a biscuit crumb from his mouth, "where were you last night?" He's looking at me with that scary look again. And to think that he was growing on me late yesterday afternoon. After all, he did save my life at one point. Today, he is quite different towards me and I can only guess that it is because I left the house and worried the life out of Ryan.

"Yes, we were so worried, Susie," Amber chimes in. "Where were you all night?"

No matter how much she has apologised, I just can't warm to the girl and would seriously like to deely-bop her, right at this minute. Worried? Sure, she was. "I went to the village and parked up by the park," I say.

"And?" Amber prompts me.

"And... I slept in my car all night."

"That could have been very dangerous," she says, eyeing me with raised eyebrows.

"I know," I say, "I realise how silly it was now."

"You are lucky that you didn't get pulled for drink/driving," says Reg. "You were knocking that wine back at the table."

I freeze and stare at him aghast.

"My old mate, Derrek, would have had you – he detests the drink/drivers. You're lucky you got away with it."

I'm so relieved that I don't have a Brussels sprout in my mouth at this moment because I think I would be capable of firing it across the room at full pelt. "I... I..." I look round at Ryan, my eyes wide with panic. "I... I never thought about..."

"My mate Derrek works in the village station – he's got the record for the most drink/drivers caught." Reg rubs at his chin, thoughtfully. "It's only a small village but you'd be surprised how many young-ones pass through, on their way home from the town."

"I think Susie realises how potentially dangerous her decision to go was. Let's not keep reminding her. Like you said, Dad, she's back and safe and that's all that matters now." Ryan places an arm around my shoulder.

"Here, here," he says, raising his coffee mug. "Drink up and be gone with you. Safe journey and all that."

I smile waveringly and try to sip my coffee. I'm too scared to drink it properly for fear of choking on it. My throat has clammed up, my eyes are about to explode out of my head powered by a bucket full of tears, swelling behind them and I'm incredibly nauseous again. My life might as well be over if Derrek was one of those policemen who arrested me last night. I can't cope with anything anymore. Oh my God…

We're ready to go and the last to leave. Amber said a short and curt goodbye before pulling Rob out of the lounge. Now it's just me and Ryan. "Right, we'd better set off home," says Ryan, rising to his feet. There's been an awkward silence since the others left and I'm relieved to be going now.

"Good to see you, Ryan. Come again soon," says Reg.

Gracie rises to her feet and stands beside her husband smiling. "Yes, it's been nice to see you, Ryan – and to meet you Susie. I'm sure that next time we won't have quite so much drama. I've hardly got to know you."

"I do apologise, again. And I'm quite sure that there won't be any drama next time. Thank you for letting me stay in your beautiful house."

Gracie nods at me but says nothing.

Ryan extends a hand towards his dad which Reg accepts. They have a very quick handshake and then Ryan kisses his mum briefly on the cheek, but she does not show any emotion and simply nods at him like she did to me. "Thank you and goodbye," I say, unsure of what I'm supposed to do at this point. In normal situations, I might have shaken Reg's hand and or hugged them both or even pecked them on the cheek, but the thorny atmosphere is not normal, so I simply smile at them both and raise my hand in a small wave.

"You can see why I don't talk about my family much now, can't you?" Ryan says as we pull out of the car park. "What a 24-hours that has been."

Twenty-four hours? Is that all it has been? It feels more like 24 days, weeks, months. So much has changed. My whole life has changed. It's just that Ryan doesn't know it. I can't even begin to get my head around what has happened and how I am going to deal with it – let alone deal with the court case next week. There is only one person in the entire world who I trust enough to talk to about this. I need to talk to her as soon as we are home... or as soon as Ryan is out of earshot. She'll know what to do. "It seems a lot longer than that," I say.

"Huh – it would for you, babe. Sleeping rough is no holiday. Meeting my parents is no fun either." Ryan jumps out of the car and presses the intercom on the gate. "Thanks Jethro... yes, good to see you too, mate... yes... we'll definitely see you again sometime." I hear Ryan say.

The gates swing open and Ryan climbs back in. We're off – heading back to normality where I'm hoping that all this drama will fade away and become not real anymore. "Your parents aren't that bad," I say, as we pull on to the main road, heading back to the village. I sink down in the seat – I'm a criminal in that village – no one can see me. "And Rob was OK too, but I hardly said two words to your mum."

"Hmm," Ryan mumbles. "They're just weird, don't you think? And Mum doesn't say two words to anyone anyway – she's the weirdest."

Huh – I'm not sure that they are that weird. I think I'm the weird one. I've put myself into this nightmarish situation and as we drive further and further away, it's becoming more apparent that I am the total oddball. I mean, who gets into messes like mine and then has got to spend their entire time trying to cover up their actions because they can't tell the truth in the first place. Me – that's who. "They're OK, really," I say, sliding further down the seat.

"When we get home, we'll start afresh, what do you think?"

"Afresh? Why?"

"With the 'Jett' situation. Let's just forget any of that stuff, with Amber, happened and move on. And if you need some time to yourself on New Year's Eve, please tell me. I will totally get it. I'm far more understanding than you think, you know."

I smile weakly. "Thanks, Ryan. I don't know how I'm going to feel – I knew him a long time."

"Exactly. If you need me or want to talk about any of it, I'm here to listen but if, on the other hand, you want time on you own, just tell me. Our relationship should be secret-less from now on..." He lets out a little laugh, "Unless, of course, it's a Christmas or birthday present secret – those ones you can always have."

I snort a sort of half-laugh and bow my head as we pass through the village. I'm holding my breath for fear of someone recognizing the car, or worse still, me. I'm a criminal now, after all. An image of a newspaper headline flicks through my mind, *'Arrested for being drunk in charge of a vehicle – Susie Satchel gets life!'* Oh God, I hate myself.

*** 31 ***

Hi bestie, sorry it's late but I hope you had a wonderful Xmas. I meant to text you on Xmas day, but I was a bit blown away when Ryan gave me my present first thing in the morning. Since then, I've met his parents, stayed in their mansion and got myself in a right mess. I mean, a BIG mess this time. No, an ULTRA mess even. I need to talk to you when you can, but I need it to be when Ryan is not around. Could you let me know when you are free to talk? You are the only person I can tell, and I trust you. Lots of love from your ever-faithful, useless, stupid friend who just won't learn how to stop being so bloody irresponsible, Susie xxx

I give a heavy sigh as soon as I've sent the message. She will know what to do. Clair is wise and sensible. I'm in the bath, as we are going out for a meal this evening – it's our fresh start. The journey home was tedious and long as I'm sure every road-user in the country must have been travelling to or from somewhere today, so I welcome this bubbly soak before we head out. Ryan has been such a dream all the way home and since we've been back, I'm sure this fresh start means a lot more to him than it does me. After all, he *can* have a fresh start, whereas I cannot – my life is on hold until the court date. It will only be, if I get away with the charge (upon further inspection, I noted that they have given me an option to provide my mitigating circumstances statement, so they obviously think I might not be that guilty), that I will be able to have that fresh start in my mind too.

Happy Xmas to you too. Don't feel bad, Suse, because I was just as useless as I also got blown away, by Archie! He asked me to marry him! Can you believe it? I was going to text (you beat me to it) and tell you, by this evening – I swear. So, questions: What did you get from Ryan that blew you away?

OMG, that second part of your text sounds ominous – what the hell have you been up to now? Please don't tell me you dropped another one of his phones down the toilet or you tried to poison him again! I'm at work until 10pm but could call you after that or tomorrow, if you're free. We have 5 days off from New Year's Day, so we could even come and see you!??? Love your bestie, Worried-Clair! Xxxx

I'm out of the bath now and sitting on the edge, wrapped in a towel. Oh gosh, yes, yes, yes – I want to see Clair so badly. A rush of excitement surges through me as I reply to her. She'll know what to do. She'll be able to get me out of this mess. The court won't want to charge me when they know that I have an upstanding best friend who is a nurse – will they?

OMG – that would be amazing if we could see you guys. Yes, yes, yes, come and stay with us. A massive CONGRATULATIONS to you both! And yes, that second part of my text was ominous, but I'd rather talk to you about it than tell you in a text message. Can I call you tomorrow morning? I'll tell Ryan I'm going to my Mum's for some reason (that will just be a little white lie) xx

Yes, tomorrow morning will be fine. Oh dear, what have you been up to, Suse? Xxx

Tell you tomorrow xx

OK, call me around ten – I should be alone then as well xxx

Thanks Clair – I don't know what I'd do without you sometimes xx

To be honest, I don't know what you would do without me, either. Lol xxx

"Who's driving?"

My heart skips a beat. "I... I don't know where we're going..."

Ryan smiles. "I'll drive – I thought we could head out to a nice little restaurant in the countryside. What do you think?"

"Sounds fab," I say.

"It's a bit further on than the one where we went, when my old phone got wet, somehow. Remember?"

I nod, sheepishly. "Yes..."

"I still can't fathom out what happened to it... but I certainly won't ever go there again..." he breaks off thoughtfully. "It's a shame though – it was a nice place." He lets out a small laugh. "Do you remember how you ended up going in the wrong toilets?"

I smile and nod. "Huh – yes, you came and rescued me, thank goodness."

"It still makes me laugh," says Ryan, taking my hand and pulling me out of the front door. "You have always had a funny way that makes me laugh. You're kind of quirky."

"Thanks," I say, sarcastically. "Clair always used to say that."

"Have you heard from her?" We climb into Ryan's car.

"Funnily enough, I messaged her while I was in the bath..." Look at me – I'm telling the truth – it feels good. "You won't believe what's happened."

Ryan hesitates before putting the key in the ignition. "Oh dear, what?"

"Nothing bad, don't worry. They're engaged. Archie asked her to marry him. Can you believe it?"

Ryan nods. "I'm not surprised. They make a nice couple."

"And..." I say, as Ryan pulls away, "they have some time off, from New Year's Day, and would love to come and see us – what do you think?"

"That would be good. We don't go back to work until the 4th. Cool – we could spend a few days with them."

"Exactly my thoughts."

We have had one of the most romantic evenings ever. Ryan is an expert at making me feel good about myself. He's so complimentary and when I don't think about the dreadful things going on in my life, I believe everything he says to me, about me. He's so sexy and charming that I cannot wait to get him home and that's the first time that I've felt like that in quite a few days. The fear of meeting his parents really put a damper on things recently. We've gazed into each other's eyes, this evening, like a newly-hitched couple, waiting patiently for that opportune moment to make a move.

The restaurant is quaint and filled with sparkle and an oversized Christmas tree, squeezed into a corner, by the side of an open fireplace. It's in a dangerous spot, if you ask me. If it toppled over it would be in the fireplace but, as I'm not a fire safety officer, it's really none of my business and I should take it at face value. It's a typical Christmassy scene and does the job of making one feel cosy and romantic.

"I'm full to the eyebrows," says Ryan, gazing at me, over the top of the candlelight.

"Me too." I place the spoon into the bowl, wipe my mouth on the napkin and drink the last bit of wine. Ryan insisted that I have a couple of glasses after what he says I've been through over the last two days. I didn't argue with him and felt I needed the drinks. Huh, if only he knew what I've really been through, he'd let me gulp down several bottles then.

Ryan leans over the table, pushing the candle to one side. "I want to get you home now and make passionate love to you."

Oh gosh – me too. I feel my face flush. It's exactly what I want to do too but when he says it like that in his sexy voice, it makes me become all unnecessary. "Let's go," I say, throwing the napkin on to the table. "Fill your boots."

***

Luckily for me, Ryan has nipped into school to sort a few things out. He said he would much rather go in today and then have more time off when Clair and Archie come. It's lucky because I don't have to pretend that I'm going to my mum's now because I couldn't think why I would have been going there without him and it would have been yet another lie. I pick up my phone and dial Clair's number.

"Hi Suse."

"Hello, Clair and congratulations once again." I smile to myself. She deserves happiness and I know that Archie will give her lots of that.

"Thank you – I'm so excited. We are going to get married in the summer of 2019."

"Wow, that's amazing. I trust we will get an invite –"

"Invite?" Clair cuts in. "You're going to be my chief bridesmaid, if you'll accept of course."

"Oh my God – I do accept. I can't believe..."

"Well, who else would I ask? You are my bestie and you will have to look after me on that day. I can already feel the nerves." She lets out a giggle. "Mind you, with your track record of late, I might have to look after you – but I guess it will keep me distracted enough to not get quite so nervous."

I let out a long sigh. "I think I need someone to look after me."

"So," says Clair, her tone of voice turning serious, "what have you done now?"

"I..." Oh God, how do I tell her this? She seems so much more grown up than me – she's getting married. But she is the only person I can share this with. If I don't share it, I think I might so insane. "I... I got arrested on Boxing night –"

"You what?" I hear her shriek and can just imagine the expression on her face – somewhere between shock and despair.

"I got arrested –" I whisper. I have no idea why I'm whispering down the phone but somehow it makes it sound less bad.

"What the hell for? Suse, why doesn't Ryan know about this if you were with him?"

"Well, I wasn't with him when it happened? I left his parent's house on my own, in the evening. "

"On your own?"

I roll my eyes. "Yes, on my own."

"Why? Where was Ryan? What did you get arrested for? Seriously, Suse?"

That's the only problem with Clair. When she wants to know something, I can't get a word in quick enough to explain, before she fires a million questions at me like a machine gun. "It all started when – "

"When? Yes? Go on, tell me."

"I'm just going to tell you if you'll let me."

"God, I wish I was there," she utters, with a sigh.

"I wish you were too. I need you. I don't know what to do."

"About the arrest?"

"About everything..."

"Right, Susie Satchel, start at the very beginning."

"It was all Amber's fault, I guess – "

"Amber? What the hell does she have to do with it? I thought you went to Ryan's – "

"We did go to Ryan's parent's – they live in this stupidly big mansion. He's super rich, you know, not that I care about that because I am not one of those gravedigger types – "

Clair roars with laughter down the phone. "You mean a gold-digger."

"Whatever... Anyway, to my complete horror, Amber was there..." I pause, waiting for a reaction but nothing comes. "Are you still there?"

"Of course, I'm still here – go on. So, Amber was there..."

"Aren't you surprised by that?" I ask, puzzled as to why Clair wouldn't find that shocking.

"They work together don't they? Or are you going to tell me that she was stalking him?"

"No, she wasn't stalking him. But just because they work together, why would you think she would be at his parent's house?"

"I don't know – is she a friend of the family?"

"No... I mean, yes... no... oh I don't know. Sort of... now she is, I guess."

"You're not making much sense at the moment. Can't you just tell me why you were arrested? Do you mean proper arrested?"

"Yes, proper arrested. I've got to go to court and all that stuff."

"Suse?"

"Yes?" I say. I want to scream, I wish she was here and we could have a real conversation, face to face. I need her.

"What the hell have you done?"

"I got done for drink/driving."

"Oh God, no."

I nod, knowing full well she can't see me but it's hard to talk with a lump stuck in my throat. Now I've told her, it has become so much more real to me.

"And you've been charged? Like properly?"

I nod again.

"Suse, are you there?"

"Yes," I say, tears welling in my eyes. "It's real. I have to go to court on the 4th."

"Oh no, Suse... Why the hell haven't you told Ryan?"

"I can't..." I manage to say as a tear plops on to my cheek and I wipe it away quickly.

"Why can't you?"

"Because I've already lied to him – I can't go and change it back now. He was already annoyed with me for telling lies about Jett."

"He knows about Jett now?"

"Yes," I say.

"So, you trying to – I don't mean to sound nasty here, Suse, and I don't want to upset you but – you trying to poison him was a waste of time because he knows anyway."

I burst into tears. That's one of Clair's strong traits – she will always come straight to the point about anything.

"Yes," I say, weakly.

"And how do you think that you are going to hide this charge from him?"

"Well," I say, wiping my nose with the back of my sleeve, "if I get points on my license or a slapped wrist, he doesn't need to know that, does he?"

"Oh my God, Suse..."

"And I can write a statement detailing my mitigating circumstances, so it should be OK."

"Suse, do you have any idea what the penalty might be for drink/driving?"

"Ah, but I wasn't driving at the time."

"What?" I can hear the exasperation in Clair's voice.

"I was parked up when the police found me. It was only because I was sleeping in my car that they arrested me. OK, so I was parked across the entrance to the police station, but I didn't know it was the police station car park, did I? I don't live around there."

"Oh my God, Suse." I hear Clair laugh. "You were blocking the entrance to the police station, asleep in your car and drunk. I have really heard it all now. Only you could do that. Only you could get arrested in that way. Oh dear, oh dear," she squeals with laughter, "you are not even capable of getting arrested in the proper, normal way. Suse – you are unbelievable."

"I know it sounds totally ridiculous. "

"Ridiculous? It's absolutely preposterous, Suse."

"OK, calm down, I'm sure it won't turn out that bad in the end," I retort.

I hear Clair make a deep sigh and I bet that she is shaking her head despairingly too – she does that when she gets agitated. "Susie," she says, in her adult, serious voice. "This is not going to turn out good. I don't think you realise what the consequences will be."

"I know it can be bad. I do understand that, but I am going to put my mitigating circumstances case forward and see what happens."

"OK... have it your way." She sighs again, but louder this time. "I'm not sure it's going to help you though – you've been found guilty, I'm guessing, by a breathalyser test, is that right?"

"Yes... I was two and a half times – "

"Over?"

"Yes," I say with another pointless nod.

"Oh my God, Suse."

"Anyway," I start with an optimistic tone in my voice, "I was wondering if you would come to court with me. I'm supposed to go back to work on the 4th but I won't be able to as that is when the court date is. I'll have to pull a sickie and hope that Ryan doesn't find out."

"I cannot understand why you won't tell him."

"It's too late for that, I can't tell him now. I can't say to him, 'Oh, by the way, I forgot to mention to you, Ryan, that I was arrested while we were at your parent's house', can I?"

"Hmm," Clair breathes down the phone. "OK, whatever, at the end of the day, it's your mess, Suse. I will come with you though – that shouldn't be a problem."

"Well... there is a bit of a problem... it's near Salisbury."

"What?"

"That's where I've got to go to court."

"But that's a two-hour drive away from you."

"I know. My case is at eleven twenty-five. We could leave around nine and I'm sure we'd be back by two or three o'clock."

"Then I'm going to have to tell Archie."

"Oh no, are you?" I say, the optimistic tone having vanished instantly.

"I'm not getting into a whole string of lies with him. It's not fair."

"But if he doesn't ask anything, you're not actually lying to him," I say.

"Don't you think he might wonder where I've gone for the entire day? Especially if we're having a break away together and staying at yours. I can hardly leave him in your flat all day – alone."

She does have a point there. I hadn't thought of that. "OK, plan two – can you come on New Year's Day and be gone by the morning of the 4th? That way I could go on my own and I'll just have to get through it alone."

"How are you going to get there?"

"Ah, well Ryan bought me a new car for Christmas, so I could brave the trip and drive there."

"Suse – when you are banned from driving, how will you get back home?"

"Banned...?"

*** 32 ***

Banned. That's what Clair thinks will happen. A driving ban. What does she know? However, I've decided that I can do this, and I will travel on my own. That way, Clair doesn't get caught up in my web of lies. I really should have thought things through more clearly before I involved her in it. Thankfully, she has now agreed to come to us on New Year's Day and leave early on the 4th. That way, she doesn't need to say anything to Archie.

I've also made the wise decision to go by train. In hindsight, I'd probably be too nervous and worried to drive anyway and the time alone on the train will be good for me to reflect upon the situations I get myself into and how I will endeavor to lead a lie-free year, next year. I can do it. I have got to do it. For everyone's sake.

Hi honey, are you back yet? Did you have an enjoyable time meeting Ryan's parents? Love Mum xx

Hi Mum, yes, it was OK. I say OK because it turned out that Amber goes out with Ryan's brother and she was there! She opened her big gob during the meal and Ryan now knows about Jett but he's OK with it. He was just a little peed off that I hadn't told him the truth. Apart from that – Oh my God, Mum – they are a super-rich family and live in a ridiculously big house which is so posh, you wouldn't believe it! I never knew Ryan was so rich either (not that that has anything to do with my feelings for him). Anyway, it turned out OK because Amber apologised for being such a bitch so everything's rosy xx

I press send and stare at my phone – huh – rosy indeed. There's nothing 'rosy' about my life at this present moment. Clair's words keep ringing through my ears, 'banned, banned, banned', surely, she cannot be right.

Oh, my goodness, honey. I'm relieved to hear that Ryan took it well but I'm not surprised at all. He's a good man. That might teach you to always be honest about everything though. It's not worth telling lies, honey, or withholding the truth as things just escalate and you can find yourself in a right mess. I'm sure that Ryan loves you enough to deal with anything about you – let's face it, it was all in the past anyway. Stop worrying your pretty little self over everything. Anyway, honey, I'm glad that he knows and I'm sure he would understand if you came with us on New Year's Eve to a little memorial service which Malcolm and Doreen have arranged in their local church. Would you like to come? Xx

Oh gosh, OK, I'll come. We're not doing anything as Ryan thinks it would be inappropriate to go out on that evening but guess what? Clair and Archie are coming on New Year's Day to stay with us for a few days! And another guess what?? They are going to be getting married next year – he asked her on Christmas day, so they are now engaged! Woohoo! So, sorting the spare room out for them will help to take my mind off other things (i.e. Jett) xx

That's wonderful news. I bet Clair is excited about it. Your day will come, honey. Anyway, I'll let Doreen and Malcolm know that you're coming. I'm glad you are – your dad will be going too. I expect that Malcolm and Doreen will want to invite us over for nibbles afterwards. Would you like to come to that too? Xx

Would it be bad of me if I didn't? xx

No honey, if you'd rather go home afterwards, that will be fine. Service is at 3pm. Come to ours and we can go together xx

OK, I will Mum. Love you xx

Love you too, honey xx

Hi babe, I should only be another hour and a half and then I'll be home x

OK, no problem. See you soon xx

Oh good, Ryan won't be home yet which gives me a little time to write my mitigating circumstances statement. Here goes –

Dear Mr Judge...

Hmm... how do I start one of these? I have absolutely no idea. Thankfully, it's not something I'm familiar with.

Dear Mr or Mrs... or Miss Judge...

Miss Judge – ha, you certainly have misjudged me.

Dear Judge_____

Maybe I'll be able to find out what the judge's name is, just to give it a more personal touch.

Sadly, I have been misjudged and I am not guilty of the crime of, drunk-in-charge-of-a-vehicle. Fair enough, I was drunk, and I suppose I was in charge of my vehicle but...

But what?

... but I wouldn't normally do something like that. It was only because I was upset and left my boyfriend's parent's house in a thoughtless moment. I was desperately trying to get away from the humiliation that one certain person inflicted upon me. I'd had a terrible afternoon and almost died by choking on a Brussels sprout, so I am sure you can imagine how desperate I was to get away from the glares and mocking.

I am a good citizen and I work in a school, teaching children daily. I've never been in any trouble (unless you count the time when I bunked off school with a friend, but I was duly punished for that and also, I apologised to my teacher profusely). So, I beg you to be lenient in this case as I can't possibly be without my brand-new car which my boyfriend bought me for Christmas. I haven't told him about this, in the hope that it will be all forgotten about as I think he would be mad at me. After all, what is the point of getting a new car for Christmas when you can't drive it (a friend of mine warned me that the penalty can often be a ban from driving)? If you let me off this heinous crime I promise to drive my car at the correct speed limits for the rest of my life.

Could I also add that I don't live in the area, so I wasn't aware of parking across the Police station car park – I'm extremely sorry about that. And, I was stationary when I closed my eyes for a few minutes. I'm sure it would have been much worse if I had actually been driving, when I closed my eyes for a few minutes. I was not intending on staying there all night – just for a few minutes, that's all. Please forgive me and I promise that I will never do anything like this again.

Yours faithfully
Susie Satchel xx

Oh shit. Without thinking, I have automatically added two kisses after my name – and it's in pen! This is the only mitigating sheet I have. *Tipp-Ex* – I need *Tipp-Ex* – like right now.

I've never written to a judge before, so I have no idea whether my statement is suitable or not – and I can't get any advice from my mum or dad either. I've read it over and over again and I think it sounds OK. I also managed to find an old bottle of *Tipp-Ex* and was able to scrape the last remnants from the bottom of the bottle with a cocktail stick, as the brush was completely solid. The sheet looks a little messy at the bottom but I'm toying with an idea to explain it. So, here goes again...

Sorry about the smudgy mess here...

I draw a small arrow, pointing to the large blob (I had to make it the size of a cat's paw print but you'll understand as soon as I continue to write) of white and grey goo.

...but my cat came and sat on this sheet of paper, with muddy paws, while I was writing this statement. I tried to rub her paw print off but ended up making a terrible mess, so I used some Tipp-Ex to try and make it look nicer, but the Tipp-Ex was old and dried up and I could only scrape the bits out of the bottom of the bottle which were tinged with grey. So, apologies that the correction fluid is not white but at least I tried. I am sure that some unsavoury people wouldn't have even bothered to tidy-up their mitigating statement, but I am a good, conscientious person and always like to do the right thing – even if I do get things wrong sometimes (hence, the reason why I am writing this statement in the first place!) Anyway, my naughty little cat has jumped down from the table and is cleaning her little feet now so no more muddy paws. Thank you for taking the time to read this statement, kind judge. Regards, Susie Satchel...

Gosh – I nearly did it again then.

Does that sound plausible? God, I hope so. OK, I know it's another lie but it was a case of having to think up something quickly to hide the fact that I put a couple of kisses on there (almost twice). The judge won't know if I have a cat or not – will he? Or she? Do they ask if you own a pet? I have no idea. I wish someone could help me with all of this legal stuff – I'm so out of my depth.

I read through my statement one last time and smile to myself. It does make me sound like a nice, cat-loving girl who is very sorry for what she has done – I hope the judge is a cat-loving person as that could actually tip the scales in my favour. Possible result – who doesn't like cats?

I fold the sheet of paper up, tuck it securely into the envelope with the other police paperwork and poke it down in the bottom of my bag. At least it's done, and I can forget about it for a few days.

***

Bang! Like a sledgehammer blow, I have woken up on New Year's Eve with a feeling of utter misery. Until today, I hadn't had a great deal of time to think about last year. I thought I was coping really well with the 'Jett' thing. I've been lying in bed for the past 15 minutes, reliving the tragic event while I listen to Ryan pottering about in the kitchen. Tears well in my eyes and I blink them away. What a difference a year can make. I pull myself up on the pillows and stare out of the window as a fresh bout of tears begin to fall. What a mess. How tragic it all is. Poor Jett – I loved him. Poor Doreen and Malcolm – how must they be feeling today? My hopeless sadness is two-fold. I'm feeling sorry for myself, as well as for Jett.

Ryan is being so supportive. He said that he was relieved that I was going to the service today – he thinks I should. He also said that we should have a quiet night in tonight, grab a take-away and have a few drinks, but only if I feel up to it. I'm not sure I feel up to anything to be honest. The poignant connection between Jett's grim death and my drink/driving charge is harrowingly comparable. I could have killed someone that night and today, the impact of my actions is a stark awakening.

Ryan pops his head around the door. "I've made breakfast," he whispers with a warm smile. "Are you up for it?"

I nod at him and muster up a half-smile. I've got to get through today. I will pay my respects to Jett at the service and try my best not to beat myself up about it all. I got myself in this whole mess because of my fears of my past being found out, but for what? It never was a problem in the first place. It has only ever been a problem in my head. I constantly strive to be 'nice' and when I do silly things which I determine to be 'not-so-nice', I lie my way out of them. This is going to stop. Tomorrow is New Year's Day and I will become 'new'. Somehow... Except, I can't reveal the truth about Boxing night so that will have to be kept in the old year and hopefully forgotten... one day.

***

All of them are a blubbering mess – except my dad but then he doesn't usually show much emotion and certainly not in public. I feel I should be a mess too, but for some reason I can't cry. I'm stone-cold and I don't mean that in the physical sense. I seem to connect more with the man who killed Jett than to my ex-boyfriend and life-long friend. I feel sorry for the man who possibly made a terrible, drunken mistake that night and now lives regretting it, every hour of every day, while being locked up in a cell for the next 14 years. Is that bad of me to be thinking of him? Please don't get me wrong, I have every sympathy for Doreen and Malcolm today and seeing my mum in tears is dreadful but that's about as much emotion as I can feel. Maybe, I did all my crying this morning and there are no tears left in me.

Ryan stayed at home and is giving the flat one last clean before Clair and Archie arrive tomorrow. He's such a homely guy. I gain strength from him and although he doesn't know it, I couldn't get through any of this without him by my side.

"Are you OK, honey?" Mum has just blown her nose for the umpteenth time and reaches for my hand.

I nod and shoot a cursory small smile at her. "Yes – I'm a bit numb," I whisper.

"Wriggle your bottom around on the seat – we have been sitting here for a long time."

"Not my bum, Mum. I'm talking about my emotions."

Mum peers at me, startled. "Oh, I see, well, that's to be expected, honey."

Dad pats Mum on the back. "Right, I think it's all done. Are you both ready to go?"

Mum looks at me before nodding and wiping her nose again. "Yes, we'll leave Doreen and Malcolm to have their own time here." Mum stands up, leans over the pew and places a hand gently on Doreen's shoulder. "We're going now. John and I will come around to your house at five o'clock."

Doreen says nothing but nods. She has a tissue firmly attached to her nose. Malcolm is sitting beside her with his hands clasped together and tucked between his legs. His head is bowed and, as we leave, he does not acknowledge us at all. I understand his grief. I get everyone's sadness, but I can't feel anything myself. Guilt is a powerful and destroying emotion and I am filled with it.

*** 33 ***

At around 11.30pm on New Year's Eve, I had that dreadful moment of remembrance. So vivid was the image of Jett lying in the road that it took me straight back to that time and to all the emotions which I was filled with that night. Despair, confusion and predominantly, denial, raged through me as I recalled talking to Jett on the road, trying to get a response from him. These sudden emotions wiped every ounce of guilt from their path. I relived that terrible moment several more times before we reached midnight and if it hadn't been for Ryan's supportive words, I think I might have gone off the rails. I'd only had one glass of wine, but I felt strangely misplaced, sitting in my cosy flat with the man I love. What a year of ups and downs it had been.

As the clock struck midnight and the TV program turned to views of the fireworks in London, my heart sank. It was supposed to be the time to move on, make a fresh start, set new goals and dream big with a hopeful, optimistic mindset...

How could it be that for me, with a court case looming? The only goal I could set myself was not to lie anymore but I was already failing that as the time hit 12.01am. I smiled weakly as Ryan held my hand and wished me everything I wanted for the new year. He kissed my cheek awkwardly as I wiped away yet more tears.

"Thank you for being so understanding, Ryan," I had said.

"Whatever it takes, Susie. You know I love you."

That was last night and today I've woken with a slightly more optimistic outlook, after all, it is New Year's Day and I have got to make an effort. It is not guaranteed that I will lose my license in three days' time, so I've decided that I will thoroughly enjoy the next few days with Clair and Archie, when they arrive this afternoon.

"How are you feeling this morning?" Ryan is making us a cooked breakfast as I enter the kitchen with a fuzzy, thick head. Anyone would think I had a lot to drink last night as my brain thinks it's got a hangover.

"I'm alright... I can't believe it hit me like that last night..."

"It was bound to, sooner or later." He turns a couple of sausages over in the frying pan. "He was more than just your boyfriend – you'd grown up with him."

I smile and nod. Isn't Ryan just a dream? He totally understands and yet I went to all that trouble of not letting him read that *facebook* message. How silly of me. What was I thinking? What am I thinking now? Why can't I just tell him about the arrest? OK, I know why – it's different, isn't it? It's very different. This is something which has happened since I've been with him and I lied right from the start. This is not a lie that I can undo by telling him. The damage has been done so there's no way back. So, I suppose that it's kind of like a, not-a-lie, sort of situation because I can't tell him, whereas 'lies' can be told. Do you get where I'm coming from? Perhaps I shouldn't beat myself up so much about it and anyway... like I've said before, it will probably turn out to be OK... as long as the judge likes cats. If he or she prefers dogs, then I could have a problem on my hands.

***

They are here! We haven't left the kitchen yet because we're all talking so excitedly about their engagement, about Christmas and about their future wedding. Oh my God, it is so exciting – a wedding – my best friend's wedding. I cannot wait. It's quite funny to watch Clair, the fiancée, as she constantly holds on to her engagement ring like it's going to fall off her finger and she'll lose it. Mind you, it's got a big enough diamond on it that I'm sure it would make an almighty smash and crash on the floor if it did fall off, which she would hear easily. I watch her glance down at it now and again and adjust it on her finger. She obviously hasn't got used to it yet or simply enjoys playing with it.

"It's absolutely gorgeous," I say again, peering over her shoulder. "You are made for each other."

Clair turns and wraps her arms around me before whispering in my ear. "And so are you and Ryan. You just need to sort your shit out first."

I gasp and dart my eyes across the room, checking that Ryan hasn't heard or noticed my startled expression. "I know," I mutter, sheepishly.

"We'll talk about it later." Clair winks at me and pulls me back to her, squeezing me tightly.

Ryan and Archie have retired to the living room with filled glasses of Jack Daniels and a large bowl of peanuts. Clair is here with me in the kitchen and we are busily preparing a cold meat and cheese buffet for tea. My spirits have certainly been lifted this afternoon since my bestie arrived. Somehow, I feel safe when she's around – like she'll sort out all my problems by waving an imaginary magic wand. Or maybe she'll be able to wave her jeweled finger now and create some magic. I smile to myself at the thought and pass the cocktail sticks to her.

"What are you smiling about?"

"Oh, nothing really. I was just looking at your gorgeous ring again – don't you take it off while you're doing things like this?" I ask.

"No..." she stops stabbing the pineapple chunks and holds her hand elegantly in front of her. "I can get it professionally cleaned once a year, for free."

"Can you?"

"Yes, at the jewelers where Archie bought it."

"That's good," I say, chopping the mature cheddar into bitesize chunks. "I bet it was expensive..."

Clair shrugs at me. "I haven't asked but I would imagine so. Anyway... let's talk about you and..." She turns and peers at the kitchen door which is closed. "You know... the mess you've got yourself in. What have you done about it?" she says softly.

"I'm taking my mitigating circumstances statement with me to court," I whisper. "Having read through the paperwork some more I've discovered that I'm getting five minutes of advice from a barrister for free at the court, if I don't have my own solicitor which I don't, and I have to give the statement to him."

"Oh, that's good – have you done a statement?"

"Yes, it's in my bag. I'll show you." I fetch the statement from my bag and hand it to Clair in an envelope. "Take it to the bathroom and read it, just in case Ryan comes in here."

"OK." Clair takes it from me, stuffs it up the sleeve of her jumper and leaves the kitchen.

Several minutes later she returns with teary eyes and a smirk on her face. She passes the letter back to me which I quickly stuff back into the depths of my bag. "You are not serious – right?"

"What do you mean?" I say, surprised.

She shakes her head and giggles. "Susie – you are not handing that in, are you?"

"Yes, why?" I reply, affronted by Clair's giggling.

She sucks in a deep breath and lets it out slowly. "Susie... it's... well, you can't... it's."

"It's what?"

"It won't be taken seriously... it's a bit... well, silly."

"It's not silly, it's truthful..." I break off, thoughtfully. "Well, apart from the cat bit but that was my mistake because I put two kisses at the end, when I wrote my name."

Clair bursts into laughter. "Two... two kisses... oh my God, Susie."

"I didn't mean to – it was an automatic thing. You know, like when you send a text and put kisses at the end without thinking. I don't see what's wrong with it. The..." I lower my voice, "the judge will think it's sweet and a true reflection of who I am – "

"That's what I'm worried about, Suse."

"Why?"

"Oh, I don't know. If you really think he should read it – "

"Or she," I cut in.

"OK, or she, then it's up to you. I don't think you're going to get off lightly even if you had a professionally written mitigating statement anyway."

"We will see," I say, rather annoyed by my best friend's lack of support. "I'll text you and let you know, on the day."

"OK." Clair peers at me and smiles weakly before placing a reassuring hand on my shoulder. "Come on, try and forget about it for now and let's get this food ready – I'm bloody starving."

***

What a lovely time we've had. We all went to visit my parents, on the second day, and Dad rustled up a quick fish and chip meal for us. Then yesterday, we went to a restaurant in town, for lunch, and did a bit of shopping in the sales afterwards. Then Clair and Archie left early this morning – like 5.30 this morning, which is ridiculous, but they need to get back before Clair's shifts start up again. And, obviously, I needed them to go early anyway.

So, today is back-to-school day. Well, for Ryan at least. I'm having to pretend it's back-to-school day when in fact, I texted Mr Reynolds early this morning and told him I wasn't well at all and that I had the flu. He replied, wishing me a speedy recovery which shocked me – maybe he made a New Year resolution to be nicer this year.

"I hate this time of year," Ryan mumbled over his huge bowl of cereal.

"Sorry? What was that?" I sort of heard what he said but I'm a little preoccupied with clock-watching and willing Ryan to finish his breakfast and leave. I need to get ready, but I can't exactly put my navy-blue trouser suit on while he's here because he'll wonder what the hell I'm up to. Inset days are dress down days at school, not dress up days.

"Going back to work in January... it's bleak."

"Oh, yes – I hate it."

"And especially after such an enjoyable time with Archie and Clair. They're great."

"They are," I say, glancing at the kitchen clock again.

"Aren't you having breakfast?" Ryan stuffs another mouthful in and crunches away.

"No... I'm not that hungry this morning."

Ryan peers at me and finishes his mouthful. "Are you OK? You seem a bit preoccupied – you're not worried about seeing Sarah or Jane again, are you?"

"No, no, not at all. I've just got the blues like you."

Ryan smiles. "Good... well, if you're lucky, you might even see me later. I was going to pop in this afternoon and talk to Reynolds about the activities for this year."

My heart has stopped. I'm sure it has. "To... day?" I say in a whimper.

"After our training. It might not be until four, but I guess you'll be home by then."

"Err... yes... probably... ugh..." I clutch at my tummy, feigning pain.

"Are you OK?" Ryan looks at me curiously.

"Oh gosh... I... I thought it was over but..." I dart out of the kitchen and head to the bathroom, slamming the door behind me. Moments later, Ryan is knocking on the door.

"Susie, are you all right in there?"

"Ugh... I've... been having the runs... since Clair left."

"Oh dear, no school for you then..."

"Hmm... I mutter and flush the toilet needlessly. I open the door to see Ryan standing outside looking concerned.

"Don't go in, babe. It's only an inset day."

"Hmm... I'll see how I am in half an hour."

"OK, let me know." He kisses me on the cheek. "No lips today – I don't want what you've got thanks. I'd better go." He kisses my cheek again. "Let me know how you are later."

I nod and give him a wavering smile. "I will. See you tonight, either way."

"You certainly will, I'll be home no later than five. Bye."

Phew – he's gone. I've just poked my head out of the front door to make doubly sure. Now I can get dressed, call a taxi and get to the train station in time. I'm optimistic that today is going to be a good day.

*** 34 ***

With 15 minutes to spare, I arrive at the courts with a nasty, fluttery feeling in my stomach. I wonder whether I have cursed myself and I'll end up having the runs for sure. It's that kind of feeling. I feel sick too, but I guess that could just be nerves.

I'm standing outside the magistrates' courts pondering over my next step. Do I go straight in, early? Or should I arrive at the exact time? What looks better? The building is large and foreboding. The red brick walls are joyless, and the narrow windows give no clue to what might be inside. I hate the place already. I peer up and down the busy road and thank the universe that no one is actually walking along. At least the people in the traffic might think that I am a solicitor and not a criminal.

I was pleasantly surprised earlier how well I could brush up in my old trouser suit. While I was on the train, I felt like an important business type person, commuting to work – if only the other passengers knew what a fraud I was – what a criminal I am. Supposedly.

I suck in a deep breath and blow it out slowly – I'm going in. I'm petrified but I've got to do it. I have a five-minute consultation with a Mr Jonathan Smyth in room 4 (wherever that might be). Huh – I bet his name is John Smith really and he's just poshed it up a bit. My legs are like lead as I climb the steps to the front doors and grab the handle.

Instantly, I am thrown into a panic. There are two burly security men standing at a table, right by the doors. They both look up as I step inside and the younger one of the two smiles at me.

"This way, Miss. I need to search your bag." The older one says. His po-faced expression is alarmingly unsettling.

Search my bag? But he can't. It's got private things in it. It's my bag. I clutch it to me tightly. "Do you have to do that?" I say in a tiny voice. "I mean... I don't have anything of interest in it." The older man frowns at me and extends his hand, beckoning for me to step forward, as the younger of the two lets out a sort of snorty laugh. "Please," I plead, "I don't have anything in my bag – well, not anything bad anyway."

The older man takes my bag, under some protest from me, I can tell you. I am mortified, I really am. I feel like I'm being insulted – my privacy and dignity are being ripped apart. My bag is filled with all sorts of junk, I'm not kidding you.

I watch, dejectedly, as the man empties several items on to the table, trying to get to the bottom of the bag. He removes: my court letter; a detangle comb; a packet of tissues; the old keyring which Kallum bought me for Christmas last year, still in the soap box (I don't know how it got there to be honest); an empty crisp packet and my toilet bag. Oh my God, not my toilet bag. Is he seriously going to unzip it? Yes, he is. Oh dear, oh no. Does he have to root through my sanitary towels, tampons and *Femfresh* pocket wipes like I'm hiding a miniature bomb or a gun in the bottom of the bag?

The younger man is peering at me through narrowed eyes which I'm slightly relieved about because at least he isn't looking at my sanitary products which are now spewing out of the bag. The older man is struggling to get the things back into the toilet bag (I've always had a cunning way of cramming lots of necessary items in that bag – it's like a jigsaw puzzle – there's a knack to it but I'm not about to demonstrate it to him). He gives up and places the toilet bag back into my handbag, its contents sticking out in all different angles, then he slides it along the table, away from me. What's he doing?

"Anything in your pockets?" asks the young man.

"No," I reply, my heart thumping in my chest. Are they going to frisk me now – I hope to God not?

"Jewelry?"

"Sorry?" I say, affronted by their intrusion of my personal space – *my privacy.*

"Are you wearing any jewelry, Miss?"

I point to my ears with a hint of sarcasm in my distorted smile. "Just these."

"Any other body piercings?"

"No," I reply, embarrassed that he would think I'd have piercings in other places – I know what kind of places he is thinking about.

"Could you remove them and walk through please."

Bloody hell, what is this place? Fort Knox? The man points to a small tray on the table so I remove my earrings and place them in it. I've now got to walk through a large metal detector type of archway – I assume that's what it is anyway and not an x-ray machine. Huh – it wouldn't surprise me if it was an x-ray machine. I might as well be naked as I walk through it because I feel so humiliated by the entire process...

Oh God, no.

Why?

How?

The machine is making a buzzing sound. My face flushes instantly. I feel sick and giddy. The older man calls out to someone else. A woman appears from a room to the left – I say a woman but she's quite butch looking with a square jawline and beefy forearms protruding from her rolled-up sleeves. "Are you wearing any other jewelry, Miss?" the older man asks.

I think for a moment, scanning my body, in my mind. "Err... no, I don't think so."

"Are you sure your pockets are empty?"

I fumble through all my pockets, but they are empty. "Nothing," I sigh.

"Would you step aside," says the burly woman. Her voice is deep and gruff. She ushers me into the room where she came from and the younger man carries my handbag in. "I need to search you as the detector went off and you say you are not wearing any other jewelry."

I want to die. I'm being treated like a criminal – I'm not a criminal – not yet, anyway. "I..." My mind is going around and around so fast that it's making me dizzy. I need to sit down. I want to fall down – to collapse in a heap on the floor and be swallowed up by the ground. "I..."

Oh my God – my knickers! It has just occurred to me. "I've got..." I point frantically to my groin area, unable to speak as my throat fills with a lump.

"Genital piercings?" says the manly woman.

"No!"

The younger man is staring at me bemused.

"No – not that," I whimper. "My knick..." God, I don't want to say it in front of the man. I turn away from him slightly and point at my groin again. "I've got a metal badge kind of thing on my..."

"A badge?"

I nod desperately – she's getting me now. "It's a kind of metal label, err... yes." My finger is desperately pointing down to my groin again.

"You have metal labia?"

"Sorry?" I frown and shoot a quick glance at the young man beside her. He's looking down at the floor and I swear he has a smirk on his face.

The woman flicks a menacing glare at the young man, as their eyes meet, indicating to him to leave the room. She gives an awkward cough as he disappears and turns back to look at me with a puzzled frown. "Your labia, madam. You have a metal badge piercing of some kind or do you mean they are metal-plated – is that what you're suggesting?"

"Not a piercing," I say, affronted by the intrusion. "It's a clip-on."

"A... clip...on..." she utters in a sarcastic way while eyeing me suspiciously.

"Yes, that's right – a clip-on."

"On your labia?"

"What's a labia? I don't even know what you're talking about. Please... this is ridiculous – I'm not a criminal."

Are you able to prove this to me? Can you remove the labia clip-on?" the woman asks, peering at me curiously before waving the young man away again as he peeps his head around the door. "And labia, is the correct terminology for the outer part of your... lady-bits, just to make you aware."

Oh God, I have heard that word before. Oh, dear me, I now know exactly what she's talking about. "No, no, you've got it all wrong – I don't have genital piercings... or clip-ons. It's a badge on my knickers, that's all." Oh, dear Lord, please don't ask me to remove my knickers – no. "I should be able to show you," I say desperately.

With trembling fingers, I lift my jacket and shove a hand straight down my trousers. I am going to hook out the side of my knickers even if they cut me in half, literally. There's no way I want to remove them or have that gruesome woman put her hands all over me. Luckily, I just manage to yank the side of my knickers out and show the woman the pretty, metal clasp-like label...

Suddenly, the clasp comes away in my hand and I feel instant relief in my nether regions as my pants shoot back down, into my trousers, with a ping – in two parts. The woman is nodding her head as the young man returns to the room and appears to be amused by the clasp in my hand too. I stare at it aghast. I can already feel an uncomfortable 'undone' sort of sensation underneath my trousers, between my legs.

"Thank you," says the woman, a slight smirk on her bulldog-like face. "If you would just pass through security again, then you can go on your way."

I follow both the woman and the young man back to the entrance, place my bag back on the table and the clasp in the tray and walk through the detector. Thankfully, it does not go off this time and I walk out the other side with a huge sigh of relief. The older man slides my bag, earrings and knicker clasp along the table and I collect them sheepishly. "Can I go now?" I mutter, ashamed by the ordeal.

The woman smiles and nods at me.

I turn and face the ornate staircase in front of me. There are signposts at the bottom of the stairs pointing upwards and to both passages running alongside the stairs. My mind can't comprehend anything at the moment – all I know is that I need to get to room 4 promptly. I turn back, and the two security men are staring at me with grins on their faces. Oh God, I hate it here – I want to go home. "Could you tell me where room 4 is please," I ask in a tiny squeaky voice filled with humiliation.

"Straight up the stairs, my love," the older one replies, "turn left and it's the second door on the right."

"Thank you." I scuttle off, up the grand staircase, as one side of my knickers begin to make its descent between my legs. By the time I reach the top of the stairs, I have a ball of knicker material scrunched up in my crotch – it's highly uncomfortable and I desperately hope it's not noticeable. I do not want to appear like I have got a bulge in the front of my trousers – that would be horrendous. I can hardly walk as I turn left towards room 4. I'm sure the elastic hem is now caught up in a most personal area and chaffing me with every step.

I reach room 4 which is tucked away into an alcove and puff out a sigh. There are four seats outside and three of them are occupied with young, rough-looking men – they may even be teenage men. They all gawp at me as I knock on the door.

"You, Miss Satch?" the oldest looking man asks. He's wearing a black hoodie, scruffy, oversized jeans and tatty trainers. I try not to show my distaste in his attire but surely, he should be dressed more appropriately for court.

I peer at him and frown. "Satchel," I say, noticing that one of the other men, who is dressed in a similar way, appears to be chewing gum. There is a stench of stale cigarette smoke in this cosy alcove and I wonder if he is the smoker and trying to mask the unpleasant smell.

"He just called you – bout five ticks ago."

"Sorry?"

"Geezer – in there – he called for you."

"Oh," I say, "I'm a little late." I tap on the door again.

"Someone else 'as gone in now, mate." The man eyes me up and down with a dirty grin on his face.

Trust me, I am praying to the universe at this moment, that I do not have a bulge in my trousers. I really couldn't cope with any crude comments at this time. I'm so done. The worrying thing is that he has just called me, 'mate'. Mate? I'm not his mate. Mates refer to men, don't they? I'm a woman, can't he see that? He must be able to see that. I have bulges up the top, even if I do have a bulge at the bottom as well.

I smile at him weakly and sit on the vacant chair. I am desperately trying to avoid the scrunched-up knicker-ball in my trousers, while presenting a demure façade. I'm surrounded by thugs – young thugs. I shouldn't stereotype people but they all look like typical criminals. Not one of them has bothered with their appearance and they all need a shave. I really don't fit in here. I shouldn't be here, yet I've come to find myself in the mix with a bunch of unruly adolescents who probably deserve to be here. I *do not* deserve to be here.

Moments later, the door opens and yet another, scrawny teenager leaves the room. He shoots a menacing glance at me before strutting off.

"Miss Satchel?" I hear the smooth articulate tones of another man's voice. Then a head appears from around the door. "Do come in." The well-dressed man is staring straight at me which causes me to give an involuntary shudder – he is the ugliest looking man I have ever seen. I don't mean to be unkind, but he really is ugly.

Wearing a grey checked waistcoat over a lilac shirt which appears to be about three sizes too big for him, Mr Jonathan Smyth's mismatched attire is actually the most appealing thing about him. His dark-rimmed, perfectly round glasses frame a pair of black, beady eyes and a large hooked nose. His ears, protruding from a balding head, stand out perpendicular to his face causing him to look more like a wingnut than anything else. I offer a sheepish grin as I approach the door, and he extends a hand towards me. "Jonathan Smyth, at your service."

"Thank you," I say, shuffling through the door with what I can only describe as chaffed labia by now. My knickers are twisting and dragging downwards with every step I take, like they are caught up somewhere. It's highly unpleasant, I can tell you. I shake his hand nervously and am surprised by his strong grip.

The room is very small with just a desk and two chairs, one either side. Jonathan Smyth offers me the chair nearest the door and walks around the desk to the other, more comfortable looking seat. Tentatively, I sit down, trying to adjust my nether regions discreetly in the process but to no avail – in fact, I'm sure I've made matters worse by yanking at the left leg of my trousers before I sat down.

"Miss Satchel – Susie Satchel – is that correct?"

I nod and open my mouth to say yes but nothing comes out apart from a tiny squeaking sort of sound. Embarrassed, I attempt to cross my legs to try and look demure again but the tugging in my nether regions is unbearable now, so I quickly uncross my legs and smile at Mr Smyth pathetically.

He has some papers in front of him which he begins to thumb through. Stopping on one particular sheet, he pulls it out and scans it with his bird-like gaze. "Drunk-in-charge of a vehicle. I trust you will be pleading guilty?"

"Well..." I start, "I do have this," I say, pulling the paperwork from my bag. "Can I use these mitigating circumstances?"

"You're representing yourself in court..."

"Yes, I know. What do I do with this then?" I wave the papers in front of him before he takes them from me.

I watch as he pulls out the sheet with my plea written on it. He begins to read it, then he pauses, peers at me briefly with furrowed brows and then reads it again. A minute later, his cheeks colour as he places the paper on the desk, clasps his fingers together and leans his chin on his hands.

Well? What's he staring at me like that for? He's making me uncomfortable.

He raises his head and clears his throat. "I should advice you that your statement is entirely unsuitable for court and therefore should not be presented before the judge." He clears his throat again before a tiny smirk appears at one corner of his thin-lipped mouth.

"Oh?" I mutter, childishly, "Why?"

"Judge Havers will not be interested in your love-life, friendship problems... or whether you have a muddy cat or not. I'm afraid this would be laughable in court and therefore I advise you to withhold it. I will put forward a recommendation for you to attend an alcohol awareness course – this will reduce your sentence by three months."

Three months? Sentence? Am I going to prison? I want to burst into tears, I want to run from the courts, I seriously want to rip my knickers off right at this moment. I've become all hot and unnecessary and my groin is on fire. "Does that..." I try to say, "Does that mean... Am I going to prison?"

Jonathan Smyth shakes his head and peers at me with that one-sided half-smirk which I think is mixed with a hint of pity. "The penalty for being in charge of a vehicle, whilst drunk, is a one-year ban."

I gasp and instantly feel a rush of nausea hit the back of my throat. It's true. Clair was right. How can it be – I've just got a new car for Christmas? Surely the judge will look at me – see how smart I look – and feel sorry for me. Won't he? Unless he notices a bulge and thinks I'm some kind of transvestite.

"This can be reduced to nine months if you agree to the AA course. Your insurers, in the future, will look upon your case more favourably if you have completed the course. And the course advisors can give you recommendations for insurance companies who are happy to take on convicted drink/drivers."

Convicted? I truly am a criminal? Will that change my CRB check at school? Oh my God, what have I done? And apart from Clair, not a single soul knows about this. I might as well rip my knickers off and make a run for it – I'll go commando and be a fugitive – I'm totally done for.

*** 35 ***

Judge Havers was a very homely looking man – even in his silly white wig. Why do they wear those things? Isn't it about time they moved on with the times and thought of something a little more modern, like sporting a royal-blue crop-top or something contemporary like that? Anyway, the point is that Judge Havers looked like your common, dear old grandad type and I bet he does like cats which irked me somewhat because he may have warmed to me if I'd been given the opportunity to present my mitigating circumstances statement. However, Mr Jonathan Smyth insisted that it was not appropriate, even when I asked him a second time. He simply gave me one of those, 'are you serious?' looks and shook his head slowly, several times.

The court room was just like I imagined it would be – I've watched enough *Judge Judy* and *Judge Rinder* programs to know a court when I see one. What I wasn't expecting was the stark ambience of it. They are eerie, strangely silent places with an overpowering woody smell – well, this one was anyway. There were three judgy-type people sitting up high, at the front, and the two people, either side of Judge Havers, were quite pompous in their manner and looks. I didn't like them at all.

Yet, the worst bit about the entire thing was the fact that I had to sit-in on the previous case (like a witness) and then the next person (after my case) sat in and watched mine. It was so apparent that I did not fit in to the scenario of a job-lot of drink/drivers being convicted all morning. All the others I saw, were young to middle-aged men – I'm sure there wasn't one single woman in the building, apart from me... And I suppose, the burly butch-bird in the lobby should be counted too.

It was such a humiliating and traumatic experience and all the time, I could feel my knickers twisting further and further around, cutting off the circulation in my left leg. I practically fell out of the dock, once I had been sentenced and my driving license taken away from me. Still, I now have an exciting alcohol awareness course to attend next month which only cost me £145 – a mere price to pay to get three months knocked off a one-year ban. I'm being sarcastic here (OK, I probably deserve everything I've been dealt) but in these dire times of mine, sarcasm really does help. It's either that or I break down and cry my eyes out to some stranger on the train journey home – and all while going commando.

As soon as I left the courts, with my tail between my legs (OK, it was the scrunched-up knickers between my legs), I headed straight back to the train station and hurried in to the toilets to remove my underwear. I really wasn't sure what to do with them and dreaded the thought of having my handbag searched again by someone, so I flushed them down the toilet. It was quite sad to see them go as they were one of my favourite pairs.

I'm now sitting on the train feeling slightly undressed and vulnerable to those womanly stains that happen sometimes. I wish I had worn a longer jacket. The train has left the station and we are heading into the countryside. I peer out of the window in a daydream state and can't quite believe what has happened today. I'm all alone in this dilemma and I can't see any way out of it but to tell Ryan the truth when he gets home tonight. I really don't want to do that, and he'll probably hate me, especially as he bought the car. I just don't see any other way out of it though.

As I'm watching the fields whizz by, my mind wanders to school. Do I tell Mr Reynolds? Oh God, I can't tell him. What would he say? What would anyone at school say if they found out? What would my dear mum and dad say? Everything is a blur of sorrow and I'm unable to clarify anything in my head. How am I going to do the course every Saturday, for six hours, over three consecutive weeks without Ryan wondering what I'm up to? That's another reason why I should tell him. I need to stop this vicious circle of lie upon lie. I can't cover up the fact that I would disappear for six hours every Saturday, can I? Apparently, the course only runs at weekends so that it doesn't interfere with people's work lives. But I want to do it during the week – it would be easier to cover up, wouldn't it?

I look up at the grey sky outside and the gloominess envelops me. It's no use, I realise, I am going to have to tell Ryan. There's just no other way. My heart sinks and a wave of dread and gloom washes over me. It could well be the end for me and Ryan when he finds out.

***

The rest of the journey home was shrouded in a dark cloud, even though the weather outside had brightened considerably as the train sped through the countryside. I've just stepped off the train and as I walk along the platform I feel naked and vulnerable – it's surprising how a thin pair of knickers can make you feel complete, held together and dressed appropriately. I head outside the station to the long line of taxis waiting to pick up their next fare. I raise a hand and the front cab edges forward to meet me. I jump in the back and call out my address with an exaggerated 'please' added at the end just because I don't want to sound like some kind of a knicker-less thug or a criminal.

Being back in my home town is a strange feeling now that I have been convicted of an offence. Somehow, I feel kind of dirty or tainted and wonder if it's because of my lack of underwear or because I've got to admit to some people, namely Ryan, school and my parents, that I have messed up big time. Admit that I am the biggest liar they have ever known.

I keep running the same conversation through my head, again and again and every single time, it does not end well...

Ryan, I need to talk to you about something...
Go ahead babe – what is it?
I... I've messed up...
OK, what have you done this time?
No, I've really messed up – this is serious.
OK, what's the problem? I'm imagining at this point that Ryan has lost interest already and will be flicking through the TV programs.
On Boxing night...
Yes?
When I left your parent's house... He'll nod his head at this point. *I got... arrested... for...* At this stage the whole story will come tumbling out of my

mouth at a hundred miles an hour and Ryan will sit there and gape at me. When I've finished the tale, he will snap his mouth closed and continue to stare at me disbelievingly without saying a word...

Then, once he has regained his voice it will all kick off. It will be the lies that do it. He'll be so angry and probably storm off, leave the flat and more than likely, leave me. Forever.

As I focus through the taxi window I note that we are crawling through the town centre traffic. I watch the people walking by on the pavements and wonder if they are all happy. Do any of them have convictions? As we leave the centre and head along the ring road which goes around the outside of the town centre and past the giant complex of superstores on our left, I take a sharp intake of breath.

"Stop," I shout, much louder than I expected to. "Can you pull over here, please." The taxi driver says nothing but shoots a steely glare through the rearview mirror as he swerves slightly and turns into a side road. "Yes, just here will be fine – thank you." I grapple around in my bag and quickly find my purse. Pulling a folded twenty pound note out from behind my credit card (I always keep some money safely tucked away there for emergencies like this), I thrust it forward. "Here, keep the change – thank you," I say, as my heart begins to thump in my chest.

"It's only three quid, love."

"Oh," I say, my mind racing around erratically. "Just give me ten back then, quickly – I've got to go. Keep the rest for your trouble – thank you."

The driver passes me a ten-pound note and gives me a puzzled frown. I snatch the money from his hand and climb out of the car. "Thank you, and... sorry," I say, before slamming the door closed. My heart is seriously racing now, along with my thoughts. I've got to do this – it is the only way. It's wrong but it's right. It's my kind of right.

Despite the continued chaffing, due to the rigid seam in the underpart of my trousers, my legs are going as fast as my brain is whirring around. I'm practically running down to the superstore complex now. But it's the only way that I can see out of this whole goddamn mess. It's the only way... believe me...

***

I stagger in through the front door – I've made it home in less than an hour since getting off the train. Beads of perspiration are running from every part of my body and my lady-bits are in tatters, I'm not kidding you. I just manage to close the door and careen towards the kitchen. Every excruciating step I take is enough to reduce me to tears. Once I'm in the kitchen, I hobble to a chair and sit down. Then I drag myself back up, realising I can't sit down. My rear is on fire and every muscle in my legs is screaming out. My whole groin feels like it's ablaze. A solitary tear tips over the rim of my eye and trickles down my cheek. How can things have got this bad? What have I gone and done now?

I leave the kitchen and teeter to the bathroom – I need a bath, a good, long, contemplative soak. There's plenty of time before Ryan comes home. And when I've recovered, I will make him a nice drug-free spaghetti Bolognese, just how he likes it, with copious amounts of Parmesan cheese and garlic bread. I can do this. I've got to do this. It will be OK... I'm sure it will...

***

I'm wearing my cosy pyjamas and dressing gown, and the Bolognese is simmering away on the cooker top by the time I hear the front door open. Ryan is home. Now is the time to execute my cunning plan and this time, it does not involve any kind of drugs. Several lies but no drugs. I can't tell him the truth, even though I battled with the possibility all morning – you must understand that.

I hear a cluttering sound and then a grunt before Ryan's perplexed face appears in the doorway. He shoots a puzzled glance at me and then scans the kitchen, peering around the side of the door like a huntsman. "Is someone here?" he asks in a whisper, looking behind him, back into the hallway.

"Nope – just little old me." I grin and slowly shuffle towards him in my fluffy slippers, trying to conceal my inability to walk properly.

"Then whose –?"

"Mine." I shrug my shoulders, screw my nose up and give him another cheesy grin before pecking him on the cheek.

Ryan is obviously dumbfounded, I thought he would be, to be honest. He hasn't moved from the doorway yet. "Why?" he mutters, gazing at me with wide eyes.

I shrug again and offer my cutest smile. "Why not?"

"But – "

"I know what you're going to say," I start, pulling him into the kitchen, "but come and sit down, your favourite dinner is ready, and then I will explain."

As Ryan sits at the table, my mobile goes off. We both look at it, resting on top of the table. The message has appeared on my lock screen (which is something I've been planning to stop because it's really annoying and my messages could be seen by anyone). I freeze momentarily and read through the message at speed. It's from Clair and I know that Ryan is peering at it as well.

How did you get on today? Been thinking about you xx

I snort a laugh, pick up my phone and shake my head. "I told her I was going to do it," I say. "I bet she thinks I can't do it..." I slip the phone inside my dressing gown pocket and totter off to the cooker to dish up our dinner.

"So," says Ryan, a tone of pure curiosity in his voice, "when did you decide to do this? I thought you weren't feeling well this morning."

"Oh... I've been thinking about it for a while now and I felt so much better by lunchtime, so I thought, why not go for it."

"Really?"

"Yes, you know the kind of thing – New Year, new me..."

"But I like the old you – you're gorgeous and sexy – you're perfect." He smiles and gives me a gorgeous wink.

Oh God, I really hope he doesn't want to have rampant sex tonight. I'm sorry but there's no way. I cringe at the thought of it. My poor 'bits' have been to hell and back today. I couldn't possibly expose them to another battering. I don't mean to sound crude but that's what it would feel like.

"Wouldn't you like an even fitter me? A toned me?"

"You don't need to tone – you're perfect as you are."

I carry two plates to the table, loaded with spaghetti Bolognese and a couple of slices of garlic bread on the side. "You might think so," I say, putting the plates down, "but I don't feel fit. I thought a bike would be the perfect way to get fit."

"Hmm," Ryan mumbles, tucking into the Bolognese straight away. "I would have thought a gym would be more suitable – especially in the middle of winter."

"A gym is expensive whereas, riding a bike will cost nothing. I bought a helmet too and... I've got my big bubble jacket which I can wear when it's cold."

Ryan nods. "OK, when are you going to be riding it then?"

"To work every day."

"To work? You won't manage that – not straight away anyway." He peers at me with a bemused expression. "That thing will numb your arse for a while, you know. And... what about your new car?"

"I know... err... yes, I can imagine it will hurt my bum for a while (huh, that's an understatement because already, I have bruised buttocks, and thighs that feel like they've been ripped to shreds, just by getting the bike home from the superstore and none of that accounts for the dreadful state of my other bits too – you know the ones I'm talking about), but I'm determined to do it. Some of the others at school are starting to ride in the new year so I thought it would be good to do it too."

"You've never mentioned this before..."

"Oh... I forgot to tell you, what with everything that has gone on since Christmas."

"OK," Ryan says, unconvinced, "but it will be interesting to see how long it lasts. The weather's not too bad now, apart from being freezing, but wait until it gets wet or icy – or even snow. You won't want to ride to work then."

Sadly, I won't have any choice – unless I want to spend stupid amounts of money on buses that turn up when they feel like it (or so I've heard some people say at work and incidentally, I'm sorry but that was a lie – I don't know of anyone else who will be riding to school in the new year). "We'll see," I say, with a determined smirk. "I do like a challenge."

"OK, have it your way babe," he mutters, before stuffing a slice of garlic bread in his mouth.

Phew! Ryan believes me. I may have just got away with this – I guess only time will tell.

Clair, I'm not going to tell you the outcome because then you won't ever have to lie to Archie. Love you my bestie xx

I think I can guess my dearest friend. I'm so sorry for you, Suse. I don't know what to say. Love you more xx

Susie Satchel will return soon...

Thank you for taking the time to read this book
I would be hugely grateful
if you could leave a short review on Amazon
Kindest regards
Tara Ford

Printed in Poland
by Amazon Fulfillment
Poland Sp. z o.o., Wrocław